Safe Zone: The Greater Good

Suzanne Sussex

COPYRIGHT

For Adam

Alone

I am alone. I have nothing but the dark night and darker memories as my companions. My mind is a song full of anger that is stuck on repeat.

"If you walk out that door, Stephen Alex Winter, don't even think you can come back. That would be it. We would be over."

It was an empty threat; we had both known it. In response, he had repeated that same damn line. The one he had said so many times. Too many times. Now his tone was flat, robotic. "I have to go; I can't stay here. You know it's the right thing to do."

I tried everything that night, calmly using logic and reason to persuade him to stay. I'd found old photos and mementoes from our relationship, to remind him of the good times we'd shared, I'd even flashed my boobs at him. A distraction technique that had never failed, it failed that night.

My anger had risen with the sun. My initial calm turned to rage. I had screamed and shouted. Thrown things and threatened. Nothing had worked.

Finally, he closed the expanse between us. Coming to me, cupping my face in his hands and lifting my chin so that our eyes met. He kissed me gently, and a glimmer of hope had shone through my despair.

But then he picked up his bags and opened the front door.

Turning to look at me one last time he said, "I love you, Clo." Then he had walked through the door, and I was alone.

I wonder if in years to come people will look back and say; "*I remember where I was the day the apocalypse started.*"

My world had ended that day. However, the truth is far more complicated. There wasn't a single day where the world ended and everyone died.

It had started months ago in South America. We heard stories of people getting sick and dying. Then of riots, violence and looting. Entire villages and small towns wiped from existence.

It was on the front page of every newspaper. The headline story on every news channel. Fancy infographics flashed on the screen to illustrate how quickly it could spread. Experts on panels discussed how bad things could get. All seemingly with the sole intention of scaring the shit out of anyone that would listen.The medical community called it ZN-134, but that wasn't sexy enough for the media. A series of random letters and numbers didn't strike fear into the hearts of the public. It didn't sell papers. The victim's eyes became inky black shortly before death, so the media called it the Black Flu.

But just like Swine Flu, Ebola and the Zika virus, the media soon turned its attention to other things closer to home.

The footballer's affair with the reality TV star. The tax avoidance of a multinational company. The newest scandal in the House of Parliament. Mundane and unimportant, all taking prominence in the news, and soon we forgot about the Black Flu.

Then three weeks ago there was an outbreak in a small town in Germany. Just like in South America, it started with sickness and death., then riots and violence, shops and bars looted, houses trashed and set on fire.The media interest quickly picked up again. This was Europe. This was close to home. Footage was shown over and over of the dead and dying, of streets filled with debris and bodies, of buildings ravaged by fire. Journalists gave their reports, shouting over the cacophony of the screaming and gunshots. Fundraising appeals rippled through social media, raising millions and serving only to assuage the conscience of those who were just so glad that it wasn't happening to them.

It hadn't taken long for the military to arrive in the small town and restore the peace. The media went quiet, not even taking the time to discuss the aftermath, so the public stopped talking about it once more.

That is until last week. A video posted on Facebook of a previously unseen BBC news report from the town in Germany. The story wasn't new.

The reporter was just repeating the same information, already heard a hundred times before. It was the scene in the bottom right of the picture that sparked the interest.

A young woman being attacked by two people, who appeared to be biting her. Eventually, the woman stopped struggling and became deathly still. The two attackers stopped, got clumsily to their feet and moved away.

Unaware of the scene behind him, the reporter continued his story. The woman stood unsteadily. Blood poured from the ragged hole torn in her neck, with more dripping slowly down her thighs. As she got closer to the camera, you could make out her eyes, which were an inky black, her stare fixed on the reporter.

The internet went wild, the post shared over three million times in one day. Many wrote it off as a hoax, others spoke of zombies, until the topic was being debated far and wide.

The public was reassured overwhelmingly by the media that the video was fake, a spoof; that the source of the Black Flu outbreak in Germany had been identified and fully contained; there was no risk of it spreading any further in Europe.

The media were wrong.

We didn't know it, but the apocalypse had started months ago. But my world ended the day I stared at the door, praying for it to open. So that I could say, "I love you too."

One

The setting sun cast its reflection across the calm ocean, hues of orange and pink merging to create a sense of calm, peace and tranquillity. The beauty of the early evening went unnoticed by Sam. His mind was too full of hope and excitement for what the night might bring.

Sitting at the bar on the waterfront, he was enjoying the warm breeze on his face and the cold beer in his hand. It was the last night of the lads' holiday; a group of eight men, playing golf during the day, drinking during the evening, and all in the name of celebrating Dean's impending wedding. At nineteen, Sam was the youngest of the group. He'd never been abroad before and was making the most of it.

On the first day, he'd joined the others for one round of golf, but soon tired of it. So, he had returned to the resort and spent the rest of the day drinking by the pool. When he was joined by the others in the evening, he'd already moved on to shots, and encouraged them to do the same.

The evening had been loud and messy. Sam had collapsed on his bed in the early hours, awaking the next day to the foul stench of stale beer, farts and vomit. He had taken a shit, a shower and dressed quickly.

Ready for another day beside the pool, thus, setting the cycle for the remainder of the trip.

Tousled light brown hair and chocolate brown eyes lent Sam the appearance of a boy-band member. His toned and tanned body drew admiring glances.

His natural charm and alcohol-infused confidence made women blush shyly, and be flattered that his attention was on them. He'd had sex with three different women since he'd been here, and was hoping for one last shag before they went home tomorrow.

Taking a swig of beer and surreptitiously glancing around, he sighed as he noticed how empty the resort was. "Slim pickings tonight," he complained to Trev who was sitting next to him.

"Eh, what?" Trev asked. Already married and no interest in picking up women, his mind was on a heated debate about Chelsea's new striker.

"It's so quiet, might have to settle for a fatty," Sam said, oblivious to Trev's confusion.

His eyes had settled on a group of four girls, quietly sipping brightly coloured cocktails in the next bar along. To Sam's arrogant mind, all four of them were overweight, their make-up applied by inexperienced hands, and tightly fitted maxi dresses unflattering on their figures.

He thought back to some of the other women he'd slept with. He'd had better, he'd had worse.

Plus, he reassured himself, insecure women make for easy prey.

"They'll do," he muttered.

"Yeah mate, sure, whatever," Trev replied, unsure if the comment was meant for him.

As the evening wore on, Sam began to tire of the inane football conversation. He'd been the only one drinking all day. The rest of them just needed a little encouragement to catch up. He looked around and caught the eye of a hovering waiter.

"Eight Jäger bombs please, mate," Sam expressed each word slowly to help the Spanish waiter understand, completely ignorant to how patronising he sounded.

The shots arrived and were downed quickly by the group. More orders soon followed and more shots consumed. Talk of football was quickly forgotten as the men grew louder and more raucous.

"I'm going for a piss," Sam announced. Getting unsteadily to his feet, he made his way inside to the small, dirty toilet. Inside the dimly lit bar, he noticed a group of local women, chatting and laughing amongst themselves. Sam didn't know what they were saying, but he also didn't care. They were fit.

Veering off course, Sam purposefully walked next to the table, puffing his chest out and winking at the hottest one on his way past. A much better choice than the other girls he'd seen earlier.

Rolling her eyes at the young boy, Rosa groaned inwardly. As a waitress in a local café, the attention of drunken English men was familiar to her, but it was never welcomed, particularly not tonight. She wasn't feeling well, and her head was thumping. She hadn't even wanted to come out, but it was her best friend Isabella's birthday, and she'd felt she had no choice

As her friends gossiped, Rosa's thoughts turned to her boyfriend. He'd visited his parents in a nearby village the day before.

Their elderly neighbour had passed away earlier in the day, after suffering from a nasty bout of flu. Some of the other villagers had the same thing, and he was sure his parents were coming down with it, too. He had complained of feeling ill himself earlier that day. Despite his encouragement that her plans should not change, Rose felt guilty for leaving him.

With a heavy sigh, Rosa stood up, "I'm so sorry Isabella, but I need to go home. I don't feel so good."

"But your wine…" Isabella began to protest, pointing at the glass that had barely been touched. Looking up at her friend, she noticed how tired and drawn Rosa looked, and backed down immediately, "It's cool, go home, get some sleep. We can celebrate another time." She turned to the others, "We'll go and eat now, yes?"

The ladies stood, gathered their belongings and left the bar together, the three women taking turns to kiss Rosa's cheeks, before heading off in the opposite direction.

Sam came out of the bathroom, slipping his hand through his hair. His face broke out into a cocky grin.

Rounding the corner, he frowned when he saw the now empty table. Never one to miss out on free booze, he headed over anyway. He looked around, confident no one was watching him, and he downed the remaining wine from the four glasses, then headed back outside.

The evening wore on, the dark night illuminated by the bright full moon. The group of men got louder. Alcohol was consumed and spilt in equal measure, more shots necked. Confidence growing, Sam decided it was time, and made his way over to the next bar. Without invitation, he pulled up a chair and sat down with the group of girls he'd spotted earlier. They looked back at him in surprise.

"Alright ladies, enjoying your holiday are ya?" he asked, smiling warmly at them.

"Um yeah, it's er … nice here, hot, you know," the girl with mousy brown hair replied, a blush creeping up her cheeks.

"So, where ya from?" he asked. Make small talk to break the ice. A basic rule of pulling, act interested in the targets.

"Oh, just a small village near Oxford," the same girl replied.

"Ah, that's lovely that is," he smiled easily, despite having no idea where Oxford is. "I'm from Maidstone, ya know, in Kent," he offered without being asked. "On a stag do," he added gesturing at the next bar. All four girls looked over so see a life-sized inflatable doll pressed against a table. Dean was dry humping it, slapping its plastic backside with every thrust.

An awkward silence followed, the four girls pointedly ignoring Dean's actions. "Drink," Sam almost shouted, startling them. "Let me get you lovely birds, erm, I mean ladies, a drink."

"Gaston," Sam called out, clicking his fingers at the waiter. "Same again over here please, and I'll take a beer."

Three of the girls cringed in embarrassment, glancing furtively at each other, sending signals, *who is this guy*? Only one was smiling, Sally, she'd never been bought a drink by a man before. This was great.

"I'm Sally," she announced, thrusting her hand forward to shake Sam's. Her enthusiasm was not lost on Sam, he knew he was in there with this one.

Gesturing vaguely in the direction of the other girls, she added, "This is Lex, Paige and Claire."

"Hi," they all said dutifully.

"I'm Sam," he replied, holding onto Sally's hand a little longer than necessary, and staring deep into her chocolate brown eyes. "Pleasure to meet you," he added softly.

~

The pounding on the hotel room door eventually stirred Sam from his slumber. "What the fuck?" he moaned, trying to sit up, but his arm was pinned under something heavy. Reaching his free hand towards the table lamp, he flicked it on and saw a naked Sally blinking sleepily up at him, her large frame trapping his arm beneath her.

"Morning," she smiled coyly up at him, twirling a strand of brown hair around her finger, "I had fun last night."

"Er, what?" Sam replied, forcefully yanking his arm free and knocking her off the bed in the process. Hazy images of the night before came swimming before him, he looked down his body and saw a used condom stuck to the inside of his thigh. "Fuck," he said peeling it off and flicking it across the room.

His head was thumping; he must have drunk a lot last night. He tried to focus, but even the walls looked like they were moving.

"You have to get up, you need to leave now," someone shouted from behind the closed door. The walls were moving from the heavy pounding on the door.

Sam angrily pulled on his boxer shorts and marched over, yanking it open.

"Now listen here, mate. We booked a late checkout... the sun ain't even up yet. I ain't going nowhere," he shouted at the holiday rep standing in the doorway.

"No … no … you don't understand, we all have to leave, it's here… we have to go."

"Go … Go where … Why … What's here …?" Sam asked confusion replacing the anger.

"There is a mandatory evacuation of all UK citizens. A coach will be leaving in ten minutes. You must be on it," the rep said hurriedly, the words trailing off as he went down the corridor to the next door.

Sam poked his head out of the door, and in the dim light he could see Dean and another one of the group, running towards the lifts.

"Oi Dean, mate, what's happening?" Sam shouted, chasing after them.

Dean repeatedly stabbed at the lift button. He glanced quickly at Sam, taking in his mostly naked form. "What the fuck are you doing? Get dressed, we have to go. Now… They… They've already got Trev."

"What... who got Trev?" Sam stuttered, his hungover brain struggling to comprehend Dean's words.

Fear cracked Dean's voice. "He's fucking dead, got attacked last night, now fucking move. I ain't waiting for you, Sam."

The fog in Sam's mind prevented him from registering what he was being told. What he did know was that his mates were leaving, and he didn't want to be left behind.

He rushed back to his room and started to dress.

"Come back to bed, Sammie … I want to cuddle," Sally said, now back in bed with the sheets wrapped around her.

"No. I've got to go; you should leave too. Something's happening," he spat at her hurriedly. He didn't really care about whether she left or stayed in the room, but he didn't want to take her with him.

Dejected and hurt, Sally huffed and stood up. She scooped up her knickers from the floor and pulled them on, while looking around the room for the rest of her clothes. "Sam, have you seen my bra?" she asked.

He turned to look at her. The expression on his face changing to one of disgust when he saw the blood on the bed.

"You dirty cow. Are you on your fucking period? You let me put my dick in you when you're on your period. That's fucking gross," Sam snarled, his alcohol-filled stomach heaving at the thought.

"No," Sally protested, "I'm not due on for a couple of weeks," she turned and looked back at small spots of blood on the sheets. "Oh," she giggled snatching her bra up from under the pillow. "No, I'm a virgin … or I guess … I was a virgin."

"Seriously?" Sam paused, his jeans around his knees and a look of joy transformed his face. "Ha! I fucked a virgin! Wait until I tell my mates." The look of elation remained as he finished dressing. He gathered the clothes scattered across the room into his holdall, and said, "Right well, see ya," as he walked out of the door.

"Wait! Don't you want my number?" Sally called out to Sam's retreating back. Pretending not to hear her, Sam sped up and opted for the stairs rather than wait for the elevator.

"It's okay… I'll find you on Facebook..." he heard her shout, as the door to the stairwell banged shut behind him.

Sam left the bright reception and stepped outside. The first light of dawn was breaking through the darkness. The coach waited as promised, the luggage compartment already full of suitcases. He added his bag to the pile and stepped up onto the coach.

He looked around for his mates, and doubt filled him until he spied them at the back. Excitement lit up his face.

"Oi, lads, guess what? I only went and fucked myself a virgin last night! Ha," he shouted, ignoring the tuts from the other passengers.

"What the fuck, man?" Dean exclaimed in astonishment. "Trev died last night, and you're bragging about fucking a virgin. What's wrong with you?"

"What the fuck do you mean Trev is dead? What the fuck happened?" asked Sam.

"After you fucked off with that bird, we went to a club," Dean explained, "but it was empty, literally no fucker there. We waited around for a bit to see if it would pick up, but it didn't. So about three, we decided to call it a night. We were walking back to the hotel and saw this fit as fuck Spanish girl, sat on the pavement, moaning. Like she was in pain or summat. Trev went up to her and checked to see if she was okay, and she bit him. Fucking bitch bit him on his fucking cheek. Tore a massive hole out of his cheek, she did. It was fucked up, man." He paused and pretended to clear his throat, while choking back a sob.

"Me and the others ran over to him, to see if he was okay, but then hundreds of locals came running at us, shouting, so we fucked off. Only, when I looked back, I saw Trev wasn't with us.

The locals were kicking him in the head. It was fucking brutal, there were too many of them. We couldn't go back; we just couldn't help him," the words spilt out followed by a loud sob.

Sam listened in stunned silence. It couldn't be real. He looked expectantly at Dean, waiting for him to laugh and tell him he was winding him up. Any minute now, Trev would jump on the coach and they would all have a laugh at Sam's expense. Instead, the tears fell down his friend's face. Dean crying freely was enough to convince Sam.

"Holy shit, so what did you do?" he asked.

Dean swallowed, "Well we hid, didn't we? Only thing we could do, mate. When they'd gone, we went over to help Trev, but he was dead. His head was… well, it was smashed to a pulp, no one could survive that. Could they?" Dean didn't wait for Sam to respond.

"We ran back here, raised holy hell at reception and got them to call the cops. Only the cops didn't answer. We were all properly kicking off at the receptionist. Then the rep came in and told us we had to be evacuated straightaway."

Sam nodded slowly, "Fuck … That's mental. Poor Trev."

"We reckon that girl had that Black Flu virus thing and the locals were just jumping on the bandwagon with the looting, the rioting, you know, like what happened in Germany?'

Sam nodded again, despite the fact he hadn't paid attention to the news in months. "Fuck …'" he repeated, not knowing what else to say.

He had only met Trev on the day they'd flown out, but he'd seemed nice enough. What a horrible way to die.

Sam had not had an easy upbringing. Expressing feelings had been actively discouraged, and now he lacked the emotional intelligence to offer any support or comfort to his friend. Instead, he turned and leant his head against the cool glass of the window. He couldn't take it in, couldn't digest the events of the morning. What the fuck was going on?

A loud bang against the side of the coach made him jump. He noticed for the first time the large group of people on the streets. There was something about them, something odd. They were stumbling along the pavements as if they were drunk.

In the early morning light, they all looked dirty, as though they'd rolled around in mud.

He stared intently at them, trying to figure out what was on their clothes. He caught the eye of a woman who seemed to be staring back at him.

Her mouth hung open, saliva dripping from her tongue. It wasn't yet light enough to see clearly, but he could have sworn that she was the fit woman he'd seen in the bar the previous night. There was something different about her. Last night she was stunning. Her hair was glossy, her makeup impeccably applied. Now, her hair hung limp and greasy. Her red lipstick looked like she'd put it on during a particularly bumpy car ride.

It coated the sides of her lips unevenly, giving an almost clown-like appearance.

He looked closer, pressing his nose against the window, and realised with shock that it was not lipstick, but blood. As he watched, the woman got knocked to the ground by the swarming crowd, and he lost sight of her.

In a bid to get away, the coach driver slammed his foot on the accelerator, and Sam was thrown back in his seat.

A woman towards the front yelped as her head hit the window. But it worked, and they soon left the crazed group behind them.

The rest of the drive was smooth, and Sam allowed the tension to ease from him. Eventually, they pulled into the airport. They were met by a man wearing a smart suit. He seemed harassed and distracted as he hurried them off the coach. When everyone had disembarked, he coughed loudly.

"Kevin Jenkins," he announced, "I am from the British embassy here in Spain. We are evacuating all tourists from this area, please follow me. Leave your luggage in the coach. It will be transported later."

Everyone immediately started talking and moaning at once, but did as instructed, and followed him.

He continued to talk as they entered the empty airport.

"We have secured a British Airways aircraft and crew for your journey. You are the last group to arrive for this flight. On this occasion, we will be bypassing check-in and security. I will be checking your names and passports as you embark."

"Er, Kev …?' Dean called from the back of the group.

"It's Kevin, and what do you want? I do not have time for questions."

"It's not a question … well not really, er Kevin, but my mate, see, my mate was bitten last night, and then a load of locals kicked him and he … well … you know … like … died. Shouldn't we be, like, bringing his body home or summat?"

Kevin stopped walking and turned back towards the group, his eyes searching for the person that had spoken, "Bitten you say? No, I'm afraid we won't be bringing his body with us."

He seemed about to add something, but instead spun around and carried on walking.

Sam stared at his retreating back. It seemed wrong that they weren't taking Trev's body home with them. What was that bloke not saying?

Realising he was being left behind, he jogged to catch up with the group. They were ushered straight through the unmanned security scanners, out to the gate and straight on to the airport concourse.

All without checking in, no one had an allocated seat, and chaos ensued as they boarded the plane. Sam chose a seat next to Dean. He strapped himself in and leant his head back against the headrest. His head was thumping with the after-effects of the alcohol consumed the previous evening.

"Oi, mate, you got any paracetamol? This fucking hangover is killing me," Sam called across the aisle to Ian, oblivious to Dean flinching at the insensitivity of his words.

"Yeah, hang on." Ian, the most organised of the group, rummaged around in his bag, found the paracetamol and threw the silver foil packet over to Sam.

"Cheers," Sam said, catching the paracetamol, popping two out and dry swallowing them. He settled back in his seat and closed his eyes. His last thought before drifting off to sleep was not of his friend Trevor. Nor of the rushed evacuation from Alicante. Instead, it was of the bragging rights he could now claim because he had fucked a virgin.

Two

I stare up at the ceiling, willing myself to find the motivation to get out of bed and start the day. The morning ritual plays itself out. The internal debate of comfort versus caffeine circles in my head. As usual, the lure of a hot cup of coffee wins out, and I push myself out of bed and head downstairs. I wrapped myself tightly in my big fluffy dressing gown. I may be out of bed, but I'm not getting dressed until I've had a drink.

Steve is in the lounge, performing various uncomfortable-looking stretches. His dark brown hair shines with the sweat that is also forming in beads on his forehead.

"Been for a run?" I ask, rather pointlessly. The sweat, the running shorts and stretching are all the clues I need. He grunts at me as I walk past him into the kitchen.

Filling the kettle, then flicking it on, I lean back against the counter and watch him through the double doors that open into the lounge.

If I'm honest with myself, I'm a little jealous of the way he can get out of bed as soon as he wakes up, and run five miles before I've even stirred. The contrast between us is stark. To say I am not a morning person is somewhat of an understatement.

I hit the snooze button on the alarm several times before I even think about getting up. Steve, on the other hand, jumps out of bed before his alarm has even dared to sound. He seems to think that his ways will rub off on me, that it's only a matter of time and I'll be running alongside him at the crack of dawn. He is wrong.

The sound of the water boiling shakes me out of my daydream. "Coffee?" I shout into the other room. Hearing a grunt in return, I decide to take that as an affirmative, and make two cups.

The lounge is empty by the time I carry the steaming mugs through, and I can hear the shower going upstairs. I plop down on the armchair and dangle my legs over the arm. Mornings are the only time I ever sit like this. Mug in one hand, tablet in the other, squashed into the chair.

It's the perfect position for catching up on the events of the world. By the world, I mean my friends, by events, I mean Facebook posts.

I scroll idly through the photographs from drunken Saturday night antics, funny memes and the usual click bait rubbish. There are a few posts that catch my eye. Something must be happening in Spain. Quite a few of my friends sending their prayers and thoughts to the injured. As usual with Facebook, an outpouring of empathy, but little content about what has happened.

My restless curiosity, a term that I prefer to inherent nosiness, gets the better of me. I switch on the TV and turn on the news.

"... and headaches. There is no known cure," states the news anchor. "In other news, George Carlton, CEO of Hillcrofts Ltd, yesterday announced that he is injecting funds to rescue the floundering J.P. Plants. Preventing the company going into receivership will save over three thousand jobs.

In a statement made last night, Mr Carlton said that when the Prime Minister contacted him to propose the deal, he knew that it was in the best interest of the public. It would support the future of the North West, an area he considers to be his second home. Employees are hailing Mr Carlton as a saint and calling for a knighthood."

I laugh out loud at this. George Carlton a saint? What a joke. I've worked for the man as his personal assistant for over ten years.

The only thing he is interested in is himself.

As for calling the North West his second home, it was only last week that he moaned about the disgusting, dirty towns, overcrowded with drunks and degenerates.

I return to scrolling through Facebook, waiting for news of Spain to come back on. Steve joins me in the lounge and takes his usual spot on the sofa. He occupies himself syncing his GPS to his phone to record this morning's run.

My phone vibrates on the coffee table next to me. I stretch forward to pick it up. There is a text from Sally, George's daughter.

I'm safe, on plane home x

That's odd. I haven't spoken to Sally since she went on holiday a few days ago. I ignore the text, assuming it was meant for her dad. I turn my attention back to the news.

"... now, a reminder of today's headlines. There has been an outbreak of the Black Flu in the popular tourist destination of Alicante. The British Embassy is arranging emergency transport for all UK citizens currently in Alicante and surrounding areas."

I immediately pick my phone up again, Sally's text making sense now. She's on holiday in Alicante. Bless her; she knew that I would be worried if I saw the news.

"...like the outbreak in Germany, official sources have confirmed that there is widespread rioting." The image on the screen changes from the newsroom to the scene in Spain. Mobs of people, throwing bricks and bottles at shop windows. Smoke rises from a building. Crowds of people seem to be fighting each other.

"Fucking pricks," I say to Steve, "Have you seen these morons?"

Steve looks up at the television, "They're just taking advantage of the situation, I bet half of them are pissed-up Brits on tour," he laughs.

"We have Dr David Smeadly from the European Centre for Disease Prevention and Control here with us now. So, Dr Smeadly, all the outbreaks so far have resulted in riots and violence. Is this a coincidence, or is this somehow related to the Black Flu?"

The doctor looks a little taken aback by the question, and he pauses a second before replying, *"ZN-134 is a particularly nasty strain of the flu virus. There is no known cure and as far as we have seen, it is one hundred percent fatal. My specialism is in diseases, not human behaviour. However, I would suggest when there is an outbreak of this nature, people get scared and react. I suspect the residents are just responding to the situation, spurred on by opportunists."* He pauses and looks directly into the camera, *"There is absolutely no medical or scientific link between the virus and the violence."*

A flicker of a reaction crosses the news anchor's face, his cheeks appearing to flush slightly.

He pauses, seems to consider the next question, then swallows, *"Rumours have been spreading, since the BBC news report that went viral a few weeks ago, that those who have died from the virus are rising and attacking people."* He ignores the doctor's stunned expression, and continues, *"Some have said that the infected are acting like Zombies."* He leaves the words hanging, silence filling the studio. Then he stands up and walks towards the camera. *"To all the viewers out there, they're hiding it, don't believe what you hear. This is far worse than you are being told, take precautions, st…"*

The TV goes blank. I stare at it for a moment until a technical difficulties message appears on the screen.

"What the hell was that?" I gasp at Steve with a glance in his direction. I'm sure I see him frown, but when he looks back at me, he is grinning.

"Ooooohhhh the dead are walking the earth, oooooohhhhh the zombies are gonna get youuuuu," he says mockingly.

"Dick," I reply.

"It's a joke, Clo; there's nothing to worry about," he says reassuringly.

He knows that I am a little obsessed with zombies. I read a lot, and my favourite genre is post-apocalyptic, specifically zombie apocalypse. Or zompoc, as I prefer to call it, just to wind him up. He hates the way everyone talks now, where everything just has to be abbreviated. I've known him block people from Facebook for overuse of LOL and OMG.

I consider what he said, and the reasonable part of my mind does know that zombies are just fiction. There are so many biological reasons why zombies cannot and do not exist.

My enjoyment of reading the genre is driven by the fascination of what could happen to a society when faced with a ruthless enemy, and left without rules and control.

This is the reason I don't join in with the online forums that discuss, in detail, what to do in a zombie apocalypse.

My preference is of the character-led books, ordinary people becoming heroes and saving the day.

So why was the TV still showing an error message? It's unlikely that a problem occurred at the exact same time as the anchor clearly going off-script. Once again, my natural curiosity drives me to flick through other channels, keen to find more references to the Black Flu.

I'm left disappointed as the other channels just show the usual Sunday morning programming. A mix of religious debates, cooking shows and re-runs of old American sitcoms.

I land back on the news channel and feel oddly comforted when I see the weather report now on the screen.

The weatherman looks relaxed and happy, as though delighted that he has the privilege to be the one sharing that fantastic news that the coming days will be hot and sunny.

"I'm going to jump in the shower," I tell Steve, who's gone back to looking at the stats from his morning run.

I don't catch what he mumbles in response.

Shutting the bathroom door behind me, I drop my dressing gown in a messy heap on the floor. I turn on the shower to let the water heat up and then, just as I do every morning, I spend a few minutes staring critically at my reflection in the full-length mirror.

I'm thirty-four, and I guess not having had children, my body isn't bad for my age and sedentary lifestyle.

Although, I pinch a roll of skin on my stomach, and suspect the firmness of youth is gradually disappearing.

I flex my biceps, and I'm pleased to see that my arms haven't developed bingo wings overnight. That day will come and, just as I do every morning, I make a mental note to myself to find and join a gym. But just like every morning, the thought is soon forgotten as I step into the steaming hot shower and feel the hot needles beating down on my skin. I lather shower gel all over my body, then leave the hot water to rinse that off as I get to work on shampooing and conditioning my long hair.

It's over an hour later when I come back downstairs, my hair now dry and straightened, and make-up applied. "Anything else on the news about the Black Flu?" I ask casually.

"Dunno," Steve replies, "I may have drifted off for a minute there, the zombie apocalypse could come and go in the time it takes you to get ready."

"Haha," I reply caustically, throwing a nearby cushion at him, and cursing as I miss by at least three feet.

"If the dead are walking the earth, you might as well just give up straightaway, with an aim like that," Steve says, grabbing the cushion and throwing it back at me, where it hits me squarely on the head. "I reckon I'll be alright, though," he laughs.

"You don't think I'm with you for your good looks and charm, do you?" I laugh back, "I'm only with you because you'd be able to protect me in a zompoc."

A look of mock indignation fills his face, "I thought you were with me because of my mind, not my army training."

"LOL," I reply pointedly. I quickly take a step back, as he jumps and lunges at me. He's too quick, and I am picked up and thrown roughly on the sofa.

My head bounces off the soft cushions that form the armrest. He pins me down, controlling me with ease. He is much bigger and stronger than me. Running and going to the gym have kept him in good shape, and his lean physique belies his strength. I start to panic as I struggle to free myself.

"Fuck off …" I groan, but it falls on deaf ears. He zones in on my vulnerability, my exposed feet, and the attack begins.

Caught between laughing and squealing, I am unable to form words, so instead kick out at him. I hate being tickled, particularly on my feet. It's my own fault, he never lets me get away with saying LOL without some form of tickle-based punishment.

I eventually manage to wiggle my way out from under him, and run to the other side of the room, still laughing.

Steve sits back on the sofa, looking smug and self-satisfied. I readjust my hair and my clothing, trying to regain some sense of composure and dignity.

"Right, I'm going shopping. Want anything?" I ask him, squeezing my tingling feet into my comfortable black pumps.

"Nope, I'm good," he replies as I lean down and kiss him on the cheek. "Watch out for zombies."

"Fuck off," I reply with a smile and shut the door behind me.

Three

Steve sighed as he heard the door shut behind Chloe. He felt guilty for not being open with her. In truth, he was worried about what they'd seen on the news that morning. So, when she was in the shower, he'd been messaging his old army mates.

Although he'd left the army over two years ago, he kept in contact with the lads in his old squadron. He may now live on civvy street, but they would always be his brothers. The time he had spent in the service meant the world to him, and he was proud to call himself a veteran.

The news coming back was concerning. The army had cancelled all leave, and ordered troops to return to their respective units.

One of his less discreet mates had told him that they'd withdrawn from all non-essential operational tours and exercises. Troops from all over the world were returning to the UK.

In his nine-year military career, he had never witnessed such measures. It seemed unlikely that the events of the last few weeks in Europe, and the sudden recall of troops were unrelated. The fear on the face of the news reporter, when he addressed the camera, was not fake. The Black Flu was a real threat.

He knew it wasn't zombies. The very thought was ridiculous. Zombies were a thing of fiction, of horror movies. They weren't real and never would be. His instincts did, however, tell him that this could be a chemical attack, the likes of which he'd trained for extensively during his years of service. The attack that had never materialised.

The more he thought about it, the more convinced he became that this was the case. Test it in South America. Learn from the test. Perfect the virus, then release it in Europe. It made sense.

A nagging doubt plagued his thoughts. If it was a chemical attack, why release it so slowly? Why allow time to create a cure or vaccination? Why allow time for countries to prepare? It made no tactical sense.

Unless… What if Germany and Spain were not the beginning of the attack. They could have been more tests, or even, small attacks to create panic and discord.

It was all hypothetical, theories that could only be confirmed if the virus were to spread quickly and widely. He'd considered sharing his concerns with Chloe, but didn't want to worry her, based on gossip and speculation. He hoped that he would never know.

For if he did, the worse would have happened and he knew the implications of that; what it would mean if a contagion with such a high fatality rate came to the UK, what it meant for him, for them.

He had never spoken with Chloe about what it meant when he left the army. That he could be recalled in the event of a national emergency. A wide-scale chemical attack would certainly qualify. He knew that it wouldn't occur to her to ask, and therefore she wouldn't worry about it. Unless the time came, he wanted it to stay that way. So, when she came downstairs after the shower, he didn't say a word about his concerns.

Four

George Carlton sat back in his unnecessarily large leather chair, behind his unnecessarily large mahogany desk, in his unnecessarily large office, a self-satisfied smile plastered across his face.

The announcement yesterday had been better received than he could have hoped. Not that he cared, he hadn't saved that company to secure the future of the North West.

George was an expert in people, and in manipulating situations for personal gain. He had become incredibly wealthy by understanding and employing the very basic of principles; it's not what you know, it's who you know.

He had built Hillcrofts Ltd from the bottom up, by applying this principle. Not many people could describe the purpose of the business.

It wasn't in the manufacturing, tourism, retail or financial services sector, but somehow had roots within all four.

With J.P. Plants, he was quick to recognise that another large employer in the manufacturing sector was struggling, and he was politically aware enough to act. The compulsory redundancy of thousands of employees would be the nail in the coffin for the Conservatives in the upcoming General Election.

The public was already lapping up the spin from the other parties, and there was a growing sense of public outrage. The question *"Why were the banks bailed out while manufacturing companies are left to rot?"* was posed time and time again. Not least because of a word in the ear of a journalist who owed George a favour. The answer was always the same; because the banks made the politicians rich.

No one took the time to provide any proof of this, or point out that if one of the big four banks collapsed, it would irrevocably damage the economy of the UK. The opposition party did not want to ruin a good story with facts. The Conservatives knew that arguing with the truth wouldn't appease the public.

They knew they needed action, but floundered around, unsure of just what this was. George had cleverly orchestrated the dissent and then capitalised on the growing pressure. He had contacted the Prime Minister and made his offer.

He would inject the cash, but before they made the announcement, the Prime Minister could visit the manufacturing plant, take the requisite tour, shake the hands of the workers, and kiss the heads of their babies.

Then he would look sorrowfully at the camera, and promise that he would personally do everything in his power to save the company. A few weeks later he would make the announcement that he had found the necessary funding.

The money George injected into the company was enough to buy him a small stake, and would keep them running for another year or so. If they didn't do something to turn their fortune around, J.P. Plants would be out of business.

He stood to lose his investment, but he could afford to. It was a calculated risk, but the reward was more than worth it. Now the Prime Minister was beholden to him; he just needed to choose the right time to call in the favour.

The possibility of a knighthood, though, that was the cherry on the cake. "Sir George Carlton," he announced out loud to the empty room. Yes, he liked the sound of that.

He flicked on the TV, ready to watch the news. An egotistical man, he relished the prospect of hearing himself being talked about in such a positive light. But as he watched, the self-satisfied smile was wiped off his face, and his blood ran cold.

The Black Flu was in Alicante. So was his daughter.

George already knew the Black Flu was a real threat, and that the media had been told to tone down their reports. His contacts had been all too willing to share the speculation and gossip; there had been more outbreaks than reported in the news, and each was followed by unexplained violence.

He just didn't think it would get to Spain, certainly not to a tourist resort like Alicante. All the other outbreaks had been small and contained quickly.

He cursed. Had this been a business deal, he would have thought through all the angles, but when Sally jetted off on Friday to her first holiday with friends, it didn't even occur to him to think of the risk of Black Flu, his mind instead, fully occupied on the announcement the next day.

Why had it not occurred to him until now that, if there were multiple outbreaks, they could not possibly be containing the problem? If they were, it wouldn't be spreading.

He knew why. There was no money to be made; therefore, he hadn't given the Black Flu much thought at all, and now his little girl was in danger.

He reached across his desk, picked up the phone and dialled a number.

Five

Sam woke a few hours later when the plane touched down with a bumpy landing. He stared out of the window as they taxied towards the terminal building. He spotted a few odd things. The sign on the terminal building clearly stated that this was Heathrow Airport. There were six or seven military vehicles parked near to where their plane came to a stop. Soldiers wearing hazmat suits and holding rifles appeared to be waiting for them.

"What the fuck is going on? We're meant to be at Gatwick. My car is at fucking Gatwick," Sam said snapped at Dean.

"Dunno, mate," Dean replied, "Maybe we've been div…" he let the words trickle off as the public announcement system crackled to life.

"We have arrived at Heathrow Airport. Please remain in your seats for further instructions."

Upon hearing the announcement, every single passenger promptly ignored it. Seat belts were unbuckled. People reached up to open the overhead lockers. Mobile phones were switched on, and the noise in the cabin rose as the aisles were filled with passengers, impatiently waiting to move.

"THIS IS CAPTAIN MILLER. I AM A BRITISH ARMY OFFICER. YOU WERE ASKED TO STAY IN YOUR SEATS. NOW SIT THE FUCK DOWN."

As if shot, every passenger promptly sat down, and there was silence throughout the plane. After a few minutes, the PA came to life again.

"Thank you for your patience. You will now quickly and quietly disembark the aircraft. You will leave in single file. You will give your name and your passport to my colleagues waiting outside. You will answer all questions in full and with the truth. You will then be directed to a holding area, where you will be told which quarantine camp you have been assigned to."

The cabin erupted with shouts of, "What the fuck?" and "Why are we being quarantined?"

"SHUT THE FUCK UP," Captain Miller's voice boomed.

Everyone did indeed shut the fuck up.

Sam waited patiently for his turn to leave, the seemingly never-ending hangover beating at his brow. Reaching the door to the plane, and at the queue on the steps, he looked out at the soldiers questioning the other passengers.

"Name," the soldier barked at him when he got to the front of the queue.

"Sam … er, Samuel Brown," he replied, thumbing in his pockets for his passport.

"Have you had contact with anyone infected with the Black Flu?" the soldier asked.

"No," Sam, watched the soldier making notes on the form attached to a clipboard.

"Have you been bitten or scratched in the last 48 hours?"

"Er what... Bitten? No... Oh, but my mate was though. Then the locals kicked him to death, brutal it was," Sam said, thinking his answer would impress the hard-looking soldier.

"Your friend was bitten, when was this? Did you touch his corpse? Did you get any of his blood on you?" the soldier fired questions at Sam in rapid succession.

"Well, er, I wasn't actually there," Sam stuttered.

"I had an early night see, didn't want to drink anymore, so I went back to the hotel." He lied, the thought suddenly occurring to him that admitting contact with anyone in Spain might not be a good idea. "My mates were there though," he added helpfully, pointing towards Dean, Ian and the rest of the group.

"Okay. Thank you. Follow the path to the right, which will take you to the processing area. You will be provided with a sleeping bag and some basic toiletries, you will take these items with you to the quarantine centre you are assigned to," the soldier said, his eyes on the lads that Sam had pointed out.

"Er, cheers mate, thanks," Sam replied, and followed the path indicated. Looking back over his shoulder to see if the rest of the gang were close behind, he was shocked to see them surrounded by soldiers pointing rifles at them.

He watched as they were escorted, at gunpoint, in a different direction from Sam.

Ushered on by the other passengers behind him, Sam stepped into the small marquee that had been set up as the processing area. It was busy, but the noise level was subdued. Soldiers stood guard, holding rifles, watchful eyes observing the crowds. He joined the back of the queue and thought about what he had just seen. Why had they taken Dean and the others away?

He thought back to the conversation with the soldier; he'd seemed very interested when Sam had told him about Trev, and it was minutes after that the others were taken away. Was that why they were taken away? Deep down he knew the answer, but wasn't prepared to admit it to himself.

"Name," the woman behind the desk asked, interrupting Sam's thoughts. He looked down at her. Her face was covered with a surgical mask.

"Samuel Brown," he replied.

"Okay then, Samuel, I'm Theresa." Her voice was gentle and reassuring. "I'm just going to check a few things with you, then we'll get you settled in. Have you encountered anyone showing any of these symptoms?" She handed him a piece of laminate card. Sam quickly scanned the list;

High temperature
Headache
Blurred vision

Muscular aches and pains
Black coloured eyes

"No," Sam answered truthfully.

"Do you have any of these symptoms Samuel?" she asked

"No," he paused, "Well actually I've got a little bit of a hangover, which is like a headache, ain't it?"

Theresa chuckled softly, "Don't worry Samuel, a hangover is nothing to worry about, there's water in the quarantine tent. Make sure you drink plenty, you'll soon feel better." She wrote something on a form and handed it to him. "Okay then, I've assigned you to Tent A. Follow those signs to your right. Pick up your sleeping bag pack on your way. You'll need to give this form to the guard at the entrance." She offered the single piece of paper to him.

"Cheers," Sam said, taking the form and glancing at it. It didn't contain a lot of information. Just his name and a status of *'Clear.'* He followed the signs to Tent A, selecting a sleeping bag from the large pile he passed on the way.

The quarantine tent turned out to be a large marquee, the sort you might see at weddings, but lacking the decoration. It was lit by industrial metal lamps in three of the corners.

In the fourth corner stood two green Portaloos and what looked like a shower block. Near the front of the tent, catering tables were laid out, holding two large urns, mugs and milk portions.

There were about fifty people already spread out in groups of twos and threes, talking quietly amongst themselves as they claimed their spot in the tent. Sam hugged the sleeping bag to his chest, suddenly feeling very alone. A soldier holding a clipboard stood and looked at Sam expectantly.

"Form," he said bluntly, holding out his free hand to Sam.

Sam handed it to him, the guard took it and added it to the pile already on the clipboard.

"Er, what do I do now?" Sam asked.

"Now?" the soldier questioned, "Now you find a spot and sit there until someone tells you otherwise."

"Ah, okay," Sam replied and scurried off to a free patch of floor.

He rolled his sleeping bag out. The paracetamol Ian gave him on the plane had worn off, and his headache was back and worse than ever. Remembering Theresa's kind words, he looked around for water and spotted a water cooler a few feet away. Some water and some more sleep. When he woke, surely the hangover would have gone.

~

"Sam, Sammie, hi Sammie," someone shouted, jolting Sam from his sleep. He opened his eyes slowly, his vision blurry and head still thumping.

"Hi, Sammie, I can't believe you're here. I couldn't find you on Facebook." Sam looked up and audibly groaned.

"Hi Sally," he said, getting unsteadily to his feet. "Oomph," he gasped as she threw herself at him, planting a kiss on his lips. He pushed her away angrily, "Fuck off, what are you doing, you bint?" he asked.

"I thought you'd be pleased to see me, we're going to be here for days, so we'll be able to be together," she said. The hurt was evident on her face.

Sam looked at her steadily, the pain in his head seemingly getting worse by the second. His face twisted into an ugly snarl. "Look, you fucking idiot. You were a one-night stand. A one-off. A fucking hands-free wank. I'm not interested in you and spending time together, you fat ugly cow."

Sally stepped back as though she had been punched. Tears welled in her eyes. "I thought you liked me," she said quietly.

"Well," Sam replied, a cruel smirk on his face. "You fucking thought wrong, didn't you?"

"Fuck you, Sam," Sally said bursting into tears, holding her sleeping bag to her chest, as she turned away from him, and ran to her friends on the other side of the tent.

He ignored the looks of disgust and the tutting around him. Fuck 'em. He had a hangover, the last thing he needed was a one-night stand hanging around.

The marquee had filled up in the time he had been sleeping, no spaces remained on the floor. Groups of people gathered together, talking quietly, those closest openly talking about him and his outburst at Sally. Beyond them were more groups, who seemed to become more animated as he watched. Gesticulating widely and pointing in the direction of the lone guard at the entrance.

Curious now, he focused on one of the larger groups who seemed the most excitable. He couldn't hear everything that was being said, but judging by the pointing and staring at the guard on the entrance, he got the sense that people were becoming angry at the lack of information. He couldn't blame them, he had no idea where his friends were, and no idea how long he had to be here.

He pulled his phone from his pocket. He hadn't used it in Alicante. It had been an unwritten rule that what went on tour stayed on tour, and no Facebook, Twitter or Instagram posts were allowed. Now the holiday was well and truly over. To kill time, he decided he'd check out what had been happening in the last few days.

After waiting a few minutes for a signal, Sam switched it off and on again. Nothing. No signal at all. With nothing else to do, he lay back on his sleeping bag and stared at the ceiling. Just as he started to drift off again, an announcement was made through a loudspeaker.

"Sally Carlton, would a Miss Sally Carlton please report to the admin desk at the entrance. That's Sally Carlton to report to the admin desk at the entrance."

Sam's head jerked up. He turned in the direction Sally had gone and watched as she stood up and looked around in confusion.

She said something to her friends, names he couldn't remember, then walked over to the entrance. She briefly conversed with the guard, before returning to her friends, conferring for a few seconds, then hugging them. Sam continued to watch as Sally made her way back to the entrance. The guard stepped aside to let her out. She hesitated and turned back in Sam's direction, meeting his eyes. She said something to the guard and headed towards him.

For a moment, Sam's mood lifted, she might be a fat ugly cow, but it looked like she was leaving and maybe she was coming over to take him with her.

As she approached, she called out loudly, "Sam, I know it was my first time and everything, but… well... was it supposed to be over that quickly?" she turned, ran her fingers through her hair, and left the tent.

Laughter broke out from around Sam, his cheeks turning a distinct shade of crimson as he heard comments and snickers from others. One, however, was not laughing at Sam. Instead, he was watching Sally as she headed out of the tent.

A well-dressed man, who had clearly been away for business, rather than on holiday, judging by his suit and lack of dodgy tan lines that many others seemed to be sporting

He called out loudly in the direction of the guard that had just let Sally through. "Excuse me, where is that young lady going?" Other heads turned towards the entrance, and the sudden onset of noise hit Sam like a tidal wave. Voices could be heard across the room, protesting Sally's departure, and questioning why it wasn't them leaving.

A voice came through a loudspeaker, announcing that dinner would be available shortly. While this message in no way answered any of the questions being shouted out, it did serve to quieten everyone down.

Sam's stomach rumbled at the thought of food. He couldn't remember the last time he had eaten anything. He watched hungrily as trays of food were put on a long table at the other side of the tent, and he got to his feet to follow the throng of people now pushing their way to the food table.

Sam reached the queue and stood behind the well-dressed man who had shouted earlier. He watched as the man took two tablets out of a small foil packet and swallowed them.

"Ere mate," Sam said tapping the man on the shoulder, "Are they paracetamol? Can I have one?"

"They are, and no you cannot," the man replied, "I have a headache, heaven knows how long we will be in here for."

"Fair enough, I think me hangover's going anyway," Sam replied, watching as the man brushed his suit jacket off where Sam had touched it, the motion causing the sleeve of the jacket to ride up, exposing a small red stain on the cuff of the otherwise white shirt.

"Is that blood?" Sam asked.

"No," the man responded, quickly pulling the jacket back over his sleeve. "It's, um, it's ketchup."

"I like ketchup," Sam replied conversationally, "Although, I only ever have brown sauce on me bacon butties." The man didn't acknowledge Sam's comment, so he continued, "Ketchup is better on sausage sarnies. I wonder what we'll get for brekkie tomorrow. I hope it's a fry-up. You can't beat a good..."

"Please be quiet," the man interrupted Sam. "Have I not just stated that I have a headache? I do not want to get into a conversation with you about bloody breakfast options."

"Alright mate, chill out, yeah, I was just chatting, being friendly," Sam muttered in response.

Both men stood quietly and moved up the queue slowly. When they reached the front, the well-dressed man quickly piled his plate with food, and returned to where he had been standing earlier.

Sam hesitated and looked over the choices.

None of the dishes looked particularly appealing, but the pasta seemed the best option. As he lifted the spoon that was embedded in the cheesy pasta mix, he heard a commotion behind him. Sam laughed when he turned around and saw the well-dressed man on the floor, the plate of food he had been carrying adorning the front of his smart suit jacket.

"Ha, serves him right, arrogant cock," Sam said cheerfully, turning back to the food table and picking up the spoon once more. When he had piled a generous portion on his plate, he made his way back to where he had been sitting. He noticed one of Sally's friends, Paige, crouching over the well-dressed man, shaking him.

"Help, please someone, help, I think he's dead," she called out in panic, her cries muffled by the sounds of the hundreds of people talking.

Sam froze in place as he watched a large woman running over to the soldier at the entrance, gesticulating wildly at him. Then turned his attention back to the man on the floor and the young girl trying to revive him. The man jolted awake and sat up. Sam let go of the breath he hadn't been aware he was holding.

Relieved, Sam carried on his way. Keeping an eye on the scene, he saw when the well-dressed man started hugging Paige.

He was only a few metres away when she began screaming and struggling to pull herself free of the man's hold.Sam let his plate fall from his grip, the cheesy pasta mixture splattering the floor. He could see blood spurting from a wound in Paige's neck. Sam froze once more.

"Everyone move. Now," a voice shouted, causing Sam to jump. He felt himself shoved aside as the soldier from the entrance appeared and assessed the situation.

"Clear the area," the soldier shouted. "You," he pointed at two girls approaching Paige. "Move. Leave her. NOW," he bellowed the last word, and they quickly stepped back.

The squadron had been briefed on the effect of the Black Flu. That it was fatal and that one bite would transmit the disease; that the infected were dying, then rising to attack people, and that only a headshot would take an infected person out.

What he didn't understand was why it was happening in here. This was supposed to have been the low-risk quarantine area. Anyone with any risk whatsoever of exposure should have been sent to the other tents. Apparently, the man had lied.

However, his job was not to question, it was to react. The rules of engagement were clear. Anyone infected must be terminated. Just as he had been trained, he made ready and pressed the safety off.

"Clear the area now," his voice boomed through the crowd. Their reaction was instantaneous. The area was cleared. He took the shot. The head of the well-dressed man burst like a melon, splattering brain matter over a sobbing Paige.

"He was biting me," she cried, her hand clasping her neck, blood dripping through her fingers onto the floor. "I helped him. I don't know why he was biting me."

The soldier regarded the young girl. Knowing what he had to do. "I'm sorry," he whispered as he shot the girl in the head. Lex and Claire rushed over to their friend, both girls sobbing hysterically, and shouting abuse at the soldier. He responded by pointing the rifle at them.

"Stop," he roared, before continuing more gently, "she's infected, don't touch her." He kept his rifle trained on the two girls and spoke quietly into his radio. Lex and Claire collapsed onto the floor, sobbing. The rest of the crowd stood silently, no one knowing what to do, or what to say. What they had just witnessed was horrific, and they struggled to process it.

A team in hazmat suits came running in and started to clean the area. Sam watched on, hunger forgotten, as the bodies of the well-dressed man and Paige were sealed in body bags. What the fuck was going on?

Six

The cool air circulating around the car sends goosebumps up my arms. If I ask the driver to turn it off, I'm sure he will oblige, but it will get too hot in here too quickly. The problem with leather seats is that you need to peel yourself away from them the moment you start to perspire. I'd choose a slight chill over being sweaty every time.

I've been parked up outside Heathrow Airport for hours, and now I'm getting annoyed. We're in one of the bays outside the entrance to departures, usually reserved for the coaches that ferry passengers in from the long-stay car parks. Today there is no traffic.

Earlier, the airport was closed for outbound flights. A few planes still seem to be coming in to land, but not as many as would normally.

What's odd is that in the time I have been here, I haven't seen anyone. Or more accurately, I've only seen people dressed in military attire.

I can only assume the passengers aboard those planes have been shepherded straight into quarantine.

For the hundredth time today, I pick up my work phone and check my emails. I spent the first thirty minutes sitting here, replying to any that had come in since I finished work on Friday, and the next half an hour reading an online paper. Now I am bored.

Very bored. For the first time in my career, I want to hear the phone buzz to tell me that I have an email.

I'd only just got back in the shop, having battled the crowds at my local supermarket, when I received a call from George. He told me a car would be arriving soon and I was to go to the airport and pick Sally up from quarantine.

I've worked for George for so long now that I'm used to being ordered around. I don't like the man.

If I'm feeling kind, I'd call him an arrogant, manipulative bastard. Today I'm not feeling so charitable, so when Steve asked me who had been on the phone, I told him it was The Cockwomble. He knew exactly who I meant.

I stay because the money is good. Every time I've had enough and threaten to leave George just throws more money at me. So now I'm paid way more that I deserve and when I look at other jobs, the salary seems pitiful.

Sally, thankfully, is the opposite of her father. Her mother died when she was four, and she was bought up by a string of different au pairs, none of them willing to put up with George for more than a few months.

As a result, I've been the only constant female influence in Sally's life. While it's not in my job description, I spend a lot of time with her.

It was my shoulder that she cried on when she was bullied at school.

It was me that explained what her period was, and took her shopping for sanitary towels. I was even responsible for persuading to George to let her go to Alicante with her friends, which probably explains why I'm the one giving up my Sunday to collect her.

I must admit, it was pretty cool when I received the email George had forwarded to me from the Prime Minister.

I had naively assumed that it would get Sally released quickly. I was wrong. It turns out that to release someone from a quarantine centre, there are a lot of forms to fill in, and a lot of conversations required. Nearly four hours later, and there is still no sign of Sally.

The last form I completed asked for Sally's hobbies.

It was at that point I began to suspect that they were intentionally making the process as difficult as possible. Maybe they felt that being obstructive was like sticking two fingers up at the PM. I didn't have the heart to tell them that he wouldn't know I existed, let alone cared if I was delayed.

Eventually I see Sally walking over to the car. I get out to meet her half way, and as I approach I can see she's crying and my heart melts. I rush over to her and pull her in for a cuddle.

"Don't worry, sweetheart, we'll get you out of here. Did they hurt you?"

Sally almost laughs, "I'm not crying because of that," she sniffs, "there was a boy and …"

"Ah," I nod with understanding. "What happened?"

We get in the car and fasten our seat belts, as Sally begins to explain the events of the last few days. She is inexperienced for her age, never having had a boyfriend. She had only been kissed once. She was on cloud nine for ages after that until she found out it was a cruel dare. I listen intently to her story; my fists clenching in anger as I hear the way she was treated. Although my anger does abate when she tells me what she said to him on her way out.

"Oh Sal, I'm proud of you, sweetheart. I bet he feels like a right idiot now. Chalk this up to experience and move on."

Sally nods, "You're right. He was a dickhead, so fuck him."

The shock of hearing Sally swear makes me burst out laughing. Maybe this experience might help her grow up a little. Make her a little less naive. She's stopped crying now, but I sense that she's hurting deeply.

"Why don't you try and get some sleep, we've got at least an hour till we get you home." She nestles back in her seat and closes her eyes. I pick up my phone and tap out a message, first to George and then to Steve, letting them know we're on our way.

I shake Sally awake an hour later, as we pass through the wrought iron gates that signal the start of the driveway.

"Wake up sweetie, we're nearly home." She opens her eyes sleepily. "How are you feeling?" I ask.

"I'm okay," Sally replies, "Do I look like I've been crying?"

I look at her red and puffy face, "Just a little," I lie. "Why don't you go straight up to bed. I'll let your dad know you're home. It's probably best he doesn't see you looking upset. You know how he gets."

Sally chuckles, "Yeah, remember the debate team debacle?"

I laugh, remembering his face when he discovered her in the kitchen crying. "Haha, yes, his face was so red I thought he was going to pop."

She'd been crying because she hadn't made it onto the school debate team. He had marched down to the school and shouted at the Headmaster for half an hour. It had worked, Sally ended up on the team. She never told him that she'd been crying because she knew he would be disappointed in her. She hated debate and dropped out after a few weeks.

"Chloe … You won't say anything to him … will you? You know, about last night."

"Don't worry, my lips are firmly sealed," I reassure her. There is absolutely no way I would tell him that his daughter had lost her virginity on the holiday I had encouraged him to let her go on.

Getting out of the car, I hug Sally and give her a kiss on the cheek. "You know where I am if you need to talk," I say as she heads up to her bedroom.

Although I've been in this house many times, it's too vast and ostentatious for me to feel comfortable here. It feels like a museum and my footsteps echo around the hallway as I walk over to George's office and knock on the door.

I wait until I hear the familiar booming "Come," then I step inside.

"Sally's home now, but she's had a long day, so she's gone straight up to bed. Is there anything else you need from me before I leave?"

"My printer has jammed," he replies.

Taking this to mean that I need to clear the jam, I head over to the printer and get to work. It takes me half an hour to detangle the paper and get the printer working again. I'm sweating and covered in toner when I turn to George and ask if he needs anything else.

"I'll work from here tomorrow, so move the meeting with Bill to Tuesday," he replies.

"No problem," I say and rush out of his office before he asks me to do anything else.

"Thank you, Chloe," I mouth as the door closes behind me. I do not mind hard work, and I am not the type of person who needs constant praise and appreciation. However, a little acknowledgement that I had spent most of the day, say, outside the bloody airport, and then spent more time fixing his damn printer, would have been nice.

~

"About time," Steve says, as I walk through the front door. "So how was The Cockwomble?" he asks, then laughs when he notices my face. "Did you fall down a coal mine on your way, or is the cam-cream look fashionable this season?"

I spin around and look at my reflection in the hallway mirror. My face is covered in smears of printer toner. I wipe it with my sleeve. "Printer toner. He was the same as usual. I swear if that man ever had to do anything for himself he would fall to pieces."

Seven

During rush hour, over five hundred tube trains thunder across the London Underground network. Seasoned commuters suffer the daily torture of crowded, hot trains. Their bodies press together to allow as many people to fill the carriage as possible.

Long ago, marketing companies capitalised on the numbers that would spill out of the stifling underground stations into the fresh air. They would offer a free trial of a new product or give away a product that would proudly display their brand. Even the most hardened of commuters will accept the proffered freebie. Their pace not slowing, their eyes still staring straight ahead, they hold out their hands for the goods that they are entitled to as the busy, hardworking people that they are.

On this warm Monday morning, the promotion of choice was bottled water. A new brand that offered advanced science in water filtration; electrolytes that would boost the immune system and add a spring to your step.

Most did not read the label, did not even look at the brand. Some opened the water immediately, taking large gulps to combat the thirst that the morning commute brought. Others put the water in their bags and carried on with their day.

Just another day in the life of a London commuter.

The first sign that anything was amiss did not occur until the evening, and the same journey in reverse that would take many to their homes; even more to mainline stations, where they could board an overground train to hundreds of destinations around the country.

The first to show signs of infection was a woman who boarded the tube at Bank Station. She was sweating profusely, her movements slow as though every step caused her pain. She leant her head against a glass partition and rubbed at her temples to soothe the pounding headache.

The momentum from the tube pulling out of London Bridge station knocked her to the ground. A solitary fellow commuter knelt to check she was okay.

The woman didn't respond to the concerned words offered to her. The good Samaritan called to others for help, but the request was met with silence, as though the pleas were not being spoken aloud.

Every commuter knew that you did not press the emergency stop button on a tube train. It was an unwritten rule. The use of the button would inevitably cause unwelcome delays. Far better to wait until the next station, where she could be removed from the train, so everyone else could get home.

Commuters pressed tightly together, taking care not to look or stare at the woman on the floor, or at the kind person offering her help. Someone falling ill on the underground was not unusual.

It didn't spark much interest or concern. Until a scream reverberated around the carriage. This was cause for concern. This was different. New. Exciting. This was worth staring at.

While many might have regretted their decision to look, the outcome would have been no different.

The good Samaritan was clutching at her arm and wailing, blood pouring through her fingers, and spilling onto the dirty floor of the train. The woman who, just moments ago, had been comatose, now got to her feet, her mouth ringed with blood. She lunged at the closest person. Another scream, more blood.

The tube came to a stop outside Borough station. The announcement about a red light that was holding them went unnoticed. Another scream penetrated the air. Commuters turned their heads to look in the direction of the new sound. It had come from the opposite end of the carriage from where the woman had fallen.

The tube was held at a red light for a matter of minutes. Inconvenient and annoying on most days, deadly on this one. More screams sounded. Blood spurted from a severed carotid artery, the sticky fluid painting the window crimson. The floor became slick and slippery. People pushed each other out of the way in a bid to escape the threat, not knowing that another would be close by.

As the tube doors opened at Borough, bodies spilled out onto the platform, the screams and shouts of alarm combined. All the carriages had experienced a similar order, and chaos and mayhem ensued.

Those that stood patiently waiting to board found themselves knocked over by others fleeing from the carriage. The extra space that the platform offered gave some the opportunity to fight their attackers off, some escaping with small bites, other dying from the sheer amount of blood that they had lost. In the carnage, no one noticed them get up again.

An attacker lunged and knocked a teenage boy through the gap between the train and the platform. He avoided slipping under the metal beast but couldn't prevent the teeth that sank into his arm. Other passengers rushed over to help and pull him up to the platform, only to receive a bite from his attacker as their reward.

Some that fled for the station exit were crushed to death by the throng of scared people, their bodies trampled underfoot without regard for who they once were.

Others sought refuge on the tube, praying that the attackers would follow the masses, or that the train doors would squeeze shut, bringing them safety. Their prayers went unanswered, their hopes crushed, as they squeezed together, no one wanting to be at the front.

An old lady was pushed towards the approaching attackers, and set upon, this attack buying time for others to flee.

Unwitting passengers, unaware of the carnage taking place in the bowels of the city, continue with their commute, boarding escalators that would bring them to the platform and for many, to their death.

Passengers who managed to escape the station to the perceived safety outside, found that their nightmare was not over.

They were greeted by a massacre, representative of what was happening deep underground. Those not yet directly affected by the events, looked on with amusement, assuming this to be a flash mob, a marketing ploy. They stopped and watched with morbid fascination. Selfies were taken, videos shot and posted across social media.

Riot police arrived and formed a barricade. They trapped those fleeing for their lives within the same confines as those that intent on taking them. They watched in silent horror the scene in front of them, powerless to help. If the barricade should break, all would be lost. They didn't know that this was not an isolated incident, that the slaughter they saw before them was being played out across the capital.

Underground services, on all lines, were quickly suspended. Police resources were directed from across the country to support their London colleagues.

To get as many people out and away from the city as possible, the trains from mainline stations were not stopped until later in the evening.

Aboard the trains leaving the city, strangers held muted conversations. As they talked, some sipped water to ease their throats, sore from the shouting and screaming earlier in the day. They were grateful for the free bottle they'd been given that morning. Others nursed their injuries, the bites and scratches, while some sat in silence, images of what they had witnessed flashing through their minds.

Without exception, all were relieved to be going home to the comfort of their loved ones.

Eight

The office chair lets out a soft groan as I lean back and stretch my arms skyward. It's almost five and time to log off. As work days go, this was not a bad one. I love it when George works from home, because it means I don't have to make the commute into the city. The morning was busy, scheduling various meetings for George, mostly with journalists requesting interviews with him. I did my best to accommodate them in his schedule; I am all too aware how much he likes positive publicity. Although I may have accidentally deleted the email from the person who would; *"Simply love to get inside the mind of our new modern day hero."* Oops.

The calls and emails petered off in the middle of the afternoon.

I made the most of the rare opportunity to catch up on some admin tasks I've been putting off for weeks. The laptop screen turns black, and I am finished for the day.

My thoughts turn to dinner. I have about an hour before Steve gets home, so plenty of time to nip to the local supermarket and start preparing our meal. Mexican tonight, I decide. Steve's favourite, because of his love of all things hot. My favourite, because of my love of all things easy to cook.

The supermarket car park is packed. It is usually busy at this time, but today there are no spaces available. I drive aimlessly around until I see a young couple loading up their car. I wait until they leave and pull into the now vacant spot. If I thought the car park was busy, it was nothing compared to the supermarket itself. It's heaving. The week-before-Christmas kind of heaving. I pick up the basket and mentally plan a route that will get me in and out of there as quickly as possible.

First stop is the fruit and veg aisles, peppers and onions my targets. I reach past a man who is piling bags of potatoes into his trolley, and I cannot resist taking a quick peep inside. Checking out what other people are buying is like a game for me. I try to work out a bit about them based on their shopping. I guess this guy is a science teacher and tomorrow's lesson is potato clocks. Either that or he has a serious love of potatoes.

I battle through the steady stream of trollies to get to the meat aisle. It is a bit strange that no one else seems to be carrying baskets. There must be a special offer on today, as most people are pushing trollies loaded so high they are struggling to steer them.

Bargain hunting annoys me. I know that some people need to be frugal, but I've seen people literally shoving each other out of the way to grab a packet of cream doughnuts reduced by ten pence.

It's not the need to save money that bothers me; it's the utter lack of dignity and respect people show each other when there is something to be had for cheap. Although, the way Steve and I shop, we probably could do with a bit of bargain hunting. Neither of us is very organised, so we tend to shop for food daily, which ends up costing us a fortune.

Fajita mix, chicken breast and various sauces acquired, I head straight to the self-service checkouts. The area is surprisingly quiet. I guess no one on the planet has the patience to put a trolley load of goods through those annoying machines. There are queues in and out of the car park. This is ridiculous. What the hell is going on?

Steve is unlocking the front door as I pull up to the driveway.

Upon hearing the engine, he turns towards me. He is silent as he holds the door open for me to step through. There's a strange look on his face. Sad and weary, as though he has the weight of the world on his shoulders. His eyes, normally such a piercing blue, are dull, almost to the point that they are now grey. A sure sign that he has something on his mind.

"Are you okay?" I ask.

He says the words that no one ever wants to hear, "Chloe, we have to talk."

He never calls me Chloe. Always Clo. I laugh nervously, "Oh my God, it sounds like you're breaking up with me."

He just looks back at me and doesn't say a word.

Cold hands grip my heart and the shopping bags drop from my hands and burst open on the floor. I watch an onion roll out of the bag and come to rest at the foot of the stairs.

He bends down and starts putting the shopping back in its bag. I follow him to the kitchen and just stand there in silence, watching him as he puts the food away. I don't want to talk. I don't want to hear what he will say.

Finally, he speaks, "Have you seen the news today?"

I shake my head. What has the news got to do with him breaking up with me?

Taking hold of my hand, he leads me to the lounge, gesturing for me to sit down. He takes a seat next to me on the sofa and turns the TV on. The screen bursts to life with the sounds of screams. Riot police shoot a water cannon at mobs of people fighting each other. A reporter tries to shout over the din.

"Is this Alicante?" I ask Steve. He shakes his head but doesn't say a word.

The scene changes to another reporter in a different location. The word *"Live"* flashes in the top right corner. This reporter stands outside the Royal Exchange, right in the heart of the Square Mile. The realisation that this is happening in London hits me, and I watch in silent horror. All around him are scenes of carnage and destruction.

People are screaming and running. It's plain to see the reporter is anxious, and he's gesturing behind him as he speaks. A woman knocks into him, and he stumbles. His experience takes over, and he quickly regains his composure. He continues with his report, then his eyes go wide, his mouth opens in a silent scream. The camera falls to the floor, rotating the image ninety degrees. The screen now fills with feet running past the camera. Then it goes blank. Just like yesterday. Only this time it's not a technical error message that is displayed. Today the message is telling us to stand by for an emergency broadcast.

"It'll be on in a minute," Steve says, "they've been playing it every so often for the last couple of hours."

"What does it say?"

"Just wait."

Patience is a virtue that I do not possess, but I can tell by his tone that he wants me to see it for myself. So, I stay silent until the Prime Minister's face fills the screen.

"I have just received confirmation that the outbreaks of violence taking place across London are related to the virus known as ZN-134. Similar outbreaks are reported in all major European and American cities. The source of the outbreaks is unconfirmed. This virus is unlike any we have seen before in the United Kingdom.

I will now hand over to Dr Eric Smeadly from the ECDC to explain the virus and the precautions I implore you to take."

The picture changes to the man who was on the news yesterday. Pearls of sweat are visible on his forehead, he is wearing a suit, the top buttons of his shirt undone, his tie askew. It's as if he was not prepared for this broadcast.

"ZN-134 or, as you may know it, the Black Flu, is highly contagious. It has a one hundred percent mortality rate, and ..." He shifts in his seat and straightens his tie, "within moments of death, those infected with the virus are reanimating and ..." He coughs and has the decency to blush, "attacking and biting those not yet infected."

He looks decidedly uncomfortable. As he should, given that only yesterday he had flat-out stated that the violence and riots were unconnected to the virus.

"While ZN-134 is highly contagious, the virus is not airborne. It is passed by fluids, including saliva, blood and semen. Anyone who has been in contact with an infected person should isolate themselves immediately. From what we have learned from earlier outbreaks, the incubation period can vary between twelve and forty-eight hours. This may be dependent on the victim's health, age, gender, and many other, yet to be determined, factors. However, the virus may have mutated. At present, we have little information, and there is no cure."

He coughs again and wipes his forehead with his sleeve. The image returns to that of the Prime Minister.

"I recognise that this news is unsettling. However, I can assure you that we will get this situation under control. We have deployed our armed forces in key strategic locations to control the outbreak in London. I am today calling upon all military veterans, who sit within the standard age brackets for the Regular Reservists, to re-enlist to support this effort. Given the nature of this crisis, we do not have the luxury of time to follow the formal recall process; however, I trust that those affected will do the right thing." He pauses for long seconds and looks meaningfully at the camera, before continuing, *"for everyone else. Please stay in your homes. If you encounter an infected, do not approach them, even if it is a family member or friend. Please remain calm. We will get this under control."*

The screen goes blank. It takes me a few seconds to compose myself, and think about the impact of what I have just heard. It's too much to process. I can't find the words. Reanimated corpses. Zombies. It's happening. I jump to my feet.

"What should we do?" I ask, "Do you think we should board up the windows, oh my God, have we got batteries? I'll go and find the batteries. Tins, yes, we need tins of food. Bottles of water."

I know I'm rambling, but I feel perversely excited. I'm not even talking to Steve anymore. My mind is racing. Planning. I don't hear him say my name until he yanks my hand, making me fall back to the sofa.

"Clo," he says, still clasping my hand. "I need to go."

"To get tins and water. Yes. I know he said not to go out, but …"

"No Clo, I'm a regular reservist. I need to re-enlist."

Just like that. Four little words. All it takes for my world fall apart.

Nine

The mood in the quarantine camp was subdued throughout Sunday night. Few people talked, and those who did, held conversations in hushed whispers, scared by what they had witnessed, and relieved that it had not happened to them. By Monday morning the shock had given way to anger. Tension built in the camp and people were demanding answers. None were forthcoming. Lack of information led to rumours and speculation. Four soldiers now stood guard at in the entrance. They did not engage in conversation with anyone, and stood alert, eyes constantly scanning the crowd for threats.

By Wednesday, the mood seemed to shift to quiet acceptance. Anger abated, and boredom reigned. Groups of people gathered together, chatting and playing games.

No one had spoken to Sam, worse, they treated him like he was not there. Over the past few days, rumours had flown around the camp of the young man laughing as another man died. Sam had heard people talking about it, and he wanted to defend himself. To tell them that he thought the man had just fallen over. That he had been rude to him, but every time he spoke people turned away.

He had given up trying to get a signal on his phone. By Monday night he had drained the battery trying.

So he sat, and he waited. He was lonely. Lying in his sleeping bag the previous evening, he had vowed that today, he would make someone talk to him. It had taken him until lunch time to pluck up the courage. Now he was ready.

He scanned the room, searching for a kind smile, a sympathetic smile.

Any indication that someone would be willing to speak to him. Nothing. Then he spotted Lex and Claire. They were sitting together, not part of a wider group. Maybe they would talk to him. Nonchalantly he made way over to them. Now he was closer, he could see their tear-stained faces. This might be a terrible idea, but he was desperate for some company.

"Hi," he said.

They looked up at him, surprise evident on their faces, "What do you want?' Lex asked.

He should have thought this through. "Er, well I just wanted to say, you know, sorry," he stammered.

"What for?" Lex asked, "being a prick?" Her cheeks flushed, anger rose to the surface, and the colour clashed with her fiery red hair. Her feelings towards Sam were clear, and he took a step back. Talking to them had been a mistake.

"No … well … for your friend, that must have been proper horrible to see."

"Thank you," Claire replied graciously.

"You're still a prick," Lex added, scowling up at him.

"I know. I was proper mean to Sally. I was hungover, and you know, well it was supposed to be a one-night thing …" he paused and let the words hang in the air. Apparently, that was not the right thing to say. The two girls glared at him.

"Well, anyway, sorry about your mate," he said and turned away.

"Wait," Claire called out.

Sam turned to face her, "What, so she can call me a prick again?" He asked, tilting his head at Lex.

"No, I just wondered if you had heard anything about what's going on." she replied, ignoring the daggers Lex was sending in her direction.

"Nah, nuffin," Sam replied. "No one has said a word to me in days. Have you heard anything?"

"Everyone is talking about what happened to Paige …" Tears welled in her eyes. "That man bit her. They are saying he was a zombie," Claire said.

Lex snorted but remained silent.

"Ha, zombies." Sam laughed, then noticed Claire's obvious distress. "Sorry. Um no, it can't be zombies. I reckon that bloke got confused and attacked Paige by mistake."

He gestured over at the soldiers standing guard at the entrance. "That squaddie knew she would get the Black Flu. See, it's contagious ain't it? I bet they couldn't risk passing it on to everyone else."

"Okay," Claire said, drawing the word out, "I guess that would make more sense. What do you think?" she turned to Lex, wanting to engage the other girl in the conversation.

"I still think he's a prick, but I think he's right. Zombies don't exist. They can't exist. It's impossible," she replied, "There is something that I don't understand, though. I thought the Black Flu had an incubation period of up to forty-eight hours."

"A what period?" Sam interrupted.

"Look," Lex huffed. "just sit down for a minute. Looking up at you is making my neck hurt." She ignored the smile on Sam's face as he took a seat next to her. "An incubation period is the time it takes for a pathogen, like a virus, to show symptoms."

Sam nodded, "Okay, so?"

"Well," Lex said, "if the incubation period is up to forty-eight hours, that means that we could be infected without showing any symptoms for two days."

"Right," Sam said knowingly, "er … so?"

"So, we left Alicante around six on Sunday morning. Anyone infected would have shown symptoms by now." She looked expectantly, first at Sam and then at Claire, as though expecting something.

"Yeah, I guess," Sam said, "oh, I see, we're not infected. That's good, innit?"

"It is, but if we're not infected, why are we still in a quarantine camp?" Claire asked.

"Exactly," Lex replied.

"Ah," Sam's confused expression turned to one of realisation. He thought for a second. "Ere, can you get a phone signal?" he asked. "Maybe we can call someone. The papers or summat to tell them we're being held captive."

"Nope, neither of us have had any since we landed," Claire answered.

"I'm not sure the papers would really care about us, either," Lex added, "I wouldn't mind phoning Sally, though." An uncomfortable silence fell on the group at the mention of Sally's name.

Eventually, Sam spoke. "Um, why?"

"She told us that as soon as she got home, she was going to get her dad to get us out too," Lex said.

"Oh, well, I'm sure she's trying," Sam said, not really believing his own words. If Sally's dad had managed to get her out so quickly, surely, he could have got these two out by now.

The conversation stalled, each lost in their own thoughts.

Sam broke the silence, "How do you know all this smart shit?" he asked Lex

"I like science, that's all," she muttered, as though ashamed of the admission.

"Ha," the laughter lit up Claire's face. "That's a bit of an understatement. Lex is a complete science nerd. She's going to be a doctor."

She leaned over and gave Lex's hand a squeeze to show that there were no hard feelings.

"I didn't do good at science when I was at school. It was too hard." Sam said. 'In fact, I didn't do good at much at school."

"Well," Claire said.

Sam waited for her to continue. When she didn't, he prompted, "Well what?"

"You didn't do well at school. Not you didn't do good," she corrected him, "Saying you didn't do good is a poor use of English."

"See, I've already learnt more sat here for five minutes that I did in years of school," he grinned.

This prompted a conversation about their school years, and they spent the afternoon talking. Sam found out that the two girls had been friends with Sally and Paige since their early school days, although it didn't sound like the four of them had been very popular.

In fact, they were the types of people Sam and his mates would have taken the piss out of when he was at school. Studious, serious and talented.

In contrast, Sam had been very popular, he'd had a large group of friends and his pick of the girls. Yet he had left school with no qualifications and a bleak future, whereas, Lex, Claire and Sally were all at college, studying hard to get into university, and ultimately into their dream jobs.

The afternoon turned to evening. Eventually, Sam yawned and stretched,

"Right, well, erm cheers. It's been nice. You know? Chatting. I guess I'd best leave you to it."

"Actually Sam, you're alright when you're not acting like a prick," Lex said.

"That's Lex's way of saying goodnight," Claire said, smiling.

"Oh …, er … right, well, goodnight," he replied and trundled across the other side of camp to his sleeping bag.

He zipped himself up in his sleeping bag, the conversations of the afternoon replaying in his head. It had been nice, talking to them. He couldn't remember when he had just sat and chatted with girls without thinking of ways to get them in bed. He drifted off to sleep with a small smile on his face.

~

"Sam … Sam …" His name being called penetrated his dreams and made him fidget in his sleep. It was the motion of his body being shaken that eventually roused him. He opened his eyes sleepily, and peered into the darkness, trying to make out the owner of the hand on his shoulder.

"Sam, wake up." It was Claire, who was still shaking him.

"Gerroff," he groaned, "what time is it?"

"Around four I think," Claire whispered.

"Something strange is going on," Lex interjected, startling Sam. He rolled in his sleeping bag to see her on the other side of him. "The soldiers have gone." His eyes now adjusted to the darkness, Sam could see that she was pointing in the general direction of the entrance.

"What do you mean, gone?" he asked, "maybe they've gone for a piss."

"I don't think so," Lex said, "I got up to use the loo a couple of hours ago, and they were gone. They haven't been back since."

"So?" Sam asked, his sleep-addled mind failing to grasp the problem.

Lex sighed as though the answer was obvious, "So, why would they just sneak off in the middle of the night? Surely they should have just waited until morning and let us all go home?"

"Oh yeah. Good point. Um … well, maybe they …um, it could be …" Sam tried to think of a logical reason but his mind came back empty, "I dunno, maybe we should see if they're outside somewhere?"

Another sigh from Lex, "Good thinking, genius. Why do you think we woke you up? We didn't want to go on our own."

"No need to be like that," he said. "I'm still half asleep. You could have just fucking said that."

"Look." Lex snapped. "Just go back to sleep. We'll manage on our own."

"Sorry," Sam replied, "I'm a bit of a grumpy dick in the mornings. Course I'll help. Just gimme a sec to wake up." He made as though to stand, but he forgot he was in his sleeping bag. He lost his balance and tumbled down, knocking over Lex who was still crouched next to him.

Unable to help herself, Claire let out a loud laugh.

"Ssssshhhh," Sam and Lex chorused. A few sleeping bags rustled nearby, the occupants shifting in their sleep.

Sam added in a whisper, "We don't want to wake the rest of these grumpy fuckwits. They'll all be wanting to come." Trying to make as little sound as possible, he untangled himself from Lex, then extracted himself from his own sleeping bag.

Claire's phone emitted enough of a soft glow to allow them to navigate through the sea of sleeping bodies. They reached the entrance without incident. A table held two half-empty mugs of coffee, a clipboard and a torch.

"Torch," Sam exclaimed unnecessarily and picked it up. "This might come in handy." His hands moved to the coffee cups. "Cold," he said.

Lex rolled her eyes behind him. "Well, if they left a couple of hours ago the coffee would be cold, wouldn't it?" She hissed. "Seriously Sam, is there no end to your genius?"

"Sounds like I'm not the only one who's a dick in the morning." Sam retorted.

"Prick," said Lex.

"Dick," replied Sam.

"For goodness sake, you two, pack it in," Claire hissed. "Now are we going or not?" All three of them turned towards the entrance of the marquee. Yet none of them took a step towards it.

"What if it's locked?" Sam asked, suddenly nervous at the thought of leaving. The soldiers could be on the other side.

"Oh, my God," groaned Lex. "It's a bloody marquee. How on earth would they lock it?'

"Oh, erm yeah … good point." He felt the blush rise up his cheeks. He turned to Lex, "Well maybe you should go first."

"Me?"

"Yeah, you're the brains, makes sense for you to go first, you know, assess the situation."

"You're a man. You should go first, make sure it's safe." Lex countered.

"What happened to equality?" he said.

"What happened to being a gentleman?" she countered.

He tried a different tack. "What good would I be against soldiers with guns?" As soon as the words left his mouth, he knew he had said the wrong thing.

Even in the dim light of the tent, he could see the red flush of anger surge across her face. "So, you're saying it's okay for me to go and got shot, but not for you?"

"Well, I'm not going first," Sam stated, folding his arms resolutely.

"Well, neither am I," Lex said, mirroring him.

They stood and glared at each other, neither willing to be the one to concede.

"Are you two coming or not?" Claire called out quietly. Lex and Sam turned in the direction of her voice. She was standing at the entrance, holding open the door, grinning.

It had been daylight when they'd entered the quarantine tent on Sunday. Now it was dark, very dark. No moon brightened the sky. No lights twinkled in the distance.

"It's dark," Sam said

"You have a torch." Lex said, adding *"genius,"* under her breath.

Sam laughed, "Oh yeah," the tension from minutes ago having eased now that he knew he was not about to get shot. He flicked the torch on, but he was disappointed to see that it did little to penetrate the consuming darkness.

"Wasn't there different zones or summat?" He asked, trying to remember what he had seen when he first arrived at the quarantine camp.

"Yes," Claire replied. "We were in Tent A. Which implies that there must be at least a tent B.

"There must be. They took my mates somewhere else. We should go and find the other tents."

"Okay," Claire said, "good idea."

They edged forward slowly until eventually, they came across a sign pointing back the way they had come for tent A, and ahead for tent B. As they got closer, the outlines of another marquee started to emerge from the darkness.

"Turn the torch off, someone might see us," Claire whispered. The urgency in her voice prompted Sam to act quickly, and the darkness engulfed them once more.

Claire led the way, keeping a slow pace so the others could keep up. She frequently turned to check they were still behind her.

At the entrance to the marquee, she paused. The tilt of her head implied that she was listening for something. Apparently satisfied, she said, "It's quiet, let's go in."

"Okay," said Sam, relieved that Claire was taking charge. He would never admit it, but he was more than a little scared. This way he didn't look like a chicken.

Claire slowly unzipped the entrance. Holding the thick canvas material in one arm and pulling her phone out with the other, she whispered, 'I'll use my phone for light, it's not as bright as the torch."

She pointed the phone at an angle in front her, so that they could be confident they would not step on anyone or anything as they edged deeper into the marquee.

Then Claire stopped abruptly. "Oh, my God," she said.

Sam peered over her shoulder, "Why are they all sleeping zipped into their bags? It's not that cold in here," he laughed, at the same time as Lex let out a small gasp.

"Sam," Claire said, "turn the torch on."

"But we'll wake them up," he protested.

"No," she said slowly. "I don't think we will."

Sam turned the torch on and pointed it immediately in front of him, realisation dawning. He stepped forward and peered down. "They're not sleeping bags, are they?" he asked.

"No," Lex said, kneeling in front of one of the still forms, and unzipping the bag to reveal a pale white corpse. A bloodied red hole in the centre of the forehead, contrasting with the ivory pallor. "They're body bags."

Sam aimed the torch left, then right, straight ahead into the distance, then immediately in front. He let out a low whistle. "There are tons of them."

"Hundreds," Claire confirmed.

Sam knelt next to Lex and shone the torch at the half-exposed corpse. Before he could stop himself, he reached out a tentative finger and poked at its cheek. The skin felt cold and firm. Disgusted and slightly freaked out, he pulled his hand away sharply. The momentum knocked him off balance, and he fell backwards to land on another body bag.

The torch rolled across the floor but was promptly snatched up by Lex. Sam scrambled to his feet and bolted out of the marquee. The sound of him vomiting permeated through the stillness of the night.

Lex groaned, "Claire, could you go and check if he's okay, please?"

"Don't you mind being left in here alone?" Claire asked, shuddering involuntarily.

"They're just people. I want to take a look at a few," Lex said, already unzipping another bag and shining the torch at the face.

"Er … okay … well if you're sure,' Claire said and fled from the tent.

"Mmm," Lex said, absorbed in her thoughts. She checked another bag; all three corpses had been shot in the head. Of course, she was assuming that it was a gunshot wound, but she could not think of anything else that would cause that type of injury. She unzipped the bag all the way. Exposing the entire body. There was an open wound on the calf. A chunk of skin and muscle had been ripped from the leg, exposing the bone. She continued to check each bag.

The next four were all a variation on the same theme. A gunshot wound to the head. Another injury somewhere else on the body.

The fifth bag she opened was different. A gunshot wound and another injury were both present. It was the face that was different. It was covered in blood. Lex reached into her pocket and dug out some tissue.

She spat on it and then used it to clean the face, hoping to find a cut that would explain why the blood was there. Nothing.

She moved from bag to bag. Unzipping each. Taking a quick look before moving on to the next. She found more with blood on their faces, but still no evident sign of an injury that would have caused it to be there.

Chewing on her bottom lip, she processed this information. What it meant was obvious. Yet she could not accept it. She opened more bags and gave the encased bodies nothing more than a cursory glance, as she thought it through.

Sam came back into the marquee. "Lex … can we get out …?" his words fell short as he eyes settled on one of the exposed bodies. "No…" he whispered, 'it can't be …' hearing the distress in his voice Lex turned to him. He had turned a ghostly shade of white.

"What's wrong?" she asked. In the few hours she had known Sam, he had not given her any impression of emotional depth, yet now as she stared at him, he looked lost and vulnerable. She joined him next to the body he was looking at. "Did you know him?" she asked.

"Yeah, he's my best mate... Dean, we were on his stag in Alicante… He's. He was getting married." Sam said, his voice breaking. A thought occurred to him, and he started frantically searching the other bags.

It wasn't long before he found Ian and the other four lads that he had spent the weekend with.

"I'm so sorry, Sam," Lex said softly and put her arm around him. Unused to displays of affection, or to being treated with empathy, the act caused Sam to flinch as though her touch burned him.

"Don't fucking touch me," he exploded. She recoiled, uncertain of what she had done wrong. "Don't try to make me feel better. My mates are dead. All of my mates are fucking dead. And you're fucking sorry? Do you even know how that feels?" The words gushed from him, an uncontrolled torrent of abuse. "You don't even like me, so don't go around pretending that you care. Just leave me the fuck alone."

Anger bubbled up within her throughout his tirade. When he had stopped shouting she raised herself to her full height and stood with her face inches from his.

"How dare you?" She said. "A few days ago, I saw one of my best friends get shot. Right in front of me. So don't you dare tell me I don't know how it feels." Her tone was indignant and challenging.

"What the hell is going on?" Claire asked, having run back into the tent after hearing the shouting. "What's happened?" Sam and Lex stood glaring at each other. "Right fine. If you're not going to answer me, then at least start moving. I don't like it here, it's creepy."

"Fine," said Lex.

"Fine," said Sam and stalked towards the exit.

"Hang on,' Lex said, her voice returning to a normal level. She rushed back to the bodies and zipped up all of the bags she had opened. Sam stared at her, refusing to give her the satisfaction of asking what she was doing. "Just out of respect," she mumbled in response to the question that hung unsaid in the air.

Sam was still angry. In his heart, he knew that Lex had done nothing wrong. Had she called him a prick and told him to man up, he would have just shrugged it off. It was the comfort and sympathy she offered. His mind could not differentiate between empathy and pity, and he had lashed out. Now he was angry at himself for his words, yet he could not find the words to apologise. Instead, he turned on his heel and left the tent.

Watching him storm through the opening, Claire asked in a quiet whisper, "What happened? Why were you arguing?"

"It doesn't matter," Lex said. "Some of his friends are in here … he didn't take it well." While she was fuming with Sam, at his words and his behaviour, she knew that he was upset and lashing out. So she would not repeat his words to Claire.

"Okay, but why …" Claire started, sensing that Lex was holding something back. It occurred to her that if this were the case, then Lex would have a good reason. So instead she changed the subject. "Why were you looking at them?" she gestured towards the rows of bodies.

"Ah… I have a theory!" Lex said, her face coming to life as she remembered the conclusion she had reached. "So, every one of the bodies …'

Claire interrupted. "We should probably wait until we've caught up with Sam."

"Fine," said Lex sullenly.

The sky had lightened as night turned into early dawn. It was easy to make out the form of Sam sitting on the ground ahead of them. He held his head in his hands and even from a distance it was easy to see that he was crying. The two girls approached him.

Lex stood back a little, arms crossed, glaring down at him. Claire crouched next to him and put her hand gently on his shoulder. "Lex told me about your friends. I'm so sorry Sam, I can't begin to imagine how you are feeling," she said gently. Sam looked up at her, his tear-filled eyes meeting hers. Her concern was genuine, and her words were heartfelt.

"They're gone …, all of them," he said, his voice thick with emotion. A solitary tear rolled down his face. "I think it might be my fault."

"Oh Sam, of course it's not, how could it be?" she said, wrapping both arms around the sobbing young man.

"I told those squaddies about Trev … That they had seen him get bitten… then they… they took them away," he sobbed.

"Bitten?" asked Lex, her curiosity getting the better of her. "What happened to him?"

"Well, I don't know. I wasn't there... But Dean said that some locals came and kicked him to death. Kept kicking him in the head. But they didn't go near him, so if he was infected, they wouldn't have caught it. I don't understand why they took them away." Sam replied, the tears making his eyes shine in the dawn light.

'In the head… hmmm… That's interesting.' Lex said.

"Fucking interesting?" Sam said. "How the fuck is that fucking interesting?" Realising her insensitivity, Lex looked shamefaced.

"Sorry Sam, I didn't mean it like that." she said, her tone softening. "It's just that I have an idea about what might be going on … I get a bit carried away."

Sensing another argument brewing, Claire stepped in, "Look, guys, we need to work out what to do next. Lex, why don't you tell us your theory, it might help us decide."

"Okay," Lex said. "That guy in the suit bit Paige, right?" She continued without waiting for an answer, "some of the people in the other tent looked like they'd bitten people. Your mate, Trev," she nodded at Sam, "was bitten."

'Yeah... so?' Sam said, failing to grasp Lex's point.

'Ah,' Claire said, "You're saying that something is making people bite each other. It would be too much of a coincidence otherwise."

"Exactly," Lex nodded enthusiastically. "I think it's safe to assume that it's the Black Flu and it is passed by being bitten.'

"Why?" Sam asked looking confused.

"Because the soldier shot Paige, even though she wasn't attacking anyone. The only reason he would have done that is because he knew that if he didn't, she would start biting people too. Which also explains why everyone in the other tent had been shot, they all had injuries, which could have been from being bitten."

She looked at Sam, who seemed to process the information before nodding slowly.

"Right, that makes sense," he said, relieved that he finally understood what Lex was talking about. "So you're saying they are zombies then?"

"What? No, of course not."

"There is an infection. The infected bite people. They die by being shot in the head. Zombies." Sam's face lit up in a grin.

"That's absurd." Lex states matter of factly. "Firstly, while the people in there were shot in the head, they might equally have died if they'd been shot anywhere else. Secondly, zombies are reanimated corpses. We have not seen anyone die and rise from the dead. Therefore, we have insufficient evidence to draw a conclusion."

"Bet ya it's zombies," Sam replied.

"Although, suit guy did collapse before biting Paige. How do we know that he didn't die and reanimate?" Claire added.

Lex opened her mouth to respond and then closed it again. She had forgotten that.

"See, it's totally zombies," Sam said, the delight at beating Lex to the conclusion evident on his face. Then the realisation hit. "Oh shit. Zombies."

"Maybe," Lex conceded.

"What I don't understand is how suit guy got infected in the first place, and why he was in with us," Claire said.

Sam thought back to his conversation with suit guy in the queue for food on Sunday night. He had been rude, not getting involved in the conversation about bacon butties. About whether to have brown sauce or tomato ketchup.

"I know," Sam announced. "I talked to Suit Guy in the food queue. He had a red stain on his shirt. He told me it was ketchup. What if it wasn't what if it was blood and he had been bitten?"

"How big was the stain Sam?" Lex asked.

"Er ...' he paused thinking back, "It was tiny. About the size of a pound coin. Why does that matter though?"

"If it's a bite it would be likely bigger than that," Lex replied absentmindedly. She went quiet for a few long seconds. "What if it was a scratch though?" she finally added.

"What if you could become infected by being scratched?" She didn't wait for an answer. "It must be bodily fluid. Saliva from a bite would get direct into the bloodstream, but a scratch … any residue from the nails would get into the blood stream too. Although …" she paused again, "It might take a bit longer."

Sam looked at Claire, who shrugged her shoulders at him. "You get used to it," she said in response to his unspoken comment. "She goes off at tangents every now and then. What I think she's saying is that the infection is passed by bodily fluids. So saliva, blood, etc." She turned to Lex, "Right?"

"Yes, exactly," Lex replied. The sun was now dawning on the horizon, the sky now light. "We'd better get back before anyone realises we're gone. I don't want to tell anyone about this until we know more."

"Why?" Sam asked, the familiar look of confusion back on his face.

"It will cause panic. We don't know these people, and don't know what they'll do if they are scared. I'm worried that they'll start a riot. Let's go back to our tent and figure out what to do next." Lex replied, already heading back to their tent. "We might not have much time, though."

"Why?" Sam asked again. Lex was really smart and in comparison, he felt like an idiot.

"Because I don't think those soldiers are coming back, and it won't take long for people to start asking questions." She replied as she opened the entrance to the marquee and tiptoed quietly back inside.

Ten

Chloe,

Well this is weird. Writing to you I mean. I can't even remember the last time I put pen to paper to write an actual letter. Although is this a real letter? It's not as if I can pop to the local shop, buy a stamp and expect the Royal Mail to deliver it to you. So why am I writing? I don't know. I don't know if you'll ever read this. After what I found out today, I can't even be certain you'll survive the week. Wow. Sorry. That's harsh. But I am worried sick about you. And there is nothing I can do about it.

Except write to you. It makes me feel closer to you, like we are having a conversation. You may never read this letter, but knowing it is intended for you does give me some comfort.

Anyway, I got here yesterday morning. I don't know what I was expecting, but the drive here was alright.

A little quiet on the roads but after what we watched on TV, I was foreseeing some sort of Mad Max experience, but it wasn't like that at all.

As soon as I got here, they put me on a condensed training course. Mostly refreshers on what I learnt in Basic all those years ago. I've got to do quite a lot of PT (Physical Training), which has been great.

Well, for me at least. Some of the other Reservists here - well, to put it kindly, they haven't put quite as much effort into staying fit and healthy as I have. There was this one guy who I thought was going to have a heart attack, and that was just on a one-mile run. The problem is while we all know we could be called up, no one expected it to happen, and the excesses of civilian life have taken hold of some of these guys.

Weapons training, or Skills at Arms, as they call it, was interesting. We're all basically retraining ourselves to take head shots rather than the centre of mass. I guess these things really are zombies. Hah! Maybe your zombie obsession will come in handy.

So anyway, we're being assessed, and there seems to be an abundance of clipboards. I guess it's to be expected, we're definitely not a fit group. It would have just been nice if they'd told us what they were looking for. We didn't even know if we'd all be allowed to stay. I've been living on civvy street a bit too long and forgot how little we actually get told in the military.

But we didn't have to wait long. We had a briefing this afternoon. This was the first time I had seen any of the men currently serving that had been in the thick of it. Jesus, Clo, you should have seen some of their faces.

These lads must have seen some hideous things on operational tours, but whatever happened out there must have really freaked them out.

There was still the typical banter, but I don't know how to explain it, they just seemed frightened.

If this was a real letter, I couldn't tell you what was in the briefing, but as you'll never read it, here goes.

Turns out it was a terrorist attack. The virus was released in all major European and American cities. They, you know, the powers that be confirmed that the South America and other earlier outbreaks were trial runs. Get this, they believe it was contaminated water given to commuters. It scares me to know how easily it could have happened to you. But Jesus, how did we not know this was coming? The planning that must have gone into simultaneous attacks around most of the western world. Jesus.

Sorry, I'm digressing. We heard dire warnings about how this was unprecedented and unlike anything we've faced before. Yeah, no shit. What was fucking scary though, thirty-seven percent of the population of Britain is infected. In only two days.

More in the big cities. London is at eighty-two percent. That's six and a half million people infected in London alone, and it's getting worse by the day. The funny thing is, other than a few frowns, there was no real reaction around the room.

Well, that is until they told us that we hadn't had any military casualties yet. That got massive cheers.

I guess the numbers are too vast to comprehend, but no military causalities, now that is something we can all relate to.

The officer giving the briefing pissed on our parade quickly, he made it clear that it's not going to last. He even used the words extinction level event. Seriously, he used those words. I suspect the plan was to scare the shit out of us. Needless to say, it worked, well it did for me anyway. He then went on to tell us about how it is our responsibility, the army that is, to create a safe environment to ensure the survival of the British Empire.

Then he dropped the bombshell of a plan on us. The mission. We're going to be creating safe zones, all over the country. Areas that will start small and then expand out until we create a sustainable living space. That's right. They aren't talking about stopping or containing this. Sure, we'll fight it, but only to create the safe zone.

The zone we're assigned to is Zone E. At its heart will be Linthem Barracks. Everyone who is here will join the guys already posted there.

Basically, we need to secure the safe zone, eradicate all presence of infected in the area. Then create a secure perimeter. Secure, but it will need to be movable for when we expand. Then lastly, we'll need to build a liveable and sustainable living environment. So yeah, quite the task!

I'll be honest, I'm shocked that we aren't going to be fighting back and regaining control of the country. It feels like we've given up before we've even tried.

We just don't have the resources to spread ourselves out across the country, so we start small and get bigger. It's logical. It's sensible. It's utter bullshit. Civilians already living in the areas will be used to help with the third part of the plan. Civilians not in the area will just need to fend for themselves until the safe zones are big enough to include them. So yeah, basically we're leaving people to die.

I can tell you that did not go down well. One guy started kicking off. He'd left his wife and two kids to re-enlist. Like me, he assumed that this would be easily controlled and over quickly. He did get invited to leave and go back to his family, he even stood up ready to go. Then the officer said, and I quote, "Intelligence suggests that failure to secure areas will ultimately result in total annihilation of the population of the UK within twelve months. However, by following this plan, we can achieve up to a forty percent survival rate."

The guy that kicked off didn't leave. Total annihilation of the UK versus forty percent survival? You can't argue with that. If everyone one of us left, the plan would fail. Everyone would die.

We then got told why we'd been assessed over the past couple of days. Everyone is staying.

The less fit guys are assigned to some shitty tasks, like clean up and disposal. I'm lucky, at least I think I'm lucky. I'm assigned to front line infantry. Hopefully, I can make a difference. I need to make a difference.

I need my decision to leave you to mean something. If I'd only known how bad it would get so quickly, I wouldn't have left. No, that's not true. I would still have left, but I would have taken you with me.

Before the end of the briefing, we got told just how different this enemy is.

I am going to quote this again; "The days ahead are going to be difficult. This is a new type of enemy. He does not sleep. He does not love or hate. He has no pity or remorse. He will not listen to reason. He could be your mother, your little sister, your grandfather or your best friend. So tonight, do whatever you need to do to relax, because tomorrow, we are going to war."

Quite the motivational speech!

I love you, stay safe.

Steve xxx

Eleven

I'm angry. In fact, no scratch that. I'm *fucking* angry. I'm really fucking angry. At myself. How is it possible to have been so stupid?

When Steve left on Tuesday morning, my anger was directed at him. I spent ages drafting messages on my phone, only to delete them and start again. I spent so much time writing those damned texts, by the time I'd finished, my anger had abated. Whether I liked it or not, he had done the right thing by leaving. The army needed him more than I did. They would get this thing sorted, and he would be home before I knew it. I could not articulate in so few words, that I understood now, could not bring myself to admit that I had overreacted and had been selfish with it. So, in the end, the text that I sent was simple.

I love you xxx

He still has not replied.

I called in sick to work that day. We had been up all night, talking and fighting.

I just couldn't bring myself to face anyone, even remotely. I rang George and was so relieved when it went to voicemail. I knew that I would cry if he asked me what was wrong. I had made myself a promise a long time ago; George Carlton would never witness me cry. The cold bastard would probably take pleasure in it.

I spent the rest of the day wallowing in my self-pity. I came to accept Steve's decision, but I was still selfishly thinking of myself. The events that had led him to leave took a back seat. All I thought about was me.

Stupid.

It was only late on Tuesday evening when I became bored of moping, that it occurred to me to find out what was happening.

Who would have guessed how quickly the world would descend into chaos when the dead started walking the earth? Well, me for one. I should have known. I should have least considered it. I have read so many zombie novels, and seen so many films. Even when I first watched the news with Steve, my reaction was to plan and prepare. Instead, I did nothing.

I guess somewhere in the back of my mind I had assumed that it would all be sorted quickly. Just like it had been in South America and Germany. I did not consider the fact that containing a virus in a small village is relatively straightforward. Containing it in cities, cities with transport links to the rest of the country, is an altogether different matter. So, by the time I'd switched on the TV, I was shocked to discover just how bad things were.

Many channels were showing a particularly unhelpful emergency message. Advising viewers to stay in their homes. Warning us not to approach the infected.

All the other channels that were still broadcasting were only showing the news. Except for E4. They were showing reruns of *"The Big Bang Theory".'* A smart move, why let the apocalypse get in the way of good viewing figures?

The news was grim. Aerial footage of London showed horrific scenes. Fire raged throughout the city.

The cameraman, safe in a helicopter, zoomed in to show crowds of people fighting, each other, as well as with the infected.

Censorship seemed to have gone out of the window. The images were graphic. Close-ups of bodies being torn apart by hordes of undead. Text scrolled across the bottom of the screen, listing the cities affected. It would have been quicker to list the cities that were not. It wasn't just the UK either. It seemed like most of Europe and America were under siege.

I stayed up all night watching the news. Morbid fascination, I guess. Sitting there in the comfort of my own home, it did not feel real. It was like watching a movie. It was actors and special effects, not real cities, not real buildings, not real people.

I phoned in sick again on Wednesday. Voicemail again. I did not even bother to get dressed, and just spent the day watching the news. It was as though I was binge-watching the latest box set. I could not get enough of it.

Which is why, on this grey and cloudy Thursday afternoon, I am so fucking angry with myself.

This morning, I decided to go food shopping. I grabbed my handbag and car keys and left the house. Sat in the car, ready to start the ignition, I cursed and got back out of the car. I had forgotten to take carrier bags. Since the introduction of the 5p charge, I had successfully remembered to bring them with me on a grand sum of two occasions. It's not that I mind paying for them. It's that I feel ashamed that I have to ask. I feel like the cashier looks at me in a way that suggests I am single-handedly destroying the world, one bag at a time.

So, when I remembered to pick some up before leaving the driveway, I was extremely pleased with myself.

Stupid me.

The short drive to the supermarket passed without incident. Lost in thought, I hadn't even noticed how empty the roads were, or even that the car park was unusually quiet.

I just parked up and walked over to the shop. That is when I noticed something was amiss.

To start with, the automatic doors did not slide open as I approached. They did not need to. They were now just metal frames, and the glass that had once sat within, now lay in shattered fragments around the entrance. I stepped through cautiously.

The only lights were from the refrigerators at the back of the store. They cast an eerie glow and sent a shiver up my spine. I could not see or hear anyone else.

I wanted to turn around, to get back in the car and go back home. But I have no food in the house, so reluctantly I carried on regardless.

My local supermarket is massive. It is one of those stores that sells everything from screwdrivers to underwear. To optimise sales, they make you walk through the household goods section to get to the groceries. However, I just walked past empty shelves today.

In Electrical, not a single TV, laptop or tablet. Even the various accessories, power cables and USB sticks were gone. I walked on through to the homeware section.

Toasters, kettles, blenders, also gone. Part of me was disgusted. This clearly was not a massive sale. This was looters. Scumbags. The other part of me was feeling increasingly uneasy. This thing only started on Monday. I do not live in a big city, just a small town. We are not affected by this. Are we?

I sped up, almost running through the rest of the homeware section towards the food. I breathed a sigh of relief when I saw that the shelves were still well stocked. It must mean that it was just opportunistic looters. If we were in any danger, if the virus was here, then surely the food would have been the first thing to go.

I started to collect a few tins of beans, then cursed. In my haste to get in and out as quickly as possible, it had not occurred to me to pick up a basket or trolley.

I ran back through homeware and out of the store. I found a £1 coin and slotted it into the trolley lock, then wheeled it back to the front of the shop. It took me a few attempts to lift it over the static metal frame that used to be the door. Once back inside, I raced back up the aisles, pushing the wonky trolley ahead of me.

It felt like I was on *Supermarket Sweep*. I actually laughed when I got back to the tinned food aisle. It felt good. I hadn't laughed or even smiled since Steve told me he was leaving.

I selected a variety of tins, then headed to another aisle to get pasta. Milk, coffee and some cereal bars soon joined the rest of the contents, and I was finished. The trolley was half-empty. I probably could have just used a basket.

I made my way over to the checkout area. As the shop was officially closed, there was no one to pay. The self-service checkouts were all switched off.

I felt like a thief as I walked past the tills, vowing to come back when this is all sorted out to pay what I owe.

Leaving the store, I realised my mistake. It had been hard enough getting the trolley over the door frame when it was empty. There was no way I was going to be able to lift it when it was half full. Remembering the carrier bags that were screwed up in my handbag,

I pulled them out and started packing them with food. I had two bags packed and on to the last one when I heard a noise.

I looked up. Someone was walking towards me. Another shopper, I figured. For a second, I went back to packing while my brain processed what it had just seen. Clothing.

The person stumbling towards me was wearing a dressing gown. Just a dressing gown. My eyes flicked back up, and I took in the image. The dressing gown was flapping open. Saggy tits hung down the woman's chest, and a thick mane of unkempt pubic hair covered her pelvic area. Embarrassed that I was staring, I diverted my eyes to her face and stepped back in fright. Half of her cheek was hanging off, her yellowing teeth exposed by the gaping hole. Her eyes were inky black.

I came to my senses quickly and assessed the situation. The woman was heading straight for me, I had no weapons, but I needed that food. Discarding what remained in the trolley, I grabbed what I had packed, and ran for my life.

I made it about one metre.

I'd forgotten about the static frame of the sliding doors, so instead of hopping over it, I kicked it, tripped, and face planted the pavement. I lay there stunned for a few seconds. I cannot remember the last time I fell over. It is a strange sensation. One minute being upright, the next flat on the floor.

I lifted my head and could see the bare feet of the woman stepping awkwardly towards me, the groaning noise she emitted sending a shiver down my spine. I jumped up, grabbed the shopping bags and once again ran for my life.

Holding the bags in one hand, I let my handbag drop from my shoulder to the crook of my arm and used my other free hand to fumble for the car keys.

When I reached my car, I threw the shopping across the passenger seat and jumped in, slamming the door shut behind me. I looked back in the direction of the supermarket.

The woman was still coming towards me. She was ungainly, her movement awkward, as though she didn't have full control of her body. She wasn't fast, and I reckon I could probably out run her.

But she wasn't particularly slow either.

I suspect if it came to a race, the deciding factor would be who has the most stamina.

It had taken my trembling hands a few attempts to get the key in the ignition. By the time I had, the woman was at the car. Her hands were slapping against the window. By this point, I was shitting myself. I don't know how I managed to get the car moving, but I did. I looked back in my rear-view mirror and saw another six or seven people stumbling around. They had the same awkward movement as the woman. Probably infected too. Not hanging around to find out, I sped off through the car park and out onto the road.

That was about an hour ago. Now anger has taken over from the shock. How could I have been so stupid and naïve? It's been four days since this started and all I've done is watch the news. Why did I automatically assume that my home town would be safe?

Stupid. Stupid. Stupid.

It hadn't taken me long to accept that fact that Steve had left. I'd rationalised his decision by believing he would be back soon.

Now the cold hard shock that I might never see him again knocks me for six. I had believed the Prime Minister when he said that it would all be over soon, that the military would get control. It occurs to me that he hasn't made another appearance on TV since Monday.

In fact, thinking about it, all that has been on the news has been harassed and frightened looking news anchors, regurgitating the same information.

There's been nothing useful at all. Not even any suggestions about how to defend yourself against these things. I can't quite bring myself to say zombies. Zombies are the stuff of fiction. What I saw today at the supermarket was very, very real.

I need to act. I need to do something productive. An idea pops into my head, and I jump up and head to the kitchen. I flick the kettle on as I dash past on my way to my office. Selecting a notepad and pen, I return to the kitchen and make a cup of coffee.

I sit down at the kitchen table and start to make notes, sipping the hot coffee, when I pause to think.

Occasionally I get up and open cupboards to take note of what's inside. When I'm finished, I put down my pen and stare at the page in front of me.

Food
4 tins beans/ spaghetti
4 tins tuna
4 chicken breasts
1 pack microwave rice
1 pack pasta
8 cereal bars
Weapons
kitchen knives
golf clubs
~~drill~~
hammer
Defence
board up windows

"Oh crap," I say out loud, "I am screwed."

I read the list again, hoping for inspiration, and that I'll think of other way to defend myself; that I would remember a stockpile of food and supplies that I had forgotten. Nothing.

"Coffee, coffee will help," I say, then groan. Great, on top of everything, I have started talking to myself. I really need some company.

A pang of sorrow rushes through me and I miss Steve. Shaking my head as though to banish the emotions, I go back to the kettle and turn it on. The light doesn't come on. I check the plug, but it is switched on. I lift the kettle up and put it back down on the stand, the kettle version of rebooting. Nothing. A thought occurs to me, and I open the fridge. No light shines out. I must have tripped a fuse or something.

The fuse box is in the garage, which is connected to the house by a heavy fire door in the hallway. I pull open the door and step in.

Without thinking, I flick the light switch. Nothing.

The fuses in this house do trip on occasion, although I thought there were different fuses for different things, that the lights were on a different fuse from the kitchen power. Maybe I've tripped the master.

The only source of light is coming from the small crack under the garage door.

If the fuse box were next to the door, it might have been enough. Unfortunately, it's on the back wall, as far away from the door as it's possible to get. I stare into the blackness, thinking about where we keep the torch. Remembering, I run back to the kitchen, root through the junk drawer, and pull out a small head torch. Then I go back in the garage and use the torch to navigate through the variety of boxes and suitcases scattered around the floor.

Reaching the fuse box, I shine the torch at each of the fuses. None of them have tripped. I stare, confused.

With nothing better to do, I flick the master off and then on again. Nothing happens.

The realisation dawns on me. The power is out. Shit, that was fast.

The torch is still on in my hands. I quickly switch it off, realising I'll need it, and don't want to drain the batteries. "Twat," I flick the torch back on and step quickly through the obstacle course that is our garage floor, turning off the torch as soon as I reach the house.

Back in the kitchen now, and I really want a coffee. The hob is gas, maybe that will still work.

I press the knob, turn and twist, relieved to hear the faint hissing sound that indicates gas is coming out. I press the ignition button, but nothing happens. Doh, that obviously will not work. It's electric.

I pause and think before opening the junk drawer again and find a packet of matches. I light one, then quick hold down the knob again, and the flame ignites. As I fill a saucepan full of water, the thought occurs to me, how long will the water last?

I settle the saucepan on the hob, and while the water boils, I go through the kitchen cupboards and pull out every bottle, glass and pan that I have and fill them with water. Just in case.

By the time I am done, the water in the pan is bubbling away. I make my coffee, then look at the water left in the pan. I like coffee. I drink far too much of it. Not only is boiling the water on the hob a pain, but it will also use up my precious matches.

I empty the cold water out of two flasks that I had just filled and replace it with hot water. That should keep me going for the rest of the night.

I take the coffee into the lounge and sit down on the sofa. Reaching for the remote control and turning the TV on, I wonder how long it will take me to remember that there is no damn power. I throw the remote across the room, and it hits the skirting board with a crack.

My thoughts turn to my phone. I have a power bank somewhere, I'll have to find that later. Hopefully, it's got enough left in to give the phone at least a couple of charges. Although will the mobile networks still work if the power is out? Picking up the phone I hit the home button, and it obliges by lighting up. I have two text messages. I quickly open them. One is from George. Shit; I forgot to call in sick today. Should one phone in sick during an apocalypse? The other is from Steve. My heart leaps as I open the one from Steve first. The message is brief.

Get to George's house, should be safer there. I love you xxx

My initial reaction is one of pleasure. He has text me. I feel like a singleton that has just received a text from a hot guy.

It doesn't take long for my smile to turn into a frown. George? Why the hell would I want to spend the apocalypse with George?

Steve knows I hate that man. Is he taking the piss? I stare down at the phone, thinking of the reasons why Steve would suggest going there. It is probably safer, because it's remote, and the long driveway is secured by wrought iron gates. But surely Steve would know that being holed up with George for days on end will drive me insane. It's been quiet here. Surely, I'll be fine at home. The logical part of my brain kicks in. Steve is at an army camp, so he will know more than me. He probably isn't allowed to say anything. My heart sinks as I come to the conclusion that I need to listen. I need to get to George's.

Remembering that I have a text from George as well, I open it, and read the message. It changes everything.

Chloe. Sally has gone back to Heathrow. It is not safe out there. Help her.

Twelve

Sam glared at Lex. "*Does she have to be right all the fucking time?*" he thought. Lex glared back, asking herself, "*Why am I always right? I hate being right all the time.*" Claire was holding her head in her hands and gently rocking back and forwards, thinking "*We are so going to die.*"

The three of them were crouching behind the tills in W. H. Smith, jumping in unison as a loud bang sounded from close by. The banging persisted for a moment, then was replaced by the noise of glass shattering, followed by the whoops of people who had gained access to one of the stores. A scream echoed around the large terminal building, although it wasn'tclear which direction it had come from.

"What shall we do?" Sam whispered to Lex.

She shrugged, "I don't know, maybe if we stay here for long enough they'll get bored and leave."

"Great fucking idea," Sam hissed at her.

"They could be here for fucking hours. Have you seen the size of this place?"

"I'm scared," Claire whispered, ignored by Sam and Lex.

"Do you have a better idea then?" Lex directed the question at Sam. He glared at her for a few seconds then shook his head. "No, well then, shut up. It's your fault we're in this mess."

Earlier that day, they had snuck back into their quarantine tent. No one appeared to have noticed their absence. They had crawled back in their sleeping bags, but only Claire slept.

Sam stared up at the ceiling, thinking about Dean and the rest of his friends. When the tears started to flow again, he had hidden his head inside his sleeping bag and sobbed quietly into the polyester lining.

Lex had also lain on her back, but she stared unseeing at a small black mark on the roof of the tent. Why had suit guy collapsed before biting Paige?

Having not been popular at school she'd avoided social media.

The platform made it too easy to be targeted by bullies and trolls, so the account she had when she was thirteen had been quickly closed and she had never reopened it. As a result, she hadn't seen the video from Germany that had gone viral. Had no idea that for a few days everyone was talking about zombies. To her mind zombies were a thing of fiction, and there had to be a more logical explanation for what was happening.

She thought back to Sam saying that his friend had been kicked in the head after being bitten.

What did that mean? Was it linked? She chewed on her bottom lip, thoughts were spinning around in her head, and when the rest of the camp began to stir she was no closer to understanding if suit guy collapsing was important or not.

The occupants of the quarantine camp were so absorbed in their own troubles, the guards had become just background fixtures, irrelevant and unnoticeable, like an old piece of furniture.

It took longer than it reasonably should have for many to notice their absence. It was only when the food wasn't brought in at eight-thirty, like it had been every day, that anyone noticed anything was wrong. Murmured grumbling at the delay quickly turned to loud, angry voices. A woman stormed to the entrance of the tent, ready to make a complaint to the soldiers that stood guard.

Lex had watched in amusement as the woman stopped short.

She looked at the entrance, then left and then right, before turning around and looking back in the direction she had come from, as though she might have missed the soldiers on her way. Lex wondered if she felt as silly as she looked, and judging by the quick retreat the woman made to her group, she guessed so.

The news of the lack of guards had undulated through the tent like cascading dominoes, the noise steadily increasing as more and more people turned and stared at the entrance. Talking to their new friends. What was going on? Where was the food?

Were the soldiers on a break? Would they be back soon?

The noise had prompted Sam to emerge from his sleeping bag cocoon, and he hurried over to Lex and Claire. They sat together in silence, observing the growing anger, frustrations and fear that emanated throughout the camp.

By lunchtime, the tension was thick, almost tangible. Groups of friends joined with other groups, and factions formed, as struggles for leadership started in the individual groups and then spilt out, with each vying for overall dominance.

"It didn't take long for it to get like Lord of the Flies in here," Lex observed.

"What the fuck have hobbits and wizards got to do with anything?" Sam looked puzzled as he stared at Lex. Claire burst out laughing, earning angry stares from the closest group.

"Moron," Lex said, rolling her eyes, a slight hint of a smile on her face. "Not Lord of the Rings." She had gone on to explain the difference, but was interrupted as a fight broke out amongst two groups.

"I think it's time to get out of here," Claire interrupted. The rest of the camp watched the fight, giving them the opportunity to sneak out unseen.

Outside the tent, they viewed their surroundings. The terminal building was close by, and in the distance, across from where they stood, a faint fence line could be seen. Sam started to walk towards the terminal.

"Hang on a minute," Lex called, Sam stopped and turned to face her, "maybe we should head over that way," she pointed towards the runway.'

"Why?" Sam asked.

"Because, eventually, the people in there," Lex nodded her head towards the tent, "are going to come out and they are going to head straight for the terminal building."

Sam, saw the logic in the suggestion. Yet it looked so far away, and the terminal was right here. Stubbornness set in, and he resolutely refused to agree with Lex. After much debate between the two, Claire made the decision for them and started walking towards the terminal.

"I'm hungry," she called out, leaving the other two no choice but to follow her, Lex, scowling, Sam, smiling.

It was eerily quiet inside the terminal. Their footsteps echoed through the big empty building, which looked as though it had been hastily evacuated. Suitcases and bags lay scattered across the floor, half-eaten meals sat rotting on tables in restaurants, and boarding passes lay casually discarded.

Lex was keen to get out of the airport as soon as possible, but Claire insisted that they find food first. They walked through an empty restaurant and found the kitchen. Opening fridges and storage cupboards, they found plenty of food.

They picked up tins of beans, slices of ham and a loaf of bread. Back in the bar area, they took some bottles of water from the fridge. Choosing one of the few clean tables, they ate their meal in silence.

"Sam, have you got a car?" Claire asked when they had finished eating.

"I have," Sam replied, a note of pride in his voice, "I've got a Ford Fiesta."

"Great, have you got the keys?"

"Yeah,' Sam said. Digging them out of his pocket, he dangled them in front of Claire's nose.

"Good, I wouldn't have wanted to go back into the tent to get them. Where are you parked?"

"Parked?" he asked, frowning in confusion. "Why does that matter?"

"Well …" she had elongated the word. "So, we can work out the best way to get to it."

"It's fucking miles away. Not sure it will be that much use to us."

"It can't be that far. It should be easy to get to even if it's in one of those off-site airport parking places."

"Nah, fuck that, I ain't walking to Gatwick."

"Gatwick?"

"Yeah, Gatwick. That's where I parked."

"Oh, for God's sake," Claire huffed, "why did you say you had a car?"

"I have," Sam said again. "I've got a Ford Fiesta."

"Right, well, this has been a truly fascinating conversation." Lex interrupted. "How about we grab some food and drink to take with us? Looks like we've got a long walk ahead of us."

"I ain't walking to fucking Gatwick. I already said that."

"No Sam, we aren't walking to Gatwick. I suggest we go to Oxford. It's closer. We'll find a way to get you home from there," Lex's words were slow and patronising.

"Fine," Sam said.

In their haste to get out of the quarantine tent, all three of them had left their bags behind. They decided to find rucksacks. Only a few shops still had their doors open. They found one that sold luggage, and stepped inside to look around for something suitable.

As Sam was trying out a small navy blue bag, a group of people from the tent sprinted past the shop.

"Come back here, you wankers," someone shouted. Within seconds a chair was thrown, narrowly missing the woman at the back of the group.

Sam peered out of the shop in the direction of the voice and the chair. He quickly ducked his head back inside, as a dinner plate went soaring past.

"They've gone fucking mental. Loads of them are covered in blood." Another plate was thrown and smashed in front of the shop. "They're throwing things."

"You think?" Lex asked sarcastically. She looked frantically around. "Hide," she added and dashed over to a display of small, cabin-sized suitcases, and crouched down behind them, Claire and Sam following her.

"Jesus, not here," the small display not big enough to conceal three people. Fortunately, the braying mob ran past the shop without looking in.

"We can't stay here," Lex said, peeking her head out from behind the suitcases.

"There look," she pointed. "We'll hide behind the counter at W. H. Smiths." She sprinted and vaulted over the counter. Sam and Claire followed her again, and the three crouched silently, waiting for it to be safe enough to leave.

That had been hours ago, and they had been stuck here ever since. It sounded like the entire airport was being destroyed. Fights were breaking out in every direction, shop windows being smashed open, and the contents stuffed greedily into bags and pockets.

"I need a piss," Sam whispered.

"You're going to have to hold it," Lex hissed in reply.

"Fuck that, I'm gonna piss myself if I don't go soon. I'm gonna have to make a run for it," Sam peered over the counter, and saw there was no one in front of the shop.

He stood slowly and cautiously. Still seeing no one, he turned back to the girls, "Wish me luck."

He stepped out of the counter area just as a loud boom rang out, instantly followed by the deafening sound of a large window pane shattering, the shards falling to the floor. Sam quickly dropped into a prone position

The terminal fell deathly silent.

"Claire, Paige, Lex, are you in here?"

"Sally?" Claire asked

"Sounds like her," Lex said. She stood up and stepped over Sam. Quickly glancing out of the shop, she smiled. "Sally, we're over here," she called, jumping and waving both hands. She did not notice the men and the woman, still rooted to the spot, glaring at her.

Sally walked over, holding a shotgun. She pointed it from side to side, as though ready to shoot anyone that dared to move.

"Lex, thank God," she approached her friend. "I'd hug you, but you know …" she nodded at the shotgun in her hands.

"Er, yep, don't worry. We should get out of here," Lex replied.

Deciding it was safe, Claire stood up from behind the counter. "I am so pleased to see you," she exclaimed at Sally. "It's been a bloody nightmare."

"Claire," Sally squealed in delight, "I'm so sorry for leaving you here. I could have killed my dad when I got home."

She looked expectantly back at the direction Claire had appeared from. "Where's Paige?" she asked. Lex and Claire exchanged glances.

"I'm so sorry, Sally," Claire said eventually, "Paige died on Sunday."

"Oh shit," Sally said, earning a shocked look from Claire and Lex. That hadn't been the response they expected. Sally had always been the more sensitive of the group of friends.

She had also been closer to Paige than Claire or Lex had. The pair had discussed at length how to tell Sally, and they'd expected hysterics, not calmness. Anger, not acceptance.

"Oh shit," Sally said again. "Sorry … that sounded uncaring. It's been a tough couple of days … so many people have died. Did a zombie get her?"

"Ha," Sam shouted and jumped to his feet. "Told you." He said to Lex.

"Oh, it's you," Sally said, with evident disdain.

Sam had the good grace to look shamefaced, "Look, Sally, I know I was a t..." His words were cut off as he was shoved brutally to one side by a large bald headed bloke.

The man lunged at Sally.

Another man, taller but thinner, pushed past Lex and Claire, knocking them like skittles to either side of him as he attacked Sally from the front.

While Sally had been talking to the others, she had let the shotgun drop in front of her, but her finger had stayed on the trigger. The man coming up behind her grabbed her right shoulder, causing her to flinch and tense her body. The motion made her squeeze the trigger tightly as she tried to stay upright. The shotgun went off with a deafening crack.

Sally went flying back, she had not braced for the recoil, and it knocked her off her feet. She careened into the bald man, her hefty frame knocking him backwards. His head smashing against a metal shelf with a loud thud. Together they fell to the floor. The now unconscious man cushioned Sally's fall.

The other man was screaming, his right leg obliterated from the pellets that had been expelled at such short range. He collapsed to the floor, passing out from the pain.

Only Sam remained standing as he surveyed the scene in shock.

He went to Sally first and helped her off the floor.

"Are you okay?" he asked, genuine concern in his voice.

Sally looked at the scene in front of her, dumbfounded. She saw Sam's mouth moving but could not make out his words, her ears ringing. She turned to look at the man she had just been lying on. A trickle of blood from the back of his head was forming a pool of blood on the floor.

"Oh shit …" she exhaled. "I didn't mean to … it was an accident."

"I know," Sam reassured her. "Perhaps I should take that," he said, reaching for the shotgun still in Sally's hands. She did not acknowledge him, but did not resist when he took it out of her hands. He studied it for a second, found the safety that was neatly concealed next to the trigger and pressed it on.

Two women came running over, each going to one of the men, both screaming hysterically at the sight of their injured husbands. "What did you do?" the one standing over the bald man spat at Sam.

"Weren't me… it was 'er," he protested nervously, tilting his head towards Sally. She glared at him for a moment, then turned to the women.

"I'm so sorry… they tried to grab me… the gun went off... I didn't mean to hurt anyone," she stammered, tears welling in her eyes.

More people were entering the shop. Angry stares directed at Sam and Sally, Lex and Claire slowly edging their way over to the pair, taking care to avoid the blood that covered the floor around the man with the mangled leg.

"I think we need to leave. Now," hissed Lex as soon as she was close enough.

The crowd edged forwards, brandishing bottles, chair legs and anything else they had been using to ransack the airport.

The fights of just moments ago now forgotten, enemies now became allies as they faced a common threat. That the threat was an obviously distressed teenager, was not relevant. These people were angry and scared, pent up rage fuelling the adrenaline that coursed through them. There is safety in numbers, and they gained in confidence as their numbers swelled.

Sally, Claire, Sam and Lex slowly stepped backwards, their intention to leave clear in their action. The mob stepped closer towards them. This went on for a few steps until Sam lifted the shotgun and swept it left and right across the crowd.

"Stay the fuck away from us," he growled, menacingly. The crowd froze, allowing the four of them to gain some distance.

One man continued to step forwards. Sam pointed the gun directly at him. "I said, stay away from us. I will use this." The man stopped and retreated a few steps to merge in with the rest of the mob.

Out of the corner of his mouth, he whispered, "Walk quickly, head towards the stairs." The three girls turned and jogged towards the stairs. Sam continued to walk slowly backwards until he had gained sufficient distance for the mob to not be an immediate threat. Sally, Claire and Lex were waiting at the bottom of the stairs.

"What now?" Claire asked, a tremble in her voice giving away her fear.

"Let's get out of the bloody airport," Lex said.

"Um… that might not be so easy," Sally said nervously. The other three turned to look at her.

"Why?" Lex asked.

"Because of the zombies," Sally replied.

"Zombies. Seriously?" Lex said, ignoring the grin on Sam's face as he stared at her.

"Why do you keep saying zombies?" Claire asked.

"Didn't they tell you anything while you were in there?" Sally said, her tone gentle. She was still ashamed that she had left her friends behind. Especially now, knowing that if she had been more insistent, maybe she could have saved Paige.

"Not a bloody thing," Lex raged. "They just left last night, and we haven't seen anyone since."

"Oh, oh dear, well … the thing is … there are zombies, lots of zombies. Everywhere. Some of them saw me come in here, so I think they might still be waiting outside," Sally admitted.

"Ha, I knew it," Sam said.

Lex glared at him, "You guessed, Sam, that is very different from knowing."

"Right, so what should we do?" Claire asked.

"Let's find somewhere safe to stay the night," Sally suggested.

"Yeah," Sam agreed. "Then perhaps you can tell us what the fuck is going on." He stared accusingly at her, as though everything that had happened over the past few days was her fault.

Sally flushed with anger, "Why is he even here?"

"He's been helping us," Claire responded. Despite herself, she was growing fond of Sam. She could see through his arrogance and bravado to a scared and vulnerable young man. He had just lost all his friends. While she was still upset at the way he had treated Sally, they could not leave him alone now.

Lex smirked. "Has he? When?" She thought Sam was an idiot and a coward. She would have no qualms at leaving him to the face the angry mob.

"When … well … um …" Claire racked her brains, trying to think of an example.

"I just got rid of that lot, didn't I?" Sam added, his voice rising an octave. Fear at the thought of being abandoned pulsated through him

"Yes. With my gun." Sally retorted, holding her hand out to Sam. He passed the shotgun back to her.

"Listen, please don't leave me behind. I can help, I know how to use that thing," he gestured to the gun in Sally's hands.

"There is safety in numbers," Claire added logic to Sam's plea.

"Fine," Sally snapped. "You can come. We can always feed you to the zombies if you act like a prick."

Sam opened his mouth to respond, but then snapped it shut again, figuring it would be better not to say anything that might make her change her mind. Instead, he merely responded with, "Thanks," and the best look of gratitude he could muster.

Thirteen

The phone in my hand sits inert. Inanimate. Eventually the screen turns to black, yet still, I stare at it. It had taken me less than a second to figure out why Sally would have gone back to Heathrow. What I could not understand was why George had let her go, why he had not gone with her.

I know that Lex, Claire, and Paige are Sally's best friends. I had pleaded with George to find a way to get them out of quarantine too, but he had been resolute. There was no way the Prime Minister would allow it. He had only agreed to Sally because he owed him a favour. I suspect he hadn't even tried.

It does not surprise me that she has gone to get them. When she was younger, she had dreamed of being the knight in shining armour. Never the princess, like the other girls.

Now is her opportunity to play the hero. But what if one of those things attacks her? Would she freeze in fear or run away? Would she defend herself or be too scared?

Long ago I accepted that I have more affection for Sally than you would expect to have for your boss's daughter. However, I hadn't realised the depths of my feelings until now. She could be in danger, hurt, lost or scared. I feel a gut-wrenching terror that I've never experienced before.

I realise now that I have an almost maternal love for her. If she is still alive, I will damn well find her and protect her. I type a reply to George.

I will bring her home.

I return to Steve's message and start to tap out a response, telling him what I'm planning to do. I pause midway, delete it and start again.

The message is simple.

OK xxx

I will be going to George's once I have Sally, I reason. I haven't lied to him. If I tell him the whole truth, he will be furious. He'll tell me not to go, he might even get himself in trouble by coming to find me, I assure myself that it's best that he doesn't know.

Making the decision to go was easy. The reality of it is much harder. I cannot just jump in my car and drive to Heathrow. I need to plan, make sure I've got enough food and supplies. Weapons.

A route. The clock on my phone tells me that it's nearly four o'clock. I allow myself an hour to prepare.

First things first, clothes. I am currently wearing jeans and a vest top. I'd put them on earlier, without thinking about going to the shops.

The vest top is okay, but it would be hard to run in jeans, although I hope I won't need to run anywhere. But prepare for the worst, wish for the best. I take the jeans off and select a pair of dark green shorts out of my chest of drawers, and put them on.

I step back and view my reflection in the mirror. I look like a fat Lara Croft. Visions of being a zombie and being stuck in the same outfit forever fill my mind. It's nothing but vanity, although fat or not, I should not have my legs exposed. I quickly take them off again.

If I were a biker, I could wear leather trousers, which would give some protection from zombie bites. I am not a biker. I do not own leathers. Even if I did, I guess running in them would be difficult. Still, having something covering my legs would make me feel better.

I root through my drawers and find a pair of dark grey trousers. A couple of years ago I signed on for a charity walk up Snowdon. I am not an outdoorsy type, but I didn't want to look out of place. I had bought everything, spending a fortune on the best brands. I struggled so much, walking up that mountain, out of breath and exhausted. The words "all the gear, no idea," played in a mocking loop in my mind.

I decided that hiking was not for me. When I got home, I boxed up all of the equipment, with the intention of selling it one day. I kept the trousers because they were comfortable and I thought they might be suitable for gardening or something.

It hadn't occurred to me that "*something*" would be the zombie apocalypse.

I pull the trousers on. They are a little tight, and this time I don't bother looking in the mirror. These are practical; they will do.

Haphazardly stuffing my clothes back in my drawers, a thought occurs to me. I am not coming back, and I'll need clothes for the next few weeks. I fill a duffle bag with tops, jeans, and underwear. In the bathroom, I pick up my toothbrush and deodorant. Back in the bedroom I select a hairbrush and some hairbands and put them in the bag too. Lastly, I open my wardrobe and choose a couple of hoodies.

The bag is almost full. I sit astride it and use my thighs to squeeze it closed while I zip it up.

Clothes sorted. What next? I think back to the list I made earlier. That was supposed to be for staying at home, but I guess it would make sense to bring any food I have with me.

Carting the duffle bag downstairs, I leave it in the hallway. In the kitchen, I unload the food from the cupboard, and pack it into carrier bags. I add the water bottles I filled earlier but leave the other containers full of water where they are.

If the situation gets to the point when someone needs to break into my house for supplies, then at least they'll be able to have a drink.

Right then, weapons. I take the carving knife out of the block and wrap it in a tea towel. Hmm … might as well take the lot. I unwrap the tea towel and add the rest of the knives from the block before wrapping it back up again. I pick up the torch from where I left it, then go back to the garage.

It doesn't take long to find the box of walking supplies. I rip it open and pull out a first aid kit, utility knife, and micro fibre towel. I load these into the backpack that is also in the box. Although... the utility knife might come in handy. I take it out and shove that in my pocket. Next in the box are my walking boots, so I pull them out. Might be useful to pop them in the car, just in case.

At the bottom of the box are two walking poles. I carried them all the way up Snowdon and all the way down again, too embarrassed to use them, even though they might have made the whole experience a little bit easier. Will they help me now? I guess they could come in useful if I injured a leg or had to walk really far. Besides, they attach to the rucksack and are lightweight, so there is no harm in taking them.

Next up is the toolkit. I take out a hammer and a chisel, because you just never know when you might need to do a bit of woodwork in the apocalypse! Although I guess they might be useful if I needed to break into something. I laugh out loud at that. As if I'm going to be breaking into things. I put them in the bag anyway, just in case.

Steve's golf clubs are next to be raided. I pick up two that are big and chunky, I know they've got an official, golfy sounding name, but I can't remember what it is. Driver? Wodge? Wedge? In turn, I swing each from side to side. They are not as heavy as they look. I'm not convinced that they would do much damage to someone. I suppose it makes sense. Designed for swinging quickly at a ball, not for beating people up. They would need to be light enough to build up power behind the swing.

The club used for knocking the ball into the hole would not need to be so light as it does not get swung back. I lift it from the bag. It's a different shape from the rest, so I assume it must be the putter, and it is heavier than the others.

I swing it around; it feels much sturdier. I am not convinced how much damage it will do, but I will feel better if I have something that has a long reach.

If I have to use the hammer or the knives, it means something has got way too close to me. I put the two lighter clubs back in the bag, then quickly take them out again. It won't hurt to have all three clubs with me.

I have everything I need from the garage, but I briefly shine the light around in case I am struck by inspiration. I switch off the torch and go back into the house, where I add the rucksack, boots and golf clubs to the bags in the hall.

I pick up my phone, but there are no new messages and it's still showing a signal.

The action reminds me to get the power bank and some batteries. I put the batteries in the rucksack and the power bank with its USB cord in my pocket. I'll charge it and the phone in the car on the way to Heathrow.

I take my car keys from the top of the set of drawers, and head to the front door. I move to pull it open but hesitate.

A wave of sadness washes over me. This is the first home that Steve and I bought together. It has so many good memories. Will I ever come back? I run up the stairs and pick up a picture frame with the only printed photo I have of us together. The rest are on our phones and laptops. It shows us at a bar on holiday in Mexico. We had asked a stranger to take it for us, and just as the photo was about to be taken, Steve had whispered, "*Boobies*" in my ear, causing us both to laugh like children. We look so tanned and happy. When we got home, I made a point of getting it printed and framed.

I take the picture out of the frame, take a photo of it, so I've still got an electronic version if something happens to the original. Then I fold it in two and put it in my purse.

Back downstairs I add my purse to the rucksack.

Taking one last look around, I open the door. I'm about to burst right out when it occurs to me that I should check to make sure it's safe.

The street is quiet. Many of the neighbours' cars are missing from their driveways. I wonder where they have gone. Wherever they are, I wish them well and hope they are safe.

The silence is interrupted by a persistent thumping coming from the house across the road. It sounds like someone is trying to get out. Perhaps they need help. I consider this for a moment. A young couple live across from us. Rich and Sarah. We exchange polite nods and pleasantries when we cross paths, but I don't really know them. Rich works in London and Sarah works at a local school. They have the same front door as me. It can be opened from the inside even if it's locked from the outside. I can't think of a good reason why they wouldn't be able to get out.

I walk cautiously over to the house and knock softly on the door. "Sarah, Rich… it's Chloe, are you okay?" The steady rhythm of the thumping changes to a frantic banging. Then it is accompanied by a low, almost inhuman groan. It sounds likes the woman at the supermarket earlier. My heart sinks. They are infected. I back away from the door, which is solid and will not wield from fists banging at it. The thought of them finding a way to open the door frightens me enough to move quickly.

I run back to my house and grab the rest of the bags from the hallway. I put the clothes and food in the boot, but keep the rucksack and golf clubs in the front with me.

I shut and lock my door and get into the driver's seat. I reverse out of the driveway and see two people making their way down the road, and their awkward movement suggests they are infected.

The street was empty a few moments ago, so I assume that the loud banging has attracted these two.

I put the car into gear and set off, watching for the reactions of the infected at the noise of the engine. As I expected, they turn towards the sound. Their pace increases as they fix their eyes on my car. I stop and look out of the rear mirror, studying them. They seem clumsy and uncoordinated. Short of getting out of the car, I am not sure what else I can learn, so I set off again and soon leave them behind me. It is nearly five o'clock on a Thursday afternoon, and on a typical day the roads would be teeming with commuters trying to get home. Now the lack of traffic creates an ominous and threatening environment. I press my foot a little firmer on the accelerator, eager to get away.

Heathrow is a little over an hour away from here. It should be an easy route, join the dual carriageway, past Oxford, then on to the motorway. Hang on. Past Oxford? Fucking idiot.

I am clearly not a survival expert, but entering a city with countless zombies roaming around, is probably a dumb idea. I stop the car, but leave the engine running. I need to think about this.

I don't want to run the risk of passing Oxford, even though it's a quicker route.

I expect the motorways will be okay, but I don't know how to get there without going along the dual carriageway.

My satellite navigation system will be no help, because it will just show me the quickest way, which I already know. I don't have a road map in the car. Does anyone nowadays? I'll use my phone.

Retrieving it from my trouser pocket, I load up the map application. It looks like I can stick to country roads and avoid the cities. I'll be going through some small towns. It is reasonably quiet here, so maybe it will be the same elsewhere. I trace the route with my finger, trying to remember the names of the roads.

A loud bang rocks the car, and I jump in fright. One of those things is pressed up against the window, its hands clawing at the glass. I look back at it, temporarily memorised by its black eyes staring at me. Although, is it staring? Can it see with those black eyes or do they just go by sound? I wave my hand left and right. It continues to look at me, seemingly not noticing the motion.

It is a strange sensation, waving frantically at someone right in front of you, and them not reacting in any way.

Just to double check, I use both hands and wave them side to side. Then I realise it looks like I am doing jazz hands and stop immediately, feeling silly. I can even feel myself start to blush.

The thing at the window carries on clawing, oblivious to my embarrassment. I feel safe in here; I wonder what else I can learn about these things. I study the face. It's a woman, probably around my age. She's wearing a simple white top that looks like it could do with a wash, and a pair of black shorts. She has little gold stud earrings and a necklace with the letter L handing from it. I wonder what her name is … was.

I don't see any visible injuries on her, and I wonder how she became infected. In fact, if it weren't for those creepy eyes and the twisted snarl on her face she would look normal. Pretty. Although looking closer at her face, I notice her skin doesn't look quite right. It's very pale and has a strange sheen to it, like it's made of wax.

I'm not sure that checking the complexion of this woman or the fact her name probably begins with L will help me. I switch the engine off, and the car is now silent. I know that the daytime running lights will stay on for a few more seconds, but I want to know if it is me she is reacting to or the noise from the car. The she-thing continues to claw at the windows. It's a fruitless exercise. She is not even banging on the glass, just scratching her fingers down it, so there is no way she will get through, but she carries on regardless. I feel almost sorry for her.

I watch for a couple of minutes. Her hands on the window are making a soft squeaking noise, and I can hear her groan, muted by the window separating us.

It sounds like the moans from the woman at the shop earlier. I am making no noise, yet still, she continues to paw at the window. Did she initially react to the sound of the engine and become fixated on its source? Or can she see me?

Without warning, I hear a new noise from behind me. I look in the rear-view mirror and see another two of those things now scratching at the boot, I look around. There are five or six more coming from different directions. The groan from the she-thing continues and is joined by more voices making that horrible sound. It's creepy, and I'm starting to feel claustrophobic. I turn the key, the engine roars back to life. It is time to go.

Fourteen

The mob watched in silence as the group of crazy teenagers made their way up the stairs. They made no attempt to follow them. Instead, they held heated discussions about what to do now. Discussions turned to arguments, which turned into fights. The teenagers that had fled from them moments before were forgotten.

Sam trudged behind the three girls, part of their group, but somehow on the outside. It had been fine before Sally had shown up. Sure, Lex was a bit of a pain in the arse, but Claire was alright. At least they both included him. Now that Sally was back it was like he didn't exist.

He figured he could just fuck off somewhere, but then he would be on his own, no friends, no idea how to get home, so his fear of being alone was driving him to trudge behind the girls like an unwanted stray dog.

Claire caught a glimpse of Sam out of the corner of her eye. He was hanging his head, his steps slow and cumbersome.

Her heart went out to him, and she slowed her pace to fall into step with him.

"Hey," she said, "you okay?"

"Yeah," he replied in a tone which implied the opposite.

"Thinking about your friends?" she prodded.

"Oh, er yeah," Sam replied quickly, "yeah, can't believe they're gone, ya know?" he was too ashamed to admit that he had been thinking about himself and how he was feeling. Dean and the rest of his mates were far from his thoughts.

"I know," Claire murmured and reached for Sam's hand to give it a squeeze.

Sam felt sorry for lying to her. Claire was nice. He didn't fancy her or anything, but she seemed like a genuinely kind and caring person. "Any idea where we're going?" he asked, keen to change the subject.

"We're looking for somewhere to spend the night."

"Can't we just kip on one of those sets of seats?" Sam asked.

"We'd be too exposed," Claire explained, "anyone could see us there, and we really don't want that lot finding us."

"What about one of the airport lounge things. You know where all the posh lot go before their flights?" Sam suggested.

Claire stopped and looked at him, "Sam, that's genius. They're big enough so we'd have room to move around, and small enough not to feel too exposed," she smiled at him.

"Ooh, and they have food and drink in them. Genius!" She knew she was laying it on a bit thick. Sure, it was a good idea, but she was acting like he had invented the wheel.

Still, it was the most useful thing Sam had said since meeting him, and her enthusiasm seemed to perk him up.

"Sally, Lex," she called, "Sam has just had a great idea."

The two girls in front of them stopped and turned around. They wore matching looks of disbelief and scepticism.

"He suggested we find an Executive Lounge to sleep in tonight. Isn't that a brilliant idea?" She said enthusiastically.

Lex opened her mouth to say something, then stopped short when she noticed the hard glare in Claire's eye.

"Um, yeah … good idea, Sam," she tried to be encouraging but knew that she sounded insincere.

Sam did not appear to notice, and for the first time in hours, he smiled.

His face transformed instantly from sullen and stroppy to good natured and happy. The difference was remarkable. Sally who had been watching the exchange, felt her heart skip a beat. This was the young man that she had met on Saturday. He was gorgeous when he smiled. Her face clouded as she berated herself. He was a prick, he had used her, and she hated him.

"I suppose we could do that," she said in a tone that did little to hide her contempt. She stalked over to a map of the massive terminal.

"There are a few lounges around. We're here," she pointed to a spot on the map. "I suggest we go to this one," she tapped another point on the map. It was on the level above them, just past security.

They found the lounge easily and stopped to look at the smart British Airways sign that told them who could gain entry.

"Ah," Sally paused, "we'll need one of the BA cards to get in. I left mine at home."

"Haha, good one, yeah me too," Sam snickered, earning a look of disdain from Sally. "Oh, you were serious. You actually have one of those cards."

"I do," Sally said primly. "A platinum one," she bragged, immediately regretting it. "My dad has to travel a lot for work, so I sometimes go with him," she justified herself. "But it's at home, so how are we going to get in?"

"Powers out, innit," Sam stated, then pushed the door. It swung open, much to his relief. He would have looked a right twat if it had been locked. He grinned again, noticing Sally averting her eyes.

Sam stepped inside, "Fucking hell," he exclaimed. "It's well posh in 'ere," his voice echoed around the empty room. He took in the expensive leather chairs, the buffet area.

His eyes came to rest on a massive display of wine. Walking over he picked up a bottle, "Anyone want some?" Lex and Sally looked back at him in disgust.

Claire softly shook her head and mouthed, "No."

"Er, second thoughts, probably best not to drink. Need a clear head and… ya know," his voice trailed off. He replaced the bottle of wine in the rack and went to another fridge that held bottles of water. He hesitated and turned to Claire. She nodded back at him, he opened the fridge and pulled out four bottles. He handed one to each of girls, and they drank in silence.

"Should we … er like … barricade the doors of something?" Sam asked when they had finished.

"That's actually a good idea, Sam," Lex said, impressed and a little ashamed that she had not thought of it herself.

Pleased with himself, Sam pointed to the wooden chairs and tables, which were placed strategically around the room. "We could use those."

Lex nodded. "Yes, they'll work." She walked over to the closest table and ran a finger over it.

Sam, enjoying his moment of glory and keen for it to continue, added, "Why don't you ladies sit down and rest. I'll sort these out. It's been a long day … er, … ya know?"

The astonishment at the selfless gesture was apparent on the faces of all three girls.

"Okay," said Sally and plonked herself down gracelessly on a large black leather sofa.

The other two girls joined her. None of them noticed the frown on Sam's face. He had only offered so it looked like he was being helpful.

He hadn't expected them to agree. What had happened to equal rights?

Sam picked up a table, then put it down again. It was really fucking heavy, must be solid wood. Not like the cheap flat pack furniture he has in his flat. There was no way he could lift it and carry it over to the door. He considered pushing it, but that would make him look like a wimp. He picked up a chair, much lighter. He carried it over to the entrance and placed it in the middle of the double doors. It looked pathetic. A child would be able to move that. It would take him ages to pile up enough chairs to barricade the door; then it would take too long to move them when they wanted to leave. He walked back over to the sofa where the girls were sitting.

"Er, seconds thoughts, I don't think those chairs and tables will be strong enough … I think we should use a sofa. One of those two-seaters will fit perfect."

"Perfectly," Lex muttered quietly. "Okay," she said to Sam and then carried on with the conversation she had been having with Claire and Sally.

Sam stood there awkwardly for a few seconds, "Er … well … see … I'll need help to lift it," he said.

The girls stood and between the four of them, they managed to place the sofa in front of the double doors. Sam was right, it did fit perfectly. A sense of relaxation came over the group. It was only a small sofa, but it would be hard to push the doors open with that in the way. For the first time that day, they felt safe.

Claire took four more bottles of water out of the fridge, brought them back to the sofa they had been sitting on, and handed them out.

"Right," said Lex, decisively, "Sally, can you please tell us what has been going on out there?"

Sally gulped, conscious of the three pairs of eyes fixed on her. "It started on Monday, something happened in London, on the Underground. The news didn't really say how it started, but they showed clips of people tearing into each other. Literally, with their teeth. It was gross. Then the Prime Minister made a speech, it was everywhere across Europe and America, in all the big cities. He said not to worry, just to stay indoors and the army would get control… but I don't know what happened. The army didn't get control. It spread really quickly, and by Tuesday it was in Leeds, Manchester, Bristol, even … even Oxford." She paused, picked up the bottle of water and took a sip. The others stayed silent, absorbing her words.

"What about Kent?" Sam asked in a quiet voice, afraid to hear the answer.

"Kent?" Sally said, then remembered Sam lived there. "I'm sorry Sam, most of Kent is gone," she said, her tone softer, "It's so close to London; it was overrun with the infected by Tuesday afternoon."

"And it's definitely zombies?" Claire asked.

Sally nodded, "They haven't used that term on the news, but yeah. People are being bitten, they die, then they come back. So yeah, zombies."

Lex looked thoughtful and chewed on her bottom lip, "How long?' she asked.

"Since Monday," said Sally, biting back the frustration, had Lex not been listening?

"No, sorry, how long after being bitten do they turn?"

"Oh, um, I've not seen anyone change myself, but the news said up to forty-eight hours."

Lex nodded. "That explains suit man and Paige."

"What happened to her?" asked Sally.

"This guy collapsed. Paige tried to help him, but he woke up and started biting her. The soldiers shot them both in the head."

"So she didn't turn?" Sally asked. Lex shook her head. "Good, it was a horrible way to die, but I'm glad she didn't become one of those things."

"Must've been the same in the other tent then," Sam said, "I guess the soldiers didn't shoot the people that turned quickly enough.

"The other tent?" asked Sally.

"Yeah," Sam nodded, "there was another tent. I think they put the people that had been exposed in Alicante in there. My mates were in there. Everyone had been shot. Hundreds of dead bodies there was."

Lex let the grammatical error slide, "There must have been a few people infected in there. I assume that they turned at the same time," She trailed off and chewed on her bottom lip.

This morning it had felt like a bit of a game, that she was investigating a murder, playing detective. It had not occurred to her that this was everywhere. Even Oxford … Oxford. She lives on the outskirts. Are her parents okay?

"How did you get here?" she asked, the hope evident in her voice. If Sally had made it here alone, then it can't be too bad out there.

"I took a bus," Sally stated.

"You took a bus?" Lex questioned, "the buses are still running?" She laughed. "Thank God, it can't be that bad if the buses are still running." A weight lifted from her shoulders. Public transport would be the first thing to be cancelled if there was a crisis. Sally must be exaggerating.

"It is," Sally insisted. "I didn't catch a bus. I took one. Literally stole one. The mini bus from the village school."

Sam laughed, his respect for Sally increased tenfold. She stole a bus. "Ha, ha, that's fucking hilarious."

Lex glared at him. Hope smashed away. Now it felt like her heart had been torn from her body, stamped upon and forced back in, the wrong way. "Prick," she said, before getting up and running to the other side of the lounge.

"Her family live in Oxford, Sam," Claire said when Lex was far enough away.

"Oh … oh shit … I didn't mean to be such a dick," Sam cursed himself. He had just felt that he was being accepted and now he had fucked it up by laughing when Lex was clearly in pain.

"I'll go talk to her," Claire said.

"No," Sam stood as he spoke, 'I will, it was my big gob.'

He walked hurriedly over in the direction Lex had gone. He passed a fridge on his way that held chocolate bars and snacks. Grabbing a selection, he carried on walking. As he approached, he saw her sitting on the floor with her back to a sofa. Her arms wrapped around her knees, which were pulled into her chest. He could see her shoulders heaving and hear the anguished sobs. Lex had seemed so strong and confident. She was the smart one, the rational one.

To see her like this broke something in Sam. All his teenage years he had been selfish, only concerned with the effect situations had on him. Trev dying had meant that he could not brag about Sally. Dean and the lads dying; his first thought had been that he would need to find new friends. Kent being overrun had meant that he probably wouldn't get to go home to his belongings.

Witnessing the raw emotion pouring from Lex, made him, for the first time in his life, think of someone else's feelings and not his own.

He stood awkwardly behind her, not knowing what to say. Lex sensed the presence of another person and looked up, expecting to see Sally or Claire.

"Go away, Sam," she said wearily. No trace of anger in her voice, just pain.

"I'm so sorry, Lex. I … I can't imagine what you are going through right now." He used the words that Claire had spoken earlier this morning when she was comforting him. It had made him feel a little better. Surely that would work with Lex.

"Why? Why can you not imagine, Sam?" she shouted, the anger returning.

"My family are in Oxford and are probably dead. Your family are in Kent and are probably dead. You should be able to imagine exactly what I am going through now. Not joking about Sally stealing a bloody bus."

She knew her words were blunt and cruel, but she didn't care. She wanted to lash out, to make someone hurt like she was.

"My family are dead," Sam replied, keeping his tone neutral, "they died when I was twelve, my mum, dad and little brother. Car accident." He stopped, unable to continue.

"Oh," Lex said, the anger leaving her instantaneously. "Who brought you up?" The shocking statement made by Sam had made her forget her own fears. There was still hope for her family. Sam had lost his when he was so young.

"My uncle took me in, but he got fed up with me and kicked me out when I was thirteen. Then it was foster homes for a few years, till I was eighteen then the council gave me a flat."

"Aren't you worried about your uncle? I guess he's still family."

"He kicked me out when I was still a kid." Sam's voice grew harder. "I was just a kid. My entire family had died, he didn't try to help or understand why I was acting out, he just took the easy option. I hope he gets what he deserves." He tightly gripped the chocolate he was still holding. The pain of those years that he had kept buried for so long threatened to bubble to the service. He took a deep breath.

"Er, I got you some chocolate. Girls like chocolate … right." He dropped the bars at Lex's feet.

She laughed, "Yes, Sam, girls do like chocolate."

She picked up a fruit and nut bar, then offered it to him. "Want one? Boys like chocolate, right?" she asked with a cheeky smile on her tear-stained face.

"Well played," he smiled as he sat down next to her and took the bar from her. "I love fruit and nut." They sat in companionable silence, savouring the taste of the chocolate bars.

"I've never met anyone that was in a foster home before, would you mind telling me about it?" she asked.

She leant her head on his shoulder as he began to talk, the physical contact offering some comfort to her, his stories helping to push the worry about her parents to the back of her mind.

Sally stood unseen behind the two of them. She watched them share the chocolate, noted the affectionate way that Lex was leaning against him.

Jealousy stabbed through her like a knife, when Sam lifted an arm and draped it casually over Lex's shoulders. She turned silently on her heel and walked away.

"Is she okay?" Claire asked Sally when she returned to her seat.

"Yes. Fine," replied Sally, bluntly. "They seem to be getting on very well."

Claire studied her friend's face. Was Sally jealous? "Um Sal," she said cautiously.

"What?" Sally asked harshly.

Claire considered what to say next, should she tell her? It was Lex's secret to tell, besides she could be wrong about Sally being jealous. "How did you steal a bus?"

Sally, letting out a small sigh of relief, had been expecting probing questions about her sudden mood swing. "Dad wouldn't let me come back to get you. We argued a lot. I even cried, and you know what he's like when he sees me crying."

Claire nodded, smiling, "Yep, I'm still scarred from the time we had that argument about whose Barbie was prettiest, you cried, and he shouted at me and sent me home."

"Haha, yes I remember that," Sally chuckled. "Well, it didn't work. So on Wednesday night when he was asleep, I got up, and stuffed pillows under my duvet, so it looked like I was sleeping. He must have hidden the car keys, because I couldn't find them anywhere. But I did find the keys to the gun cabinet. I took the shotgun and decided to walk."

Sensing Claire was going to comment, Sally added, "Stupid, I know. It took me ten minutes just to get to the end of the driveway. It would have probably taken me days to get here. So I figured I needed to find a car."

"So how did you end up with the school bus?'

"I walked into the village. It was really dark outside, creepy. I could hear these groans, you know, the sound that the zombies make?"

Claire shook her head, "No, I've not seen any of them. What does it sound like?"

"Um… it's kind of… *urrrrrrrrrrrrrrrrrr*." Sally mimicked the noise as much as she could, looking embarrassed.

"Like a dog growling. But it's constant. I had heard it on the news, but hearing it in real life is bloody scary. The school was the first building I came to, and the bus was in the car park."

"Lucky for you the keys were in it," Claire commented.

Sally looked uncomfortable, "Um … well … they weren't."

"So how did you take the bus?" Claire asked confused.

"I kind of … um … broke into the school," Sally replied, looking down at her hands and studying them intently.

"What?" Claire exclaimed, then she let out a loud snort of laughter. "You broke into a school. You stole a bus. You shot someone. What happened to sweet, shy Sally?" She teased. "I couldn't believe you were swearing earlier, but that's nothing compared to everything else you've done."

"I didn't mean to shoot that man," Sally protested. "But I guess the rest of it, yes, guilty," she held her up her hands in mock surrender. "I don't know, since Saturday, you know … Sam," she said awkwardly. "Well, that and quarantine and all those people dying … I guess we're all going to have to adapt if we want to survive this."

"Is it really that bad?" Claire asked gently. Being in quarantine had protected her from everything else that was going on. She was still half expecting that she'd go home tomorrow and see her family, sit down for a welcome home meal and talk about her adventures.

"Yes," Sally muttered, studying her hands again.

"It's bad. It's really bad. Do you remember Rita, our cleaner?" Claire nodded.

"She came on Tuesday as normal, but she wasn't well. She died in the kitchen. I didn't know anything about it until I heard yelling, then loud bangs... Dad hit her with a frying pan ... said it was self-defence ... that she was attacking him."

Claire gasped, "That's awful ... was she?"

"I don't know. I ran downstairs when I heard Dad shouting. Her body was on the kitchen floor. There was blood everywhere. Before he shoved me out of the room, I saw her eyes. They were black. The news said that happened when they turn. So she probably was infected." She gulped in a breath of air, trying to keep the tears from falling.

"Dad took her body somewhere, he was only gone for half an hour or so, but when he came back, he was different. Quiet, pale and, I guess, sad. Probably even more so than I remember him being when mum died." A fat tear rolled down her cheek, and she wiped it away with her sleeve.

Claire reached over and squeezed her hands. "That's terrible, you must have been so scared."

"I was, but that wasn't the scariest thing I've seen," she said, glad of the comfort of Claire's hand holding hers.

"What was?" Claire asked.

"At the school, I broke in through the office window, figured that's the best place to find the keys." She paused, anticipating the next question.

"I threw a big rock at the window. It smashed, but the noise was so loud. I used the torch on my phone and found the keys quickly. They were hung on a rack, and they were even labelled, so I was only in there for a few minutes but when I climbed out of the window, the groaning sounded really close. I shined the torch around, and saw children. They can't have been older than five or six. They were coming towards me. Their eyes … the groaning," she shuddered, reliving the memory. "They were so close. The closest one grabbed me, but I punched it."

Claire had been listening with increasing fascination exclaimed, "You punched a child?"

"Yes, but they're not people anymore, not really. If I hadn't, it would have bitten me. It didn't seem to hurt it, but it fell over, and a couple of the other kids tripped over it. I sprinted for the bus before they could get up again."

"Bloody hell," Claire exhaled.

"When I turned on the ignition, the headlights came on. There were dozens of children. Everywhere I looked, these kids, with those awful black eyes, were heading towards the bus."

"Jesus, what did you do?"

"I … They were everywhere … I had no choice …"

"Oh," Claire said, understanding what Sally seemed unable to say, "You did the right thing, Sal," she added reassuringly. "You said yourself, they're not people anymore."

"I know," Sally nodded.

Both girls went quiet, lost in their own thoughts. Despite her words to Sally, Claire could not help but feel shocked at her friend's actions. Running over children. Could she have done the same? She admired Sally's bravery and strength. It just did not seem real. Surely things cannot be as bad as Sally is suggesting.

The silence between the two became awkward and uncomfortable. Sally sensed that Claire was judging her actions, but she did not know. She had not been there. Those children had shown no fear as the minibus sped towards them. They made no attempt to move. No screams as the heavy wheels snapped their bones. Just those groans. She'd had to do it. If she hadn't, she would have become one of them, and she would rather die than let that happen.

Footsteps echoed around the room as Lex and Sam walked back over to them. The change in the pair was noticeable. Lex was laughing at something Sam said. He was grinning with delight at making her laugh. They seemed comfortable together. Friendly. Sally felt the ugly twinge of jealousy flow through her again, but pushed it aside. It was out of place after the conversation they had just had.

"We brought chocolate," Lex announced. Dropping a pile of chocolate bars on the table. "What did we miss?" Oblivious to the tension, she plonked herself down onto the sofa.

"Sally was just telling me about how she stole the bus," Claire said, relieved that the silence had been broken.

"Ooh," Lex said, "I was wondering about that?"

Sally explained again. She left out the part about the children this time and Claire had the sense not to mention it.

"Fucking hell, Sally. You're a legend," Sam exclaimed when she had finished.

Sally's cheeks went pink with pleasure at the compliment from Sam. Then she remembered that she hated him. "Whatever," she said dismissively.

"You said earlier that some of those zombies followed you here. What happened?" Lex asked.

"There were some outside, just sort of milling around. When they heard the bus, they started coming towards it. So I got as close to the airport as I could, and they were still following me. I didn't want them to follow me into the building, so I parked outside one entrance and then ran to another. I left the engine running and the radio on, hoping that they would be more interested in the noise than in me."

"Were they?" Lex asked.

"Yep," Sally confirmed. "I was really quiet, though, and parked at an angle, so they probably didn't see me get out. We'll need to work out a way to distract them again, so we can get back to the mini bus tomorrow."

"Um … Sally …" Sam paused, "We won't be able to use the minibus tomorrow."

"Why not?" Sally snapped at him. "I've still get the keys."

Sam really didn't want to be the one to say this, but the other two girls didn't seem to have picked up on the problem and were staring at him in confusion.

"You left the engine running and the radio on?" he asked as politely as he could muster.

"Yes, I just said that, to distract the zombies," she snapped back.

Lex finally grasped what Sam meant, "Oh, Sam's right. The battery will be dead. Even if it isn't, there'd probably be no more fuel left," she stated, looking at Sam, who nodded back.

Anger surged through Sally, anger at herself for making such a stupid mistake. The events of the last twenty-four hours were almost too much to bare, and she could no longer suppress her emotions.

"Of course you'd agree with your new boyfriend," she spat, instantly regretting the words. This morning she had run over children. This afternoon she had shot a man. Being jealous over a boy was pathetic, but the words had been spoken, and she could not take them back.

"Boyfriend?" Lex asked in astonishment, "what are you talking about?"

"I saw the two of you. Over there. Getting cosy," Sally said, her voice thick with venom. She knew she was being childish, but she could not bring herself to back down.

Sam watched on in amusement. Was Sally jealous? Of Lex and him? He thought she hated him. Interesting…

Lex laughed, "Sally, I'm not interested in Sam."

"Yeah didn't look like it." Sally retorted.

"She's not, Sal," Claire added gently.

"Thank you, Claire. When I want your opinion, I'll ask for it," she snapped back.

"I'm not, Sally. The thing is … I'm …" Lex is not often lost for words, but this wasn't how she wanted to tell one of her best friends, but Sally was almost unrecognisable in her anger. "I'm gay."

Sally's mouth fell open. Then her phone began to ring.

Fifteen

The roads are quiet. So much so that I haven't seen another car since I left the house, or at least not one that was moving. I've seen plenty of those things. As I pass by, they become animated, reaching out, only to stumble and fall as they grasp the area which was occupied by the car only seconds before. It's comical to watch.

My progress is painfully slow. I keep having to stop, not least because I need to manoeuvre around the undead, but also because I keep stopping to check the map on my phone to make sure I'm going the right way. It's taken me two hours so far, and it's now dark outside. However, by my reckoning, I'll be on the M4 in less than ten minutes. All being well, I should be at Heathrow well within the hour.

I'm starting to get a bit worried about petrol. I should have enough to get to Heathrow, as long as I don't take any long diversions, and assuming that I've got the directions rights. I'm just not sure what to do about getting back to George's once I've got Sally. Will fuel pumps work without any power?

I'm also worried about finding Sally when I get there. I'm tempted to call her, but what if something happens to me and I don't make it? What if I make it, and she's relaxed because she thinks I'm on my way, and by doing so puts herself in danger?

What if I get there and she's already one of those things? What if I'm too late? I decide not to call. I'll get to Heathrow and work out what to do from there.

I'm lost in thought, not paying attention to where I'm going. So I don't see the man standing in the middle of the road until the last second. I slam the brakes on, but it's too late.

The impact of the car sends the man flying over the bonnet. He rebounds off the windscreen, then slides motionless to the floor. I hold both hands on the steering wheel, shaking. Was that one of those of those things, or just a man, looking for help? I should call the police, that is what you do in an accident after all. I take the phone and dial the emergency number. All I get back is a busy signal. I guess I expected that. I suspect the police are too busy fighting off the infected to respond to a road traffic accident.

I cannot see the man in front of the car. Should I check? I weigh up the pros and cons, then decide, I have no choice. He is blocking the road, and I don't think I could live with myself if I drove over someone who was not infected. I open the car door, hesitate, then pick up the putter from the passenger seat. It's getting darker, but the headlights provide enough illumination for me to see the shape of the prone body.

I walk tentatively towards him. He is lying face down. His right leg bent at an awkward angle.

"Hi," I call out, feeling stupid. "Are you okay …?" I ask, feeling even more stupid. I prod him in the shoulder with the golf club. He stirs and lets out a muffled moan.

"Oh, thank God," I breathe out in relief. I haven't killed anyone. I crouch down next to him and put a hand on his shoulder. "How badly are you hurt?" I ask. He feels icy cold. I should get the travel blanket out of the boot to wrap around him.

The man groans in response and struggles to push himself up. He turns to me. His inky black eyes are looking up at me, his mouth pulled back into a snarl. The groan, no longer muffled, is loud in the silence of the countryside.

He lurches for me and gains purchase on my arm, dragging it towards his mouth. I yelp, jump back, and he loses his grip. I quickly stand up, but he grabs at my ankle. I try to shake him off but he is stronger than me, and his grip is too tight. Remembering the golf club in my hands, I smack him in the arm. Using all my strength and might but he does not even flinch. He just keeps on inching closer and closer to my leg. His groan is becoming louder and more frenzied, he is millimetres away now. I take the putter and smash it down into his head. It has little effect, and I know I am going to die. Images of Sally lost and alone flitter into my mind. I cannot let her down. I will not let her down.

A feeling of rage, unlike anything I have felt before, floods through me. I smash the putter into his head.

Again and again. I keep going. I do not notice when he lets go of my leg, nor when he stops moving, or even when his head explodes under the relentless attack. I just keep hitting him. Releasing all the anger and sadness I have felt over the last few days. I only stop when my swings become slow and sluggish. All my energy is spent. I want to sink down, curl up in a ball and cry. But I can't. Blood, skull fragments, and brain matter paint the road. It is everywhere, it is disgusting. My stomach seems to agree, and I add vomit to the grim mess surrounding me.

When I have nothing left in my stomach, and the retching has abated, I stand up straight and return to the car.

I notice that bits of his head are still on the putter, I really don't want to take it with me, but while it wasn't a great weapon, it saved my life.

Instead, I wipe it on the grass verge, and then throw it on the back seat. The desire to cry remains, but it's overshadowed by the urge to get away from this road. Away from this carnage that I have caused.

Within minutes, a sign for the M4 comes into view. I breathe a sigh of relief. The rest of this trip should be easy. I join the motorway. It is busier than the country roads were. Although not in the conventional sense. A few cars are moving, but most are stationary.

I drive slowly, check my rear-view mirror and pull up alongside one. Four people are inside. Two adults in the front, two children in the back.

They strain against their seat belts. The two closest to me claw at the windows trying to get out. It breaks my heart to look at them.

A few days ago, they were a family. Now they are trapped in that car, doomed to spend the rest of their lives in this metal tomb.

Tears threaten again, but I must be strong. I accelerate away from the family and vow not to stop again until I get to Heathrow.

The vision of the family stays with me for far longer than I would like. Do they understand their fate? Is there a part of them that knows what they have become? How long will it take for them to die? Hang on, do they die? Could this be a short-lived threat, as soon as the infected die out then the survivors are safe again?

There are so many questions. So much that I do not know. There is only one thing I do. I need to get to Sally. Everything else can wait until she is safe. I put my foot down and carry on.

The road is clear enough to drive at a solid speed.

I do need to keep changing lanes to avoid the stationary cars, but fortunately, most of them are on the hard shoulder.

Some with doors open, the occupants seemingly attempting to outrun whoever was infected in their vehicle.

The rest of the trip passes without incident.

As I get closer to the airport, my earlier decision not to phone Sally seems stupid. She may not have got there. She might have come and gone, or not made it at all. I follow the sign to departures and where I sat waiting on Sunday. I notice a lot of people hanging around as I drive closer. Actually, that's not right. There are a lot of those things around. They seem to be heading towards a small mini bus that is parked up on the pavement next to one of the arrivals entrances. Oh God, what if someone is trapped in there.

Slowly, I edge forwards. The things don't seem to notice me. My headlights illuminate the writing on the side of the bus.

It obscured by the things, but I think I can make out the words Little and something borough.

My heart sinks. Little Brickborough. That is the village closest to George's house. I reverse a little, so I'm further away from the crowd, and switch off the engine. Willing the headlights to turn off. When you get home at night and it's dark, it's an excellent idea for the lights to stay on a little after the car has stopped. Much less so when you're trying to avoid being detected by a horde of zombies that want to eat you as soon as they see you.

Within a minute, the lights go out. It doesn't look like any of the things noticed me. I pick up the phone and dial Sally's number. Relieved that the networks are still working,

I wait for her to answer, getting more antsy with each ring. She doesn't answer, and the call goes to voicemail. I hang up.

Shit.

What do I do now? Within seconds my phone starts ringing, and I answer it quickly, a sigh of relief when the caller ID flashes; *'Sally Carlton.'*

"Sally, is that you?" I ask.

"Hi Chloe, yes it's me."

"Are you okay? Are you stuck on the bus?"

"No … I'm mean yes, I'm fine, I'm safe. No, I'm not on the bus."

"Thank God … wh…"

She cuts me off, "How do you know about the bus?" she asks, confusion in her tone.

"Oh … right … yeah. I'm at Heathrow, near to where the bus is parked."

The other end falls silent.

"Sally … are you still there …?"

"Yes," there is a muffled sob. "I'm just so happy to hear your voice, Chloe."

"Me too, sweetie. Listen, where are you?"

"We're in terminal five. The airport lounge just after security. I think it's called Galleries Club," she goes quiet, and I hear her talking to someone else. "It's the North one," she adds.

"Okay, honey, I'll be there as soon as I can."

"Chloe … be careful. There were some other people in here. They were going mental earlier."

"Don't worry about me. I'll be there soon."

I hang up the phone. Awesome. Infected people are walking around, wanting to eat me, now some crazies that I need to avoid. I think about what I packed in the car earlier. The rucksack with the knife, chisel, and hammers is next to me in the passenger seat, along with the golf clubs and walking poles.

I attach the poles to the bag and wiggle it onto my back, which is not easy inside a small car. I put my phone in my pocket and grab the putter from the back seat. I take a deep breath. Okay, I can do this.

I open the car door and close it quietly. I can see a route to the terminal, but I want to avoid detection.

I take a few steps away from the car and remember the bag of clothing that is in the boot. Call me paranoid, but I do not want it stolen. I press the lock button on the key fob. The indicators flash on, accompanied by a loud beep. Fuck. Stupid car. Stupid me for forgetting that the car beeps when locked. Cars should really have a built-in apocalypse mode.

I glance in the direction of the mini bus. Every one of those things has turned and is heading in my direction.

Fuck. Fuck. Fuck.

Holding the three golf clubs, with the bag banging against my back, I run as fast as I can towards the building. At the entrance, I look back. They are still following me.

Fuck.

They are going to chase me right into the airport. I try to visualise the layout of the terminal. The check-in area is huge, but it's a large open space.

It's wide but not too long. I should be able to make it to security without them seeing me. The departure area is concealed, so with any luck they might just wander around, then maybe get distracted by something else.

I sprint across the bridge that leads into the main building. I can still hear them, but I can no longer see them. Once across, I dash past the check-in desks to security. Damn. I had forgotten about the maze of moveable barriers that mark out the queue. I duck under the first one, but the walking pole, sticking up from the bag pulls me back.

I lower myself further down, but the rope has attached itself to the base of the handle. I shimmy backwards, and the pole becomes free. I spend a second or two trying to lift the rope over the pole, but my shaking hands are working against me.

I have no choice.

I run left for about ten steps, then right for another ten, left for another ten, the finally the last few steps right lead me to the x-ray machine, which I dash through, grateful for the first time that there is no electricity.

I look back, the sound of groaning muted now by the distance I have gained. I doubt that they would manage to navigate the queuing system anyway.

To my right is a small corner that leads to the North Lounge. In front of me is the balcony that overlooks the rest of the departure area. I step forward and look over. Even from this height, I can see that the airport has been trashed.

I step back quickly, because, while I am curious about what happened, I really want to avoid the crazies that caused this mess. I go right and head towards the double doors. I push them forward, but they don't move. I tap quietly.

Nothing. I don't want to knock any louder, because I don't want to draw attention to myself. I retrieve my phone from my pocket and type in a quick text. As I watch, the message status changes to delivered. The phone switches itself off. I forgot to charge it in the car and now I have run out of battery.

Sixteen

"You should probably answer that," Lex told Sally, who was staring at her in disbelief, while ignoring the phone vibrating on the table.

Sally didn't reply, but she picked up her mobile as it fell silent. A smile brightened her face as she hurriedly dialed a number. Three faces stared at her as she talked into the phone. She paused to the check the name of the lounge with Lex. She was still smiling when she hung up.

"Who was that?" Sam asked.

"Chloe," Sally replied.

"Who is Chloe?" he asked.

"She's my dad's PA," Sally said

"Oh," said Sam. Then he turned to Lex, "So, you're a lesbian?" The cocky grin was back on his face.

Lex ignored him, "Sally …" she said tentatively.

Sally got to her feet, walked over to Lex and gave her a hug., "I'm sorry for snapping at you."

"It's okay," relief flooded through Lex as she hugged Sally back. She had known for so many years that she was different from the other girls. That she had no interest in boys, that she was not attracted to them. She had wanted to tell her friends, but she was scared how they would react. So instead she stayed quiet, forever waiting for the right time.

The time they spent together in the Quarantine camp had strengthened her bond with Claire, and she had told her a few days ago. Claire had accepted it without question. They had discussed the matter at length, and Lex shared her worries and fears about how to tell her family. She had known Claire would be supportive. She was a lovely person, she didn't pass judgement, and she could see the good in everyone.

Sally was a different matter. Throughout their school years, Sally was obsessed with the opposite sex. She constantly talked about who she fancied. Boy band posters covered her walls, and in truth, she did not think that Sally would understand. Sally's embrace evaporated that uncertainty. She understood, and she didn't reject her.

"Is Chloe here?" Claire asked.

Sally pulled away from Lex's embrace, "Yes, she'll be here in a minute." The three girls chatted amongst themselves the argument all but forgotten, Sally asking Lex the same questions Claire had asked her a few days earlier. When did she know? Had she told her family? Who did she fancy? The latter topic led to a lengthy discussion about the girls they had gone to school with. Discussing who was pretty, who was not.

Sam sat quietly, observing the interaction. Women were so different from men.

He couldn't imagine chatting his mates about which men they knew were attractive. In a way, he was pleased to know that Lex was gay.

Their earlier conversation had started a bond forming. He had shared more with Lex than he had with any of his mates. She had listened, asked questions and seemed genuinely interested in him. He wanted to be her friend. The removal of the complications that could come when a man and a woman became close means he could look at her as a sister or cousin, and not as a possible conquest.

His thoughts turned to the argument. Sally had completely overreacted. The only explanation was that she was jealous. The only reason for this would be because she liked him.

A few days ago, he wouldn't have cared, but when Sally had come back into the airport, holding the shotgun, a face full of strength and determination, she looked… well, she looked sexy.

Not in the conventional sense, slender tanned body, perfect hair and makeup. No, it was different, more raw, more honest. Even the way she spoke to him, hard, full of hatred. He was used to girls fawning over him, and not talking to him like that.

His thoughts were interrupted by the message tone on Sally's phone.

"Bugger," Sally said, "It's Chloe, she's outside, she can't get in." She turned towards the door with its sofa barricade, "We need to move that."

Together they lifted the sofa out of the way and pulled open the door. Chloe stood on the other side, her face showing pure relief.

She sped across the threshold and pulled Sally in close. Sam, Lex and Claire lifted the sofa back in front of the door. Then stood patiently, waiting for Chloe to release Sally.

When the two women parted, Chloe turned to the rest of them. She had met Lex and Claire a few times before.

She gave them both a quick hug then turned to Sam.

"I'm Sam," he said and offered her his hand to shake.

"Sam?" Chloe asked. She turned to Sally, who gave an almost imperceptible nod.

Ignoring his outstretched hand, Chloe raised her own and used it to slap him across the face.

"Ow," He moaned, rubbing his cheek, "What was that for?"

"That was for being a cock," Chloe replied vehemently. "That will be the last I say or do on the matter. But …" she hissed the last word, "you treat her or anyone else like that in the future you'll have me to deal with. Got it?"

"Yes … er yes, mam," Sam stuttered.

"Mam?" Chloe questioned, "I'm not the bloody queen. Chloe is fine."

"Okay, Chloe," Sam replied, still rubbing at his face.

"Right," Chloe said, "it's dark. There are a shitload of those things outside. We'll stay here tonight, then work out how to get home tomorrow. Okay?"

Sam wanted to reply, he wanted to tell this woman that they had already agreed on this plan. But for once, he held back. He did not want to be on the receiving end of another of her slaps.

Chloe wandered over to the buffet area. The sandwiches were dry and curling. Peanuts, crisps and chocolate bars would have to do for dinner tonight. She grabbed handfuls and brought them over to the sofas that the group seemed to have adopted as a base.

The group talked and ate. Every now and then one of them would disappear to the loo or to the fridge to get something to drink. They shared their experiences, Chloe learning all she could about the things that Sally had encountered.

Claire noticed that, once again, Sally avoided mentioning the incident at the primary school. The room got darker as the evening wore on.

"We might as well try to sleep, sounds like we've all had a bloody long day," Chloe said.

"One of us should stay awake, just in case," Lex said.

"I'll do it," Sam offered. Chloe looked at him, eyes narrowed.

"Make sure you stay awake," she said, "Wake one of us if you get tired."

"Yeah, course," He said, pleased to have a role in their little group.

The girls each chose a sofa and lay down to settle in for the night.

Lex fell asleep almost immediately a small smile on her lips. The relief at sharing her secret felt like a huge weight had been lifted off her shoulders. She felt good, she felt happy. Her family must be fine. She was sure of it. Nothing could go wrong now.

Chloe lay, eyes closed but mind alert. Where was Steve? How would they get out of the airport tomorrow? Would she ever see Steve or her home again? Thoughts rushed frantically through her mind and sleep took a long time to come.

Claire fell into a restless slumber, her dreams filled with zombies and shotguns. She fidgeted and moaned throughout the night.

Sally stared into the darkness, because every time she closed her eyes the images of all she had seen and done over the past day flashed before her. Children with inky black eyes reflected by the headlights, the man whose knee had been blown off, the look of admiration on Sam's face when he complemented her actions. Eventually, sheer exhaustion dragged her under.

Sam sat upright, the shotgun on his lap, facing the door. He was determined to prove his usefulness. He wanted to help, he did not want to be sent away.

He would stay up all night and make sure no one threatened the little group. He managed a little over four hours before exhaustion overcame him and his head dropped to his chest. He slept.

~

Chloe woke first, her growling stomach reminding her that she had not eaten much the previous day. She looked over at Sam, sleeping quietly on a chair. They should have set an alarm so they could change over every few hours. In hindsight, there was no way he was going to last the night. Choosing not to wake the sleeping sentry, she quietly got up and looked around the lounge.

She spotted a door marked private, a key card entry system by the handle. Tentatively she pushed on the door and it opened without resistance.

Inside was a small but industrial kitchen. A large stainless steel fridge stood proudly in the corner. She opened it and grinned.

Bacon.

Taking the unopened packet out of the fridge, she looked around for something to open it with. Above a food preparation area was a rack that held a huge set of shiny utensils. She found some scissors and cut open the pack. The power had been off for a few hours, but the packet still felt slightly cool. She sniffed at it. It smelt like bacon. Maybe a fridge that size took longer to warm up when the power was removed than a domestic fridge.

Rooting through cupboards, she found a frying pan. The hob was gas, so she held down the nob and pressed the ignition, hoping that it was battery operated.

She grinned as it sparked to life and a ring of blue flame shone in the dim morning light.

She carefully laid each rasher into the pan, which was large enough to fit the entire pack. Leaving it to cook, she searched around for something to have with the bacon. In a large larder style cupboard, not only did she find bread, but she also found sachets of ketchup and brown sauce. Selecting a loaf and as many packets as she could carry, she dumped them on the work surface and went back to the fridge to find spread.

The smell emanating from the sizzling pan was glorious, and Chloe sniffed the air with pleasure as she flipped the bacon over. She turned as the door opened, to see Lex walk in.

"Is that bacon?" she asked

"Yep," replied Chloe, taking pleasure at the look of delight on Lex's face.

"Can I help?"

"Actually, yeah, can you see if you can find something to put these on, please?"

Lex rooted around the various cupboards and found a stack of crockery. Selecting five side plates, she held them up for inspection. "Will these do?"

"Perfect. Thanks, hun," Chloe replied as she buttered the bread. "Do you want to go and wake the others?"

Lex left the room and returned within a minute with Claire, Sam and Sally in tow.

"Bacon," exclaimed Sam, "I fu… I love bacon."

"Help yourself, it's ready," Chloe replied, noting in amusement, that Sam had stopped himself from swearing.

They each made themselves a sandwich and took them back out to the seating area. Eating quietly, savouring the taste of the delicious bacon. "There's more in the fridge if you're still hungry," Chloe said once she finished her sandwich.

Sam and Sally rose together, then looked at each other awkwardly. Eventually, Sam shrugged and turned towards the kitchen.

"Does anyone else want more?" Sally asked before following him.

The other three shook their heads. "I could murder a coffee," Chloe said, rising to her feet.

"Don't worry Clo, we'll make them," Sally replied, glancing over at Sam who nodded his agreement.

Sam held the door open for Sally. She considered refusing to enter and insist that he go first. She dismissed the thought quickly, it would be churlish of her, and she was already embarrassed by her childish behaviour the previous night.

In the kitchen, Sam added more bacon to the pan, reignited the gas, and then started to butter the bread.

"Can you see a kettle?" he asked Sally.

"Power's out," she reminded him. "We'll boil the water in a pan." She found a large saucepan and filled it with water from the tap. She put in on the hob next to the frying pan.

Sam lit the ring as she searched through the cupboards.

"I can't find any tea or coffee."

"I think I saw some out there yesterday," Sam said, nodding his head in the direction of the lounge. "Little packets, like you get in hotels."

"Thanks," Sally mumbled and left the kitchen. Minutes later she was back with sachets of coffee, tea bags and milk cartons and dumped them down next to Sam.

"Bacon's ready," he said, taking the frying pan off the ring.

They made their sandwiches in silence, then stood to eat them, neither looking at the other. When they'd finished, they stared at the large pan of water, willing it to boil quickly, the silence between them becoming uncomfortable.

"I'm sorry," Sam blurted out.

"Cups, we need cups," said Sally at the exact same time.

"Er yeah … I'll go, er … find some," Sam stammered, turning away.

"Sorry for what?" Sally asked.

Sam paused, hesitated, then slowly turned back to face her. "For acting like a dick," he mumbled, a blush creeping up his cheeks under Sally's gaze.

"You didn't act like a dick. You are a dick." Sally said, "You were my first, and you treated me like I was nothing. I know I'm fat and ugly, I can even accept that I was a one night stand, but to talk to me the way you did… in front of so many people. What sort of person does that?" She asked, willing the tears that were welling in her eyes not to fall.

"I'm sorry," Sam said again, "you're not fat or ugly, Sally. I was a selfish dickhead. I lashed out at you, because … well … because I'm not a very nice person… but I'm trying to be better … I am," he said in earnest.

Sally stared back at him, "I'm not ugly?" she asked in a quiet voice.

"No, you're not ugly. Actually, I thought you looked really hot when you were swinging that shotgun around yesterday." Sam paused, "Although I bet the guy with one leg doesn't think so," he laughed, then stopped short. Was he being a dick again? To his relief, Sally giggled.

"No, I bet he wouldn't," she said, "I bet he's hopping mad today," She added, a mischievous glint in her eye.

Sam stared at her, then burst out laughing, "I'm trying to think of a joke to match that one … but I'm stumped."

They collapsed into fits of laughter. "Oh … it's not funny. I shot a man. I could have killed him," Sally said, trying to regain her composure.

"He asked for it Sal," Sam said, fixing a serious look on his face. "They were hurting people and smashing up shops. We were hiding from them. Fuck knows what would have happened if they'd found us. Or if they'd got the shotgun off you."

"Yeah, I suppose, I just feel bad … you know?"

"Well don't, it was an accident. You didn't do it on purpose," he said reassuringly, then added, "and if anyone says differently, well they can hop off."

Sally burst out laughing again, reassured by Sam's words. Sam grinned back at her, then started giggling himself. It felt good to laugh, even though they both knew that they should not be laughing at that man's misfortune. But the giggling fit had taken over them both, and soon they had tears running down their faces. Each time they tried to stop laughing, they would look at each other and start again.

"Oh shit," Sally hiccupped, "I think the water's boiled."

"You think?" Sam said, still laughing. "What gave it away?"

That set Sally off again. The water was bubbling ferociously in the pan, spilling over the sides and generally making a mess. She took the pan off the heat, her hand trembling from laughing so much, water sloshing around the pan. Instinctively Sam took it away from her, to stop her from scalding herself. They prepared the drinks in a companionable silence.

A stark contrast to the uncomfortable tension that hung between them only minutes earlier.

"Er, Sam… can I ask you a question?" Sally said tentatively.

"Yeah sure," he replied.

"What… um, what's a hands-free-wank?"

Sam felt himself blush, "I'm really sorry for calling you that."

"Yeah, but what does it mean?" Sally persisted.

"Well… er… it's you know… when you have sex with someone… and ya know… you don't make that much effort…"

Sam squirmed, the blush on his face turning into a dark crimson. "So, it's er… like having a wank… but without your hands, cos, see… someone else has done the hard work."

Sally nodded slowly and went quiet for a second, deep in thought. Finally, she said. "Well that's not very modern, is it?"

"Modern?" Sam questioned, confusion evident on his still red face.

"Well no, surely it should be called a Bluetooth-wank nowadays." She said, trying to keep a straight face.

Sam stared at her in surprise. Then started laughing uncontrollably again. "A Bluetooth-wank? Sally, that's fucking hilarious."

Chloe walked into the kitchen and found the pair doubled up laughing. "What's so funny?" She asked. Other people's laughter is contagious, and she soon found herself smiling.

"It started by Sally making a joke about the dude she shot yesterday…" Sam began.

"You did what?" Chloe demanded, turning to face Sally. The smile replaced with a look of anger.

"It was an accident, someone tried to take the gun from me, and it went off," Sally replied, a pleading expression on her face. "I didn't kill him. Just... well… it kind of… destroyed one of his legs."

"And you're laughing about it?" Chloe asked, still furious.

"Sally made a joke about him being hopping mad today," Sam added trying to be helpful.

"Oh, my God. What is wrong with the two of you? Losing a leg is no laughing matter. I expected more from you, Sally."

"Sorry Chloe," Sally said, ashamed of herself.

Chloe didn't respond, she picked up two cups of coffee and stalked out of the kitchen. Sally took two more cups, leaving the remaining one for Sam. He took it and rushed to the door to hold it open for Sally.

They sat and drank coffee in awkward silence. Sally searched for something to say to ease the tension, "Chloe, where's Steve?" she eventually asked.

Chloe stiffened, "He has reenlisted in the army, to help fight this thing," She replied.

"Oh, I saw they were asking for volunteers in the emergency broadcasts the other day," Sally said, "It didn't occur to me that Steve would go."

Chloe nodded curtly and sipped at her coffee.

"Steve is your boyfriend, right?" Sam asked, and she nodded again. "And he just left you alone, in the middle of a zombie outbreak?"

Sam did not mean to be insensitive, he was making conversation, trying to build a bond with Chloe. He did not realise that he had chosen a topic so tender.

Chloe slammed her mug down on the table.

"Yes, Sam. My boyfriend left me. He left because he is a man of honour. In doing so, he has put his life on the line... my life on the line, because he can do more in the army than he could if he had stayed with me. Yes, he has sacrificed himself... our relationship, but he has done so for the greater good, and I for one could not be prouder of him."

As she spoke Chloe's demeanour changed. The tension ebbed away, her body relaxed, her shoulders dropped. A sense of calmness emanated from her. As though for the first time she truly understood why Steve had left. She looked at Sam, her eyes challenging him, daring him to speak.

Steve's actions were far beyond anything that Sam could comprehend. He couldn't imagine thinking of the country before he thought of himself, so he stayed silent. Knowing that there were no words he could offer.

Chloe finished the rest of her coffee, "Right, we need a plan to get out of here," her words eased the tension that had built in the room. Four young faces looked back at her expectantly. She sighed, "Any ideas?"

"Did you come in your car?" Lex asked Chloe, who nodded in affirmation. "So, we need to get back to that then."

"Yes," Chloe replied, "it's parked right outside, but I think we have two problems. One is that a load of those things followed me in here yesterday and might still be out there. And two, I don't have a lot of petrol left, so we'll need to get some from somewhere."

"Ah okay," Lex nodded thoughtfully, "how fast are the zombies?" she asked.

Chloe blanched at the term, up until now she had been calling them things or infected. Saying the word zombie made the whole situation scarier and more hopeless. "They aren't really fast, and they aren't really slow. More like the average walking pace I guess," she replied.

"Yeah, but really clumsy," added Sally, "like they're drunk or something."

"Yeah," Chloe nodded. "So, we can outrun them, but it will be difficult to avoid them if they were to come at us from different directions. Oh, and they're hard to kill."

"Damage to the brain??" Lex asked, making the question sound like a statement.

"Yep, I think so. One attacked me on my way here, and I beat the crap out of it with a golf club, but it only died when I had … well pulverised its head."

"Okay, so we'll need weapons."

"Yes, I've got a few things with me, but not sure how helpful they'll be," Chloe said.

"We've got the shotgun," Sam added. "I'm not a bad shot, so I could use that, you know, to avoid accidents," Sam said straight-faced as Chloe glared at him. When she turned away, Sam winked at Sally, who chuckled, earning herself a hard stare from Chloe.

"Okay, so I've got a putter, a knife, hammer and chisel… oh and some walking poles."

"Fuck me," Sam groaned, "Are we going to go for a hike, then doing some DIY?"

"Well, I left my arsenal of zombie killing weapons at home," Chloe snapped.

Claire interrupted before Sam could say anything else. "We could look around here for anything that might come in useful."

"Yes," Lex nodded, also keen to keep the peace. "There must be something useful in here."

"Okay, then. What about petrol?" Chloe asked. "I don't think petrol pumps work without electricity. We'll need a way to syphon the fuel from other cars. Does anyone know how to do that?"

The four women turned to Sam, expectantly, "What?" he asked, affronted. "'Cos I'm not as posh as you lot, you think I know how to nick petrol?"

"Um no," said Chloe.

"Nope," said Claire.

"Not me," said Sally.

"Do you?" Lex asked.

"Well yeah. But that's not the point," Sam said, grinning. "We'll need a can or something to store it in, and a hose."

"Well, we can probably find a couple of catering tins around here somewhere that will probably do. Guess we'd need a funnel to get it in the car?" Chloe asked.

Sam nodded, "Yeah, but where are we going to find a hose?"

The five of them considered this. There were no grass or floral areas around the airport so there would be no need for it to house a garden hose.

"Or…" Sam said, tentatively, "We could just nick a car?"

"What, like hot wire it or something? Do you know how to do that, too Sam?" asked Sally.

"Oi, cheeky, no I don't," Sam replied in mock indignation. "But don't they have those places… you know… where they take your keys and park your car?"

"Valet parking. Yes. Of course. Great idea, Sam," Claire beamed at him.

"What, so I suppose I'll just leave my car here?" Chloe said annoyed at the thought.

"Well, unless you can think of a better idea, then, yes," Sam replied.

Chloe remained silent for a few seconds, "No, I guess you're right."

"I am, besides, I guess these places are close by, so we could take your car and leave it there. Then you can come back and get it when this is all over."

"Yeah, okay, although if we happen to find a hose lying around, let's stick to the original plan. Okay?" The others nodded. "Right. Okay, so let's go find some weapons, then make a run for it."

Sam, Sally, Claire and Lex headed to the kitchen. Chloe went to the buffet area and loaded the rucksack up with snacks and bottles of water. She paused by the large wine rack and considered for a moment. Could you make a Molotov cocktail from wine? She had no idea but suspected it would need to be a spirit. There were miniature spirit bottles, but they were plastic, and she was sure it would need to be glass. She grabbed some just in case.

In the kitchen, they found plenty of utensils, pots and pans, some knives and some scissors.

Only the knives could realistically be used as weapons, but even they didn't look like they would be much use.

Sam left the three girls to search, and went back into the lounge. The tables each had four sturdy wooden legs, judging by how heavy it was when he'd tried to lift it the night before. They might do some serious damage if swung. He tipped one of the empty tables on its side and looked at the legs.

"Er Chloe," he called out.

"Yeah,"

"Can I borrow your hammer and chisel please?" he asked.

"Are you taking the piss?" Chloe accused.

"Er no," Sam laughed awkwardly, "I really need them."

"Okay …" Chloe replied, looking at him with suspicion. She found them in the bag and handed them to him.

Sam returned to the table. Positioning the chisel at the top of the leg where it met the table top, he hit it with the hammer until the leg came loose enough to pull from the table. He repeated the action with the other three legs.

Chloe picked up one of the legs and swung it like a baseball bat, "Ha, I knew that chisel would come in handy," she said smugly. "Do you mind if I take one?"

"Nah, it's fine. I can't carry one as well as the shotgun anyway," he replied.

Sally, Lex and Claire came out of the kitchen each holding a couple of knives.

"Ere," Sam said, handing each of them a table leg. You can use this. Should be able to give 'em a good whack with one of these."

"Keep those knives, though, they might come in handy," Chloe added.

"I got one for you," Sally said shyly and handed Sam a carving knife.

"Cheers," Sam said, he secured it onto his waist with his belt. "Chloe. Do you want me to carry that rucksack for you?" He offered.

Chloe looked up at him, surprised. "Thank you, Sam, that would be great."

He took it from her and swung it onto both shoulders. Not a style he would usually adopt in public, but he needed to have both hands free to control the shotgun. Sally rummaged around in her bag. She pulled out a box of shotgun shells and gave them to Sam.

"Here you go," she said, "makes sense for you to take them."

Sam took two out of the box and cocked the shotgun. He pressed the drop leaver to put a round in the chamber, then added the two shells to the magazine.

"Right so that's one in the chamber and five in the magazine," he said, "so six shots. I can reload, but it will take a minute, so if I need to, you'll have to cover me. Okay?"

"I thought shotguns only held two bullets," Claire said.

"Some do," Sam nodded. "But, not this model, it takes a total of six, oh and they are called shells, not bullets."

"What's the difference?" Claire asked.

"Well… for a rifle or a handgun, you'd have rounds. The round is the whole thing, like the casing, the propellant and the projectile. A bullet is the projectile. But this is a shotgun, so it's a bit different. Instead of a round, you have a shell, and instead of a bullet, you have shot, which are like little pellets, and they spray out when you fire it."

"Blimey Sam," exhaled Claire. "How do you know all that?"

"I… er… one of my foster parents used to take me clay pigeon shooting. Thought it would help me calm down a bit."

"Foster parents?" Claire asked.

"Shall we get moving?" Lex interrupted the conversation, sensing Sam's discomfort.

Relieved, Sam nodded and headed towards the door. Together, they lifted the sofa away from the exit, and Sam pulled the door open quietly and stuck his head out.

"Oh shit, I hope you're ready for this," he whispered, keeping his voice low to avoid being heard by the hundreds of zombies shuffling aimlessly around the departure lounge.

Seventeen

Thursday 19th September

Chloe,

Wow! What a day. I'm writing this from my new room at Linthem. My room is basic, although that's a generous description. There are two sets of bunk beds, one small table, and a lightbulb. That's it, that is my room, and yes you guessed it, I'm sharing with three other lads. The good news is that I'm not the only one writing to someone. Jonesy, another one of the reservists, is currently sat in his bunk above mine, writing to his kids. I guess I'm not the only one that finds it therapeutic.

It's weird being back in Linthem. I was based here when I first joined the Army, so I have some great memories from this place, but it's different now. The area in the safe zone has been secured, but it's not big enough yet, so tomorrow we'll be going out and extending the perimeter.

The infantry will be playing a big role tomorrow. We've been told we'll need to take out a lot of zebs to clear the area. Ah sorry, zebs is now the new name for zombies. I guess they don't seem as scary when they sound like something out of the Magic Roundabout. Anyway, so tomorrow we are going to see some real action.

Thank God, I'm in the infantry, some of the less fit reservists are on disposal, which is basically collecting, then cremating the dead.

The enlisted guys have been great. I was worried there might be a "them and us" divide, but there hasn't been at all. Although last night we were basically given a shitload of beer and told to get to know each other. It was actually great being back in this environment. One of the best things about the good old British Army is the universal ability to have a laugh, no matter how shit everything is.

Did I ever tell you about Pinocchio, one of the guys in my platoon on my last tour of Afghanistan? He was the one that got injured when our convoy hit that IED.

When the medic was trying to stop the bleeding, he told Pinocchio that he was going to lose his right arm. One of the other lads overheard and said to him that he'd better start wanking with his other hand. Another one chipped in and told him to use his nose because it's big enough. Pinocchio, cool as a cucumber, although you could see he was in agony, laughed. A proper belly laugh and replied that it was a shame it wasn't his nose that had been injured, as he could afford to lose some of that. It's that spirit that I love about the army. The Yanks used to call us Brits crazy for constantly ripping the shit out of each other.

I don't think they really understood it, though. It's not that we don't feel fear or that we're cruel or insensitive. It's just that when the world around you is going to shit, you need to hide any doubt and put on a brave face. Just one person losing it can create a panic and bring the whole platoon down.

I've digressed a bit here, but basically, that is what it was like last night.

We'd just been told that millions of people have either died or become a zeb. That we are going to have to go outside and shoot British citizens. You can bet your arse that everyone was as scared shitless as I was, but last night could have been any other night with the lads. Someone even called for a naked bar. Luckily, I was almost out of the door, so avoided the carnage. It was a good night. A few beers are just what I needed to start getting to know the lads. I didn't get too wasted. A few years out of the army has destroyed my ability to hold my beer, and I can't keep up with the young lads.

When I got back to my room, I saw your text. Okay? Chloe, I know you too well, you're hiding something, I can't believe you'd actually want to go to George's, at least not without moaning about it. I hope you don't do anything stupid. I'm sorry I haven't text you back. It's a selfish reason, but I know how stubborn you are and it doesn't matter what I say, you'll do whatever you want to anyway.

I would rather not know. I am just going to pretend that you're with George and Sally in his big secure home, drinking wine and having a pleasant and easygoing apocalypse.

Although after today, I do wonder if it was the right decision to suggest you go out there. The drive here was insane. We rolled out at first light, I was in the back of an SV, I haven't missed how bloody uncomfortable those damned bucket seats are. I was in the first convoy. Our objective was to clear the route for the other vehicles. There were five SVs and a couple of Fox Hounds. Every vehicle was manned with a GPMG, so the combined firepower was immense. We had the sides up on the SVs and were told that if we had contact, then we were to engage from the back of the vehicle, and only debus if we became overrun with zebs.

When we first left, I thought it was all a bit excessive, and actually, just a few troops could easily have sorted it out, there were a few individual contacts, but the GPMGs made short work of them.

As we got further, things got much worse; burnt out cars, abandoned buildings with doors kicked in, and windows smashed. But it was the number of corpses littering the streets that worried me. On Tuesday all had been normal, I can't believe how much the world has changed in just a couple of days.

It was a slow trip, there were just so many cars abandoned on the road. Some of them still had keys in the ignition, so they were easy. Most of them didn't, so had to be pushed. The first zeb I saw up close was a baby. It was strapped in its carrier in the passenger seat of a car. I'll tell you, Clo, seeing that thing straining against its restraints, its snarling contorted face and those black eyes staring up at me, was probably the single worst thing I have ever seen. It didn't even have teeth, so it wasn't going to hurt anyone, but the order came to destroy it. It wasn't me that had to do it, thank God. Can you imagine having to shoot a baby in the head at point blank range?

We only had to engage once, but there were shitloads of them. I was chatting away to Jonesy, inane chatter just to pass the time and the SV stopped quickly. Someone shouted "Contact", and it was like the last few years out of the army just fell away. We all jumped up and took firing positions, aiming out of the open sides of the vehicle. I don't know what was happening on the other side, but judging by the swearing behind me, they had hundreds coming at them, just like we did. The GPMGs gunners joined in and were taking them down, but unless it was a headshot, they just kept coming. Even if they couldn't walk, they would just drag themselves along the ground.

I've seen a load of shit on my tours, but every other enemy I have faced would flee or at least run for cover when they got shot at. The zebs didn't even flinch. When one of them fell, the next one would just keep coming.

When we got the order to engage, it was the crawlers that we were told to aim for, the GPMGs would thin the herd, we would finish them off.

It was a good tactic and worked well. They didn't get close enough to be a threat, and it was over in less than half an hour. We must have killed over five hundred of them. You can imagine the celebrations afterwards. The jokes about the outfits some of the zebs were wearing, calling out women that might have been fit when they were alive. The inevitable bragging about how many each of us killed and talking about perfect head shots.

I joined in, I had to, we all did. The British Army spirit and all that. It was hard, though. These people weren't wicked or evil. They hadn't done anything wrong, they just had an infection. A nasty, shitty disease, that turned them into brainless murderous goons, but still. They're just people. Or at least they were. It's getting late, and I need to sleep, I think it's going to be another long day tomorrow and this time we'll be on foot.

I love you.

Steve xxx

Eighteen

For the first time in his adult life, George Carlton had absolutely nothing to do. By Monday night, the constant ping of emails had ground to a halt. By Tuesday, so had the calls. There were no newspapers to read, no news to watch, no deals to make, not even the financial market movement to worry about. He had run out of people to phone. Most of the calls to his political contacts had gone straight to voicemail. The ones that had rung went unanswered and eventually went to voicemail too. The few people he had spoken to did not know much. They were the dregs of his contacts. Backbenchers, yet to reach the inner circle.

Only one person could offer anything remotely useful. The Prime Minster and his Cabinet had been whisked away to a safe zone. The leader of the opposition and the shadow cabinet had been taken to another.

He did not know where these zones had been located. When George pressed him, he had suggested that they might be centred around existing military bases.

George had decided already that he needed to get to one of those safe zones. For now, there was nothing to do, other than sit and wait for Chloe to return from Heathrow, with his daughter.

Again. It did not occur to him that he should be barricading his home, worrying about supplies, thinking about weapons. The thought that he should be researching possible locations for the safe zones didn't even cross his mind. Chloe would sort it out. So instead he sat in his large office chair and stared absently at the wall.

It had taken him until midday yesterday to realise Sally had gone. Teenagers always sleep in, so when she hadn't appeared downstairs for breakfast on Thursday morning, he had quietly popped his head around the door and saw her still form asleep.

By lunchtime when she still hadn't eaten, he had used the last of the bread to make her a sandwich. A peace offering. He knew she was angry at him for not letting her go and find her friends. While he was adamant that he was right, it wouldn't do at all to spend the next few days locked in a house with a stroppy teenager while the government and the army sorted this mess out.

George didn't have any friends, he had a network of contacts instead. He never took part in any so-called leisure activities unless there was something in it for him. A golf course was the perfect place to make deals. Going on shooting weekends was a good way to impress the upper classes. He hadn't stepped into a pub since he was a teenager. Instead, he would go to award ceremonies or other such events. Occasions that were useful to meet other influential people.

There was no one alive that George particularly cared about, other than Sally, so he didn't understand why she would want to go back to Heathrow and find Claire, Lex and Paige. They were perfectly safe where they were. Protected by the army, he knew they would come to no harm. Even if they did, so what? She could find new friends. It's not as if any of the girls wanted a career in any field that might be helpful to Sally in the future. So he had not listened when she'd begged for his help. Her tears and pleas had fallen on deaf ears.

Sandwich in hand, he gently knocked on Sally's bedroom door.

"Sally, I've made you a sandwich," he said proudly. It wasn't often that he prepared food. He waited patiently, expecting her to make a joke about how she was surprised that he had known where to find the bread, but there was no response.

He knocked again, harder this time.

"Sally," he repeated firmly, "there is no point being stroppy. It won't change anything."

The only response he received was silence.

"Right, that's it, young lady," he said as he pushed open the door, seeing that she was still asleep, hidden by her duvet.

He walked over to the bed and shook her. His hand didn't meet the resistance he had expected, causing him to lose balance, and the sandwich to slide off the plate.

He pulled the covers back, and his heart skipped a beat as the pile of cushions, that had evidently been used to fool him, collapsed

He immediately retrieved the car keys from their hiding place in his underwear drawer and went out to look for her. Having no idea how long she had been gone, but knowing it would have been at least five hours, he made the decision to drive to the village, then for a few miles in the direction of Heathrow.

She'd be on foot, so she couldn't have got that far.

On Tuesday when he had been forced to kill the cleaning lady, he'd phoned the police. It was self-defence. Besides, he had a contact at Scotland Yard that owed him a favour. He wasn't worried about the implications. It didn't seem to matter anyway. The emergency services were engaged. Wanting to rid the house of the body, he had wrapped her body up in an old bed sheet and put her in the car. He had intended to drive to a hospital so she could be disposed of in the proper way. He hadn't expected to see any more of those things, they lived in a quiet location, nothing happened here. Which is one of the reasons that he had made the little village his home. The closest hospital was in Whitney, and he had to drive through the village to get there.

On his way to the village, he was just passing the local school when a child ran out in front of his car. He had slammed the brakes on, stopping in time to avoid hitting the child.

The child froze. Tears streaming down her little face, as she stared at George with a look of terror on her face. Shaken himself, George didn't see where the woman came from, but did see as she lunged at the child. He heard the screams as she was pulled to the ground; witnessed the blood as it pumped out of her neck, soaking her white blonde hair. He stared on as the little body went limp.

He watched the frenzied attack in horror, his hands planted on the steering wheel, his feet still pushing down the clutch and the brake. The attack lasted less than a minute, although it had seemed to play out in slow motion for George. When the child fell silent and stopped moving, the woman slowly got to her feet and stepped towards his car.

In fright, his feet slipped off the pedals, and the car lurched forward bumping the woman, who stumbled, fell backwards and was hidden from view.

As George turned the key in the ignition to restart the stalled vehicle, a bloodied hand slapped the bonnet. The woman pulled herself up, trying to crawl over the bonnet to get to him. She was soon joined by the small child, now with a gaping hole in her neck. Two pairs of inky black eyes stared up at him. He lifted his foot from the clutch and slammed on the accelerator. The car jolted forward, but again it stalled. The momentum had been enough to throw the two things off the car.

He quickly turned the key in the ignition again, put the car in reverse and this time lifted his foot slowly off the clutch while increasing the pressure on the accelerator. The car slowly began to move backwards.

When he was far enough away, he put the car into first gear and slammed his foot down. He drove straight at the two figures, who were back on their feet. On impact, the woman was thrown to the side of the road, her head cracking on the kerb. The child went under the car, and he felt the left tyres breaking its body as it rolled over it.

He carried on, and when he was a safe distance away, he performed a well-executed three-point turn, then drove back in the direction he had come from. The woman had once again got to her feet, so he steered in her direction. This time he hit her head on, and she, too, was crushed by the weight of the car. George did not look back but drove back to his house, shaking and pale.

As he was pulling into his driveway, he remembered the body in the back of his car. Cursing, he reversed back out onto the country road and stopped.

A small stream ran through a ditch on the right-hand side of the road. George dragged the body from the car and rolled it into the ditch.

He watched as the stream quickly turned a light pink colour, as the water washed the blood from the corpse. He surreptitiously looked around. When he was confident no one had witnessed his shameful actions, he got back in his car and drove up the long driveway home.

Entering the house, Sally was anxiously waiting for him. He didn't say a word as he walked past her to his office and locked the door. He didn't come out of the office until later that night and barely spoke until the next day, when Sally had announced her intention to go back to Heathrow.

He hadn't intended to leave the house until the army had got things back under control. He had already witnessed, and been party to, too much horror.

He didn't want to see any more.

It was with a sense of trepidation that he drove out of his driveway, intentionally avoiding looking at the side of the road, where a body lay rotting in the stream.

He entered the village and was shocked by what he saw. Hundreds of infected wandered aimlessly in the streets. At the sound of his car, they turned in unison towards him. He quickly scanned the crowd and was relieved when he didn't see Sally, but he could also not see a way through. His car would knock some down, but if it stalled or if a body got trapped in the wheels, he would be swarmed. He used an empty driveway to turn around and sped back home, leaving the infected behind him.

When he had returned home, he considered his options. Sally wasn't answering his calls. He had no contacts at Heathrow.

The emergency services constantly had a busy tone.

So, as George did when he had a problem he couldn't fix, he chose to delegate the task. Chloe would know what to do.

Now it was over twenty-four hours since Sally had gone. He had tried to phone her, but she didn't answer. All he knew was that Chloe was going to get her. He had no idea if Sally was alive or dead. If Chloe had reached her at all. He felt no guilt at sending Chloe directly to Heathrow. If she wasn't at Heathrow, he was confident that Chloe would drive back to his house, and hopefully, would find Sally on the way.

He had no concern or consideration for Chloe's well-being, of the danger she might face helping him. To him, she was a resource, someone to use as he needed. Her thoughts and feelings were irrelevant, and as long as she did her job, she would get paid well. That was enough.

Nineteen

As someone who has read more than my fair share of zompoc, I have, of course, considered what I would do in a zombie apocalypse. How I would react in situations, how I would learn to thrive more than just survive. In all my musings, I never once created a scenario where I would be trapped in a bloody airport with four teenagers looking up at me, like I'm their protector, as though I alone can keep them safe.

The truth is, I'm still a bit pissed off with Sally. To find her laughing about causing a severe lifelong disability to another human being is untenable. I'm pissed off with Sam too, but more just by his mere presence.

While secretly I'm a little impressed with his knowledge of guns and his shadier skills, which might come in useful, I can't believe that the three young women have become friendly with him.

Not after the way he treated Sally.

For now though, there are more important things to worry about, like how we are going to get out of here alive.

When Sam looked out of the door and whispered to us about being ready, I crept quietly behind him and now I'm standing on tiptoe to see over his head. There are loads of those things.

"Close the door … quietly," I whisper.

Sam does as instructed, and very slowly closes the door. When it's shut, I signal to them all to follow me, and I head further into the lounge so I can talk freely.

"I don't know if they can see with those black eyes, but I do know that they can hear," I say to the four scared faces looking back at me.

I'm trying to look calm and confident, but I'm shitting myself. "Sally, did you learn anything about them on your way here?"

Sally pauses for a second, thinking. "Not really," she eventually replies, "same as you, they are attracted to noise, but I don't know if they saw me or just heard me when they came up to me."

I nod, "So we have two choices, one, we can hope they can't see and try to sneak out. Or, two, we can assume they can see, and try to distract them somehow."

They all look at me, expecting me to decide. Silence fills the air around us, as I wrack my brains for something that could be used as a distraction if we go with option two.

"I think it's best to assume that they can see. That way, if they can't, then it's a bonus," Sally says, breaking the silence.

"Yes," Claire nods enthusiastically, "hope for the best, plan for the worst."

"But," Lex interjects, "if we distract them somehow, then it will alert them to our presence. So even if they can't see, they will know we are there. So, we don't get any benefit from assuming that they can't see. But if we assume they can't see and try to sneak past them, then find out they can see, then we're in trouble." The words come out in a torrent, her mouth unable to keep up with the speed of her logical mind.

"Er, what?" Sam blurts out.

"Maybe slow down a bit, Lex," I say. I didn't understand her either and by the looks on Claire and Sally's faces, neither did they.

Lex takes a deep breath, "Option one," she holds up one finger, "we try to sneak past them. If they can't see, that's great. If they can, we will get attacked. Option two," she holds up a second finger, "we create a diversion; we also get attacked."

"Why?" Sam asks.

"Because, they will know someone is around to have created the diversion."

"I don't think they are that clever," says Sally.

"No," Lex explains patiently, "at the moment, they are just wandering around with no purpose. Yes?" She looks at Sam, who nods. "As soon as they hear a noise, we can assume that they will head towards that. Yes?" This time she looks at me.

"Yes," I confirm.

"So," she continues, "unless we can create a diversion that keeps their attention long enough for us to get out, we can assume we will be dealing with a bunch of alert zombies. That will more than likely pick up on any noise we make."

"Assassins Creed," Sam blurts outs excitedly.

"What?" I ask him.

"Well in Assassins Creed … If you alert a guard or someone of your presence when you are on a stealthy bit of the game, then they start actively looking for you. So being stealthy doesn't help so much anymore."

"Exactly," says Lex, relieved that she is getting her point across.

"Okay …" I say slowly. "So how does this help us?"

"Well, we're fucked either way, aren't we?" Sam states.

The room falls silent again. There is no way out of this that doesn't involve us getting attacked. From the expressions on their faces, I can see that the others know this. I say brightly, "So, we create a diversion to buy some time, run like hell, then if we get attacked, we defend ourselves as well as we can with these." I shake the table leg in the air with enthusiasm.

I keep the smile on my face, trying to look sincere and not terrified. They seem to relax; my act must be working.

"Right then," I add, maintaining my cheerful demeanour, "best that we go out in single file. I'll take the lead, Sam you bring up the rear. Girls, you can be between us."

"What? Why the fuck do I need to go at the back? Why don't you go at the back and I'll go at the front," Sam asks with an edge of anger to his tone.

"Sam, you have the bloody shotgun. If they're coming up behind us, you can shoot them."

"What if they're coming towards us?" he asks.

Hmm, he has a good point there, "Then I'll shout for you to run to the front," I say, making it up on the spot. "Point is, Sam, we are heading to my car. I know what it looks like and where it's parked."

"Ah okay, fair one," he says, all trace of anger gone.

Okay, so my motives for placing Sam at the back aren't totally fair. I don't know him. I don't like him. I obviously don't want him to die, but, well, he's less important to me than the three girls are. I can feel my face going red as I process this thought, and quickly turn away.

"What can we use as a diversion?" I ask.

"How about we all take a wine bottle and throw it one by one over the balcony," Lex suggests. "That way hopefully they'll all go downstairs."

That's not a bad idea. We're on the top floor of departures near security. This floor is a mezzanine, and the balcony overlooks the rest of the departure lounge.

I don't think those things are intelligent enough to go for the stairs, but they might all head to the balcony, which at least will keep them distracted in their attempts to try and get down to the lower floors.

"Good idea, Lex," I say, and head over to the wine cabinet. I hand out four bottles of wine and grab one for myself.

What a waste of good wine.

"Right, let's go then," I add cheerfully.

I lead the way back to the door and pull the door open quietly. I turn to the others and put a finger to my lips to make sure they remember to stay silent. The things are still wandering around. The nearest one is about thirty feet away. To be able to throw the bottles over the balcony, we need to get out of the corridor that leads up to the lounge. I turn back and motion for Sally to follow me.

She steps out quietly, and I start to make my way down the corridor. A few feet from the end I press my back up against the wall. No idea why. It doesn't offer any cover from the closest infected. Sally follows my lead, as does Lex, Claire and then Sam. I turn towards them and mouth, "Ready?" and they nod silently at me.

I raise my arm and throw the bottle as hard as I can.

Shit. I throw like a girl.

The bottle smashes against the glass screen of the balcony. As one, the things - okay, I'll say it, Zombies - turn their heads towards the noise and start making their way towards the smashed bottle.

"Go," I hiss at Sally.

She takes her bottle and throws it. Shit. She also throws like a girl. Her bottle smashes against the floor a metre or so away from mine. The shuffling zombies seem to become more excitable.

"Lex," I whisper.

Lex's throw was awesome. It sailed clear of the balcony and seconds later the sound of the bottle shattering could be heard from below. Unprompted, Claire lobs her bottle, and she too clears the balcony. The zombies are getting nearer the two smashed bottles upstairs.

I chance a peek out of the corridor to the exit. I can only see a few now between us and the exit back to the check in desks.

Fuck. What if there are more?

The check-in is hidden from view. There could be shitloads out there. I run through options in my mind. There are none. We'll just have to hope for the best.

Sam steps forward and tosses his bottle. It also sails over the balcony and smashes below. Zombies are now pushing against the glass screen. There must be at least fifty of them. The concentrated noise of their groans and moans is almost too much to bear. Another sound joins the cacophony. A creaking sound.

The glass isn't strong enough to hold that many people pressing against it. It's cracking.

Instead of running for the exit, I hold my position and watch in fascination as the glass shatters, and some of the zombies plunge to the floor below.

"Sam, Claire, Lex, run back and get more bottles," I whisper excitedly. "Sally, hold the door for them. I'll keep look out."

Within thirty seconds, they were back, two bottles in each, the table legs and shotgun discarded for the time being.

"Right, throw them over the edge," I instruct. "One at a time, but closer together than we just did."

They nod and begin throwing bottles. With each smash, the zombies continue to surge forwards towards the noise. They are dropping like lemmings. I stifle a laugh. Stupid things.

When the six bottles have been thrown, there are only a couple of zombies left in view. I take a deep breath.

"Run," I whisper urgently and start sprinting for the exit. I reach it quickly and pause before going out, looking into the check-in area. I can see four zombies in the threateningly close vicinity. I turn back and see Sally and Lex have joined me, Claire and Sam are running and will be here in seconds.

I get the answer to whether they can see through those evil eyes, as Sam's being chased by two of the things, who must have spotted us.

He's running much faster than they are, so they're not an immediate threat.

I start to run again but this time at a slower pace. I head towards the closest zombie who has its back to me. It begins to turn as I get near, but I don't give it a chance to react, as I smack it over the head with the table leg. It falls to the floor, and I hit it a few times until it stops moving, its head smashed to a bloody pulp. I swallow the bile that is rising in my throat and head to the next one. It's already coming towards me, so this one gets a whack to its face. Its nose explodes, but it doesn't go down. I hit it again, but it stands firms. Holding the table leg in two hands, I jab it forwards and knock the thing off its feet. When it is down, I hit it a few times to make sure it stays there.

I look up to see Sally and Lex hitting another one and Claire going for the last one. Sam has his back to us and is aiming the shotgun at the two coming his way.

"Don't shoot," I shout.

He turns towards me and looks confused.

"You'll draw more of them."

He nods in understanding and pulls the knife from his belt. He carefully places the shotgun on the floor and then runs towards the two zombies. I sprint after him. The two infected are too close for him to take on alone. I get there as he plunges the knife into the eye of one of them. The eyeball explodes.

A mixture of pus, blood and a black fluid squirts out, catching Sam on the shoulder.

The zombie goes limp, Sam still holding the knife is dragged down with it, landing on top of the thing. The next zombie lunges forwards and crashes into Sam's back. The rucksack offers Sam some protection, and I smash the table leg across the side of the thing's heads as it bites down at the bag.

The force of the impact knocks the zombie's face towards Sam's shoulder, I quickly hit it again, this time killing it.

Sam groans and tries to move, but is pinned down by the dead body on top of him. I use the table leg to push the zombie off, then hold out a hand to pull him up.

"Cheers," he said, shaking.

"Did you get bitten?" I ask him, forcing him around so I can look at his back. He is covered in blood and the remnants of zombie eye, but I can't see any bite marks. I note a small tear in the rucksack and say a silent prayer of thanks that he was wearing it.

Looking around, there are at least a dozen more zombies heading our way. "Come on," I say, "We need to get out of here."

Still dazed, Sam nods. Together we jog towards the entrance where the girls are waiting. Like Sam, they are covered in blood. I look down at myself. Disgusting. Blood coats my arms and hands. Infected blood. Shit.

"Wait here," I say.

I sprint back past the check-in desks and enter Boots. I quickly find the antiseptic hand wipes next to the tissues and grab a few packets. Turning to leave the shop I spot tampons in the next aisle. I grab a couple of boxes, better safe than sorry. My hands are laden with goods. If I get attacked now, I'm screwed. I need something to carry this in. I look around. The cash desk is at the back of the shop, but there are baskets at the front. I pause, undecided for a second, then run to the entrance and drop everything into a basket. Pausing again, I consider the opportunity. I go back into the shop and head to the pharmacy section. I throw various drugs, bandages, plasters and alcohol wipes into the basket. What else should I get?

The scream from one of the girls makes me jump. I'm taking too long. With the basket in one hand and the table leg in the other.

I run back out of the shop and see, Sam, Claire and Lex, pulling one of those things off Sally. The zombie has her gripped tightly in its gnarly hands. I can see that she is pulling back from it and managing to avoid its mouth clamping down on her. Why aren't the three of them hitting it? I wonder then realise the answer immediately. It's too close, they would hit Sally too.

"Knives," I yell.

Sam reaches one hand down for his, but it is still embedded in the eye of a dead zombie.

Lex and Claire didn't react to my shouting, either because they didn't hear me or they are afraid to let go of the thing trying to bite Sally.

Shit. More zombies are heading their way. Too many, we can't take on that many between us. I sprint over, dropping the basket which spills its contents to the floor, and grab my own knife. I stab it hard in the ear of the thing and let go as it drops to the floor.

"You okay?" I ask Sally, who nods back dumbly. "Claire, Lex, grab that basket and the stuff off the floor."

I lean over the fallen zombie and pull the knife. It's stuck. Using my foot on its neck to brace myself, I give it another yank and it comes free. It's covered in blood and brain matter. I wipe it on the zombie's sweater, leaving a bloody mark on the grey material.

The other zombies are getting closer.

"Right, let's go," I turn to run before I even finish the sentence. I breathe a sigh of relief when I see my car is where I left it. Shit. Where are the keys? I rummage around in my pockets until I find them and click the button to unlock the doors. There are five of us, and it's only a small car. It's going to be cramped.

I open the door and get in. Sam runs around to the other side and gets in the passenger seat, leaving the three girls to squash in the back. Lex is still holding the Boots shopping basket.

I jump out of the car again, and take it off her and put it in the boot. Sam still has my rucksack, and the girls still have the table legs. All of it taking up valuable space, but I want the bag and the weapons close to hand.

The zombies from the check-in area have followed us and are slowly approaching the car. I put the key in the ignition, ready to drive away. Before I do, I take one of the antiseptic wipes and quickly clean the gore off my hands and arms. As soon as I've finished, I start the car and drive away.

"I wonder what happened to those other people," Lex muses.

"The ones from yesterday?" Claire asks.

"Yeah," Lex nods. "They might have been idiots, but I hope they got out in time."

"Well, did anyone see a one-legged zombie?" Sam quips and I glare at him. "Sorry," he mutters.

"You okay Sal?" I ask; her reflection in the rear-view mirror is pale, and she looks shaken.

"I'm fine," she nods, "I know they used to be people... those things... but, did anyone else think that was kind of awesome?" she adds.

The car fills with noise as they all begin to talk at once, sharing their experiences. I know exactly what Sally means. I didn't enjoy killing them. I don't think the others did either, but, adrenaline still courses through our bodies.

We are safe in the car. We won. It's a heady feeling. I have never felt so alive. It's like when I go on a roller coaster.

The anxiety builds during the queueing to the point where I feel sick. The ride itself is over in a blur and then afterwards I get loud and excitable and want to go again.

It's like that, only ten times more intense. I know that I'm unlikely to die on a roller coaster, but back there, we were fighting for our lives.

I bring myself back to the present as I hear Sam say my name.

"What was that?" I ask.

"I was just telling the others how you saved my life," he says grinning.

"I didn't … not really, it was the rucksack. If you hadn't been wearing that, he would have got you for sure." I protest.

"You killed him … you could have just left me there." Sam says.

I'm uncomfortable with the praise, not least because less than an hour ago I had purposefully set Sam at the back of the group to protect the rest of us. When I'm nervous or uncomfortable, I turn to humour. Which would be a much better defensive mechanism if I was actually funny.

"Next time I will leave you if you take on two on your own," I say, forgetting to smile so show that it was supposed to be a joke.

"Oh er, right," Sam says, and now he is uncomfortable.

"It's a joke," I say and plaster a mad grin on my face.

Sam looks even more uncomfortable now. I'm sure he's wondering who the crazy lady is, and remembering back to when he was younger and the stark warnings about not to get in strangers' cars.

The three girls are snickering in the back of the car as they watch Sam and me in the front seat, Sam edging slightly away from me, and the stupid smile still on my face.

"Right, erm," I cough. "Any suggestions on where to go?"

"Follow the signs for the airport parking," Lex suggests. "Bound to be a valet parking in one of the multi-stories."

I nod and slow down, looking for signs. The long-stay parking is coming up on my right. I flick the indicator on and follow the signs. Why did I use the indicator? Idiot.

It's dark inside the multi-storey car park, and my headlights automatically come on. There's movement in the shadows. Must be more zombies. Surely survivors wouldn't hang around a car park.

"Try the top floor," Lex suggests

I nod and navigate my way to the top. Lex was right. There's an office marked with the words "Private" and "Valet".

"That must be it," Sam says.

"Thanks, Captain Obvious," I reply, sarcastically.

I pull my car into one of the empty spaces. Unload everything now or wait until we've got a car?

Wait, I decide. That way if something goes wrong we can just jump back in my car. We won't get far on the petrol I have left, but hopefully, there would be enough to get us out of immediate danger.

"Sam, come with me and bring the rucksack," I order. I don't know what it is about him, but for some reason, I just keep being either mean or bossy when I speak to him. He either doesn't notice or doesn't care. As instructed, he gets out of the car and picks up the rucksack. He brings the shotgun with him too. Good idea, I think, but don't say out loud.

We walk over to the door, and I turn the handle. As I expected, it's locked. You don't just leave a door to a room that is, hopefully, full of car keys, unlocked.

"Can you get the hammer and chisel out of the bag, please?" I say, trying to be civil.

He does, and hands them to me. He stands with his back to me, holding the shotgun in both hands, ready to shoot at anything coming up the ramp.

Another good idea.

"Um, good idea Sam," I say. He's trying, he might be a bit of a prick, but he does have some sense, I guess.

I wedge the chisel in between the door and the frame and use the hammer to hit the chisel handle. The wood starts to splinter. I shift my aim from the top of the chisel handle to the side and hit it again. This time there is a crack, and I knock a big chunk of wood out of the frame. I readjust the chisel, so it's angled towards the lock rather than the frame. I give it a good solid whack and the lock breaks, leaving the door to swing open.

Stepping inside the room, I'm relieved to see rows of car keys, with neatly labelled tags showing the corresponding registration number. Okay, so what car? I step back outside and look around. There are a lot of good cars here. Something bigger that we can all fit in comfortably.

"Should we take two cars?" I ask Sam, who is still holding his position, watching the ramp.

He considers the options for a few seconds. "I dunno. It would be good to stay together, but it might be sensible to split up. That way, if one car gets in trouble the other can help out. Also, if something happens to one, like it runs out of petrol or summat, then we have a back- up plan."

"Yeah," I agree, "that's what I was thinking." It wasn't what I was thinking at all, I was just wondering if it might be more comfortable, but Sam doesn't need to know that. "Which ones?"

He takes a quick look around, before looking back to the ramp. "Four by fours," he says. "Easier to get over any obstacles. Plus, higher up on the road so we can see more."

"Blimey Sam, just how many zombie apocalypses have you been in?" I joke.

"What?" he says, clearly confused and trying to find the insult in my words.

"Keeping a look out at the point of access, thinking of contingencies, choosing sensible cars. It's like you've done this before."

"Er … no …" he says nervously. Like I'm accusing him of something.

"Relax," I say and smile to show that I am being genuine. "I'm complimenting you."

"Oh," he says, and a little tension leaves his body. "That's why I was confused. I didn't know you knew how to complement people," he adds with a cheeky grin.

I laugh as we walk out to the cars, choosing two larger models and memorising the number plates. Back in the office I find the right keys and take them off the rack. I give one set to Sam.

"Here you go, you take Sally, and I'll take Claire and Lex."

"Why Sally?" he asks, the nervousness back in his voice.

I'm confused by the tone, and I guess he has worked out that I'm protective of her. Does he think I'm trying to set him up, so he does something that will piss me off and give me a reason to kick him out of our group? "That way we have two cars with at least one person that knows the way in each car," I explain.

"Ah okay," Sam says, then nods, "makes sense."

"Let's load up and head out. I'll take the lead." I say, Sam grunts in agreement.

It only takes a few minutes to move the contents and the passengers from my car to the other two. I climb aboard the shiny silver Audi Q5 with Lex in the passenger seat and Claire in the rear. Sam gets into a white Honda CR-V, and Sally holds the shotgun next to him in the passenger's seat.

I strap my seatbelt on and take a last look at my little car, before driving off down the ramp, Sam following slowly behind me.

"Chloe...?" Lex asks then pauses.

"Yeah,"

"I want… I mean… I need to know." she stammers.

"Know what?" I ask, concerned. Lex is usually very articulate, and it's not like her to struggle over her words.

"My parents…" I glance at her and see a single tear rolling down her face.

"Okay, honey," I say soothingly, "let's take you home, where do you live?"

"Botley," she replied, wiping the tear from her face.

Oh, shit. Botley was right on the outskirts of Oxford. Going there is probably a really bad idea, I bet the place is overrun.

"Okay," I say, because there is nothing else I can say.

Twenty

The steady rumble of engines disturbed the peacefulness of the outside world. Sally sat quietly next to Sam and surveyed the scenes out of the windows. It had got much worse since the day before.

"It's bad out here," she said to Sam, "much worse than yesterday."

"It is," he said, "bad I mean. Obviously, I wasn't out here yesterday, but shit, look at that …" he points at a car, upturned and on fire on the side of the road. A blackened and charred body hung halfway out of the passenger window.

They drove in silence, following the route Chloe was taking, weaving around the debris that lay strewn on the roads. Coming up to a lay-by, Sam saw that Chloe was indicating left. Puzzled, he followed her in, and came to a stop behind her.

Chloe got out of her car and jogged over to Sam. He wound the window down, an uneasy feeling washing over him as he saw the worry on Chloe's face.

"What's up?" he asked. He kept one hand flopped over the steering wheel, his casual pose belying the tight knot in his stomach.

"Change of plan, we're going to Botley to get Lex's parents."

There was a small intake of breath from Sally in the passenger seat, "Is that a good idea?" she asked.

"Probably not," Chloe admitted, "It's so close to Oxford, it's bound to be overrun … but …" she paused, flicking her hair off her face. "She needs to know that they are okay."

"Do you think they are?" asked Sally, leaning further over Sam to talk to Chloe.

Chloe sighed, "I don't know. I hope so, for Lex's sake, but it's so close to Oxford…" She repeated herself, the words trailing off at the end.

"Okay," Sam interjected, "we managed to get out of the airport, we'll be fine." He grinned with a confidence that he was not feeling.

Chloe nodded, reassured by Sam's assurance. "Keep following me, stay close behind and if you need anything, flash your lights. Okay?"

"Yep. Although… why not just phone Sally's mobile?"

"Networks are down. It was bound to happen, with the power going off yesterday."

"Okay, just use your hazards if you want to get our attention."

"Will do," confirmed Chloe as she turned and walked back to her car.

Sam wound the windows back up and turned to Sally, "You don't like this idea, do you?" he asked.

"Nope," she replied quickly, "I understand that Lex wants to know about her parents, but Oxford… it's going to be crawling with those things, and all we have are a few table legs and a shotgun."

She looked back at Sam, her face flushing with shame as he silently studied her. "I don't know," she added. 'It just… I have a feeling something will go wrong."

"If it was your parents, what would you do?" Sam asked.

Sally tilted her head to one side and considered the question, "I'd like to think that I would want to do what's right for the group and take the safest option, but… I guess I would want to know too," She conceded.

Sam put the car into gear and slowly pulled away behind Chloe, "We'll get as close as we can. If it's too bad, then chances are they wouldn't have survived anyway."

Sally nodded and chewed on her bottom lip, but didn't respond. Instead, she stared out of the window as the countryside rolled by. Sam reached out a hand and squeezed her knee.

"We'll be alright," he reassured her. He left his hand on her leg, taking comfort in the human contact. He was scared, really fucking scared but he felt a growing responsibility towards this group. As the only man, an unfamiliar, yet deeply rooted instinct to protect them was bubbling to the surface. Still, the feel of Sally's soft leg beneath his hand gave him comfort.

Sally stared down at Sam's hand, then glanced up at him. He was staring intently in front, seemingly concentrating on driving.

Confused at this display of affection, she picked his hand up to remove it from her leg, but instead of just flicking his hand away, she found herself clasping it tightly.

Hand in hand, Sally and Sam drove on in silence, following the silver Audi. Both worried about what they would soon face, but both glad for the comfort given by the other.

~

They'd been on the move for over an hour before they started to approach the outskirts of Oxford. The going had been slow because of the cars, and in some cases, bodies, on the road. They'd seen a few infected, but Chloe had sped past them as fast as she could safely go, and Sam had followed suit.

Now as they drew closer to their destination, Chloe's anxiety increased. Claire dozed obliviously in the back seat, but the conversation in the front seat had dried up, neither women knowing what to say.

Small talk seemed pointless.

When Lex had mentioned the weather, they knew they had reached the very end of possible conversation topics and had spent the last ten minutes in silence.

"Take a left here," Lex said and pointed in the direction she had indicated.

Chloe duly obliged, glancing out of the rear-view mirror to make sure Sam and Sally were still behind. The road took them away from the lush countryside, and houses started to sporadically pop up, set back from the sides of the road. The further they went, the more houses they saw. There were no infected in plain sight, but from the abandoned cars and the smashed-out windows on some of the houses, it was clear that even this remote rural area had not avoided the carnage of the last few days.

Lex said nothing, other than occasionally giving directions. She felt sick at the thought of what she might find when they reached her house.

As the roads turned into streets, the feelings increased and she bounced her leg up and down, as though to remove some of the tension. The more populated the area became, the grander the scale of destruction. Now as well as the odd car or broken window, there were burnt-out shops, houses and cars. Front doors seemingly kicked in. Bodies scattered the pavements. Blood painted the streets, most of it dried, so she guessed that whatever had happened here had taken place a few days previously.

"Take a right here," she said and held her breath as they entered the street that she called home. She relaxed a little, maybe the fighting, or whatever it was, had not reached the side streets.

There were still signs that something wasn't right, the odd open door, a few smashed windows, but the destruction was far less apparent than it had been on the main roads.

"It's the house at the end, the one with the blue door," she pointed towards it.

Chloe followed the directions, she, too, feeling anxious and apprehensive. She came to a stop in front of a pretty detached house. It looked like it had been recently built despite the mock Tudor style timber adorning the upper half.

"Are we here?"' Claire asked sleepily, the sensation of coming to a stop causing her to wake.

"Yes," said Lex, and Chloe also nodded in ascent.

They unbuckled their seatbelt and took hold of their table legs before exiting the car. Sam and Sally also got out of their car and walked over to Chloe, Lex and Claire. Sam looked at them all holding their table leg.

"Shit," he exclaimed, "forgot the shotgun."

He jogged back to the car and opened the rear door, picked up the gun and ran back, not noticing that the door hadn't fully closed when he had pushed it shut.

"This it then, Lex?" he asked.

"Yep," she smiled. There was no sign of damage on the outside of either her house or any of the immediate neighbours'. Her parents' BMW sat proudly in the driveway. It looked like a normal house on a normal day.

She ran up the front path and rang the doorbell. "Forgot my key," she grinned as she waited for her parents to open the door.

The door remained resolutely shut.

"Maybe they're sleeping?" Chloe said.

"Or in the garden?" Sam said.

"Maybe the doorbell battery is dead?" Claire suggested, instantly regretting the use of the word dead.

Worry lines creased Lex's forehead and her smile faded into a frown,

"Hmm, maybe," she said, not indicating which option she thought most likely.

A planter full or miniature red roses stood next to the door. She rooted around the base of the plant, cursing as a thorn cut into her finger. When she pulled her hand out, she was clasping a large grey rock.

"Don't smash the fucking window," Sam shouted in alarm. Then immediately went red as he realised that Lex had retrieved a key from a hidden compartment in the rock. "Well… it looked real," he muttered in embarrassment.

Lex inserted the key in the lock and hesitated a second before turning it. Chloe rushed over to her, "Why don't I go first?" she suggested.

"Okay," Lex nodded, she looked down at her hands, where a patch of blood had welled up from a tiny cut. She wiped her finger on her jeans.

Chloe turned the key in the lock, then jumped at the sudden high-pitched screeching of a car alarm. They turned towards the source of the noise and saw the Honda's light flashing as though at a disco.

"Shit," Sam said and fumbled in the pocket for the keys.

"Shut it up," Chloe shouted over the din.

Sam pressed the buttons on the key fob, but they did not have any effect. He ran over to the car and opened the driver's door. Still, the alarm continued. He put the key in the ignition and the onboard computer lit up, showing an outline of the car, the rear left-hand door flashed red. He quickly moved to the door and slammed it shut. The alarm silenced immediately.

"Oops," he said, "didn't know that car alarms went off if the door is left open."

"Only some do, generally the newer cars," Chloe said through gritted teeth.

It was a genuine mistake, and Sam had tried to fix it as soon as possible. But that alarm was deafening and you could bet that any zombies close by were heading their way now. "We need to move quickly," she said and ran back up the path, turning the key in the lock and pushing the door open.

A foul stench assaulted her nostrils as she stepped tentatively into the house. She wasn't familiar with the smell of death, but this foul, putrid odour must come close. Lex tried to push past her as she paused in the doorway.

She turned to her and said tenderly, "Wait here a minute," then called out, "Sam, bring the shotgun and come with me."

Sam nodded and jogged up to the door, Lex had taken a few steps back and was hopping from foot to foot, trying unsuccessfully to dispel the nervous energy that was threatening to engulf her.

Chloe stepped through the open front door, and Sam followed closely behind her. She turned to him and placed a finger on her lips. He nodded in response, understanding the need for silence. He, too, had drawn the same conclusion the second he had inhaled the stench permeating the house.

The front door led to a large entrance hall, where coats were hung neatly on racks, shoes placed carefully beneath them. Unopened letters sat on a small console table. Glancing quickly at them, Chloe saw that they were addressed to Lex. No doubt left there waiting for her to return from her holidays. The hallway split off in four directions, closed doors to the left and right. Straight ahead were the stairs, and a narrow corridor leading to an open door.

Chloe slowly turned the handle of the door to the left. It opened into a small room, with a desk and a sofa. Likely used as an office for one of Lex's parents.

The room was empty and free from the overpowering smell of the rest of the house. Quietly closing the door, Chloe turned to face the door on the right.

Again, she turned the handle slowly, but this time it opened onto a tastefully decorated lounge area. A large corner sofa dominated the room, a magazine lay discarded on one of the cushions, and the sofa faced on to a large screen television, which sat on an expensive looking mahogany stand.

Chloe exhaled, two rooms checked, two rooms empty. Once again, she pulled the door shut, trying to be as quiet as possible. Turning to Sam, she indicated the open door at the end of the corridor in front of them. It, too, must be empty, they hadn't been quiet enough not to attract attention, and the open door would have meant that an infected could easily have approached them by now.

She strode down the corridor and through the door. She stopped short at the scene that was laid out in front of her. It was a kitchen, white high gloss cupboards with a grey worktop. To the right was a dining area with a glossy white table and dark grey leather chairs. An opening next to the table led out to a conservatory.

In any other circumstances, Chloe would have admired the stylish and modern kitchen, but not today. A man was slumped over the dining room table, a pool of blood formed around him. Tentatively she walked over to the man and put her hand on his shoulder, flinching at the feel of the coldness beneath her palm. She forced the body upright, for no other reason than to understand what had killed him.

A knife was protruding from one of his eyes. The other stared blankly back at her. A healthy, normal eye, no trace of the black inkiness that the infected displayed.

"He was alive when he died," she whispered to Sam.

"Er, well, yeah," Sam said, not really understanding how anyone could be anything other than alive when they died.

"I mean he wasn't one of those things. He wasn't infected," Chloe replied, clarifying her previous comment.

"Actually, I think he might have been. Look." Sam pointed to a gash that had been ripped out of the inside of his lower arm.

"He got infected and killed himself before he could turn," Chloe said, and the courageous and selfless act astounded her. What would she do in the same circumstances? Would she be brave enough to kill herself to avoid becoming one of those things?

"So, assuming that's Lex's dad …" Sam said, pulling Chloe out of her thoughts. "Where's her mum?"

They both turned towards the open kitchen door, expecting to see a female zombie coming at them. There was nothing, just stillness and silence. In unison, they released the breath each had been holding.

"Conservatory?" Chloe said, and Sam nodded in response.

Gingerly they headed through the opening into the large glass room. Wicker furniture with soft, inviting cushions adorned the room, and another TV stood in the corner. No signs of life, or of death. The room looked ordinary. If it hadn't been for the prevalent smell emanating from the corpse, it would have been inviting.

"Upstairs?" Sam asked.

"Upstairs," Chloe confirmed.

They headed back out of the conservatory, through the kitchen and then up the stairs. They came to a spacious landing.

A marble planter sat in the middle, with flowers, once colourful, now drying and wilting from lack of water.

Six doors circled the planter. All closed. Sam moved to the nearest door and opened it. He was greeted by a spotless room, with impersonal decoration, perhaps a guest bedroom. It was empty.

He opened another door. Likely to be Lex's room, judging by the books crammed into every available space, no chick lit for Lex, medical journals and biographies filled the shelves. The bed had a pretty mint green duvet cover and a collection of stuffed bears. A picture sat on the bedside table, next to a mint green lamp; Lex, Claire, Sally and Paige, arms around each other, laughing. Chloe picked it up, removed the picture from the frame and put it in her back pocket.

Back on the landing, they headed towards another door and both spotted the blood stains on the polished chrome door handle.

"Ready?" Chloe asked.

"Yep," Sam replied, lifting the shotgun and aiming it at the closed door at head height.

Chloe turned the handle and the door swung easily open, she jumped back, giving Sam space to shoot. He didn't need to. Lying on the floral bedspread was a woman, her eyes closed. She looked peaceful, as though she was sleeping. The congealed blood on the side of her face contradicted the serenity of the scene. The source of the blood appeared to be her left eye. Evidence of a stream that had flowed, like tears, from her eye, following the contours of her face, and ending as a pool on the pillow. Her arms folded across her chest, in her hands lay a photograph of the family, smiling brightly on a day out.

Sam walked over to the woman and gently lifted her eyelid. The eyeball was missing, in its place a deep wound that must have been caused by a knife penetrating through to her brain.

He lifted the other eyelid and nodded in acceptance, as he saw the ink black eyeball staring back at him.

"She must have turned first and attacked him. He must have killed her and then himself," Sam said.

"Yeah," Chloe replied, "we can't let Lex see them like t…"

Her words were cut short by Sally hollering from downstairs. "Chloe," she shouted with desperation in her tone.

Chloe and Sam reacted instantly, both running out of the room and back down the stairs. Sally was standing in the open doorway, Lex and Claire close behind her, "They're coming."

Reaching the girls, Chloe looked past them out of the door. Hundreds of zombies were staggering up the road.

"Shit. Get inside, shut the door," she hissed. "Maybe they haven't seen us," she added hopefully. "They're probably just attracted to the sound of the car alarm."

They piled into the house and Chloe pushed them through to the living room.

"What's that smell?" Lex asked, her eyes wide, darting around.

"Ssshhh," Chloe urged.

"It's my parents, isn't it? They're dead, aren't they?" Lex's voice rose, nearing hysteria.

"I'm so sorry Lex," Chloe whispered, "I'll explain later, but for now I need you to stay quiet."

Lex nodded, tears streaming down her face. She wanted to scream and shout, she wanted to see her parents, she wanted them to hold her and tell her everything would be okay. The pain was too much to bear. She collapsed to the floor, head buried in her hands and rocked to and fro.

Claire and Sally were on her immediately, arms wrapped protectively around her. Sally stroked her hair. Claire stroked her back.

Lex did not feel them; did not notice the comfort her friends tried to offer her.

She just felt the pain. But she stayed quiet. Knowing that they couldn't fight that many zombies. Knowing that she couldn't draw them here and be responsible for all their deaths. Part of her didn't care. She wanted to die. To join her parents. If she had been alone, she would have shouted and screamed and killed as many of them as she could before being taken. But she was not alone. They would not kill just her. So, for that reason alone, she whimpered quietly and didn't let the rage inside take over.

Chloe edged over to the window that looked out on the manicured front lawn. The zombies were close now. They seemed to be aiming directly for the house. They couldn't know they were in the house, could they?

She considered their options. The window would not last long if that many bodies pressed against them. They could go upstairs, less chance of being heard, but no escape route if those things got in.

The kitchen was the most sensible option, but… Looking down at Lex rocking on the floor, her shoulders heaving as she cried silent tears. They couldn't let her see her Dad like that.

Not only would it be too distressing for her, but she might also cry out and give away their position.

She cursed herself for not thinking to move the body. They were trapped there. There was only one option. She needed to protect these girls.

"Sam," she whispered and gestured for him to come over to her. He did, relieved to be away from the three girls that he had been standing next to awkwardly. "I'm going to make a run for the car, then hopefully draw them away. As soon as it's clear, take the girls to Sally's. Don't let Lex see her parents like that."

Sam looked at her, his eyebrows raised, "There are hundreds out there, how will you get through them?"

"I'll go over some of the gardens."

"Chloe. For the record, this is a terrible idea," he stated.

"I know," she snapped back at him. "I don't know what else to do."

"We could wait it out?" he suggested.

"If they hear us, they will get in. We can't fight that many off."

"We could go upstairs."

"Sam, I've thought through the options. We go upstairs, we cut off any escape route. We go to the kitchen, Lex will likely not be able to keep quiet. We stay here, they will get in, and they will kill us."

"I could go … ya know, instead of you," he suggested, the words out of his mouth, before thinking through what he was offering.

Chloe paused for a second, Sam could go. Sacrifice himself instead or her. She shook her head. "Sam, I can't do that. Even if you get through them, where will you go? You don't know where Sally lives."

"No, you're right," he agreed, trying to hide his relief.

Impulsively Chloe pulled Sam into a hug, "Thank you for offering though. I think maybe I was wrong about you."

"Nope, you were right," he said as he swapped car keys with her. "But I'm trying to be better. I'll keep them safe. I promise."

Chloe nodded at him with a smile, "You'd better, or I am going to be seriously pissed."

He walked with her to the front door, the three girls oblivious to the conversation and the plan. "Do you want to take this?" he offered her the shotgun.

"No," she shook her head. "I don't know how to use it, I'll probably end up shooting myself in the foot," she joked. "Besides I have my trusty table leg." She shook the wooden leg at him.

She turned to the door and quietly opened it, "Wish me luck." She said and sprinted to the car.

Sam watched as the indicators flashed twice, and the door was pulled open.

He closed the door only when he had seen Chloe safely in the car. As soon as it was shut, he ran to the living room to watch from the window. Sally was in the doorway, blocking his way.

"What was that?" she asked, concerned.

"It's Chloe … She's gone to distract them, so we can get away," he hurried to the window, but the view was poor.

"She did what?" Sally exclaimed as Sam moved back past her. He would get a better view from upstairs. She followed him, up the stairs and into the guest room. They both peered out of the window, staring out onto the street.

Chloe had started the car. The zombies were about one hundred yards away and had become more animated and maybe a little faster since spotting her.

Sam and Sally stared in silence as Chloe performed an impressively quick turn in the road and drove at speed towards the herd. At the last minute, she swung to the right and mounted the kerb.

Most of the infected were in the road, but the pavement was not empty. She clipped one with the wing mirror, it stumbled, then fell off the kerb, landing face down. Apparently, zombies weren't smart enough to use their hands to break their fall.

Other infected trampled over the fallen zombie, causing them to fall, and soon there were half a dozen zombies, piled up on the side of the road. Chloe carried on going, hitting a couple of the things heads on. They fell beneath the wheels, but she didn't stop. Sam and Sally continued to stare down until the Audi disappeared around the corner.

They heard a distant honking of a horn, and, as one, the massive group of zombies turned and started walking in the direction that the car had taken.

"How could you let her do that?" Sally asked Sam accusingly.

"I didn't, I even offered to go instead, but she wouldn't let me," Sam protested, holding his hands up, as though surrendering. "We should go once the street is clear, I promised … I promised her that I would keep you safe."

Sally backed down immediately, she had known Chloe for long enough to understand why she would take such a risk to protect her. It did make sense for Sam to stay with them, as he knew how to use the shotgun.

"Okay," she sighed. "We best go tell the others."

Sam followed her out of the room, but Sally paused at the top of the stairs and turned to him. "Lex's parents?" she asks.

"Mum in there," he nodded to the master bedroom. "Dad in the kitchen."

As he spoke a howl of pain came from below them.

"Shit," Sam said, running down the stairs, taking two at a time.

The sound of sobbing came from the kitchen.

"I guess she found her dad," Sally whispered to him.

He nodded grimly as he walked into the room. Lex was hugging her father, crying hysterically. Claire was standing by her, trying to extract her friend from the corpse.

"What happened?" Lex moaned.

"I … well … we … me and Chloe, see. We thought that your mum bit your dad, then your dad killed your mum, then himself," Sam explained nervously.

"Jesus, Sam," Sally hissed, "tactful."

Sam looked down at his shoes and shrugged his shoulders, maybe his choice of words was not the best. "I'm so sorry, Lex," he mumbled. "What your dad did was very brave. He must have known you'd come back here and didn't want to put you in danger."

Lex looked over at him, "Yeah, maybe you're right," she said through the tears. "That sounds like my dad, he's such a worrier… was such a worrier," She corrected herself. Almost choking on the words. She stepped away from her dad and straightened her back, "I'd like to go and see my mum now."

"I don't think that's a good idea, Lex," Sam said, trying to be more tactful this time. He adds. "She's not your mum anymore. Your mum is in heaven."

Lex snorted, "Heaven?" she said. "Do you believe in that religious tripe?"

"Well … no … but … it's what people say, ain't it? It's what people said to me… you know, when..." his words trailed off.

Lex nodded. Claire looked questioningly at Sally, who responded with a shrug. Neither knew what Sam was referring to.

"Sam," Lex said firmly. "I would like to see my mum now, please. I know it will be horrible. But I need to say goodbye."

"Okay," he said, holding out his hand, "Come with me."

He led her upstairs and to the master bedroom. "Wait here a sec," he said and quickly went over to the body and closed the eyes. "Okay, come in."

Lex stepped slowly into the room and let out a gasp. Her mother looked peaceful. Spotting the photograph in her hands, she picked it up. The tears began to flow as she looked at the picture of them taken last year.

It had been a lovely day. She remembered the sun had been shining and they had decided to have an impromptu picnic. They had settled by a stream, and after they'd eaten, they had paddled in the cooling water. Her dad had sat the camera on a log and set the timer. She smiled when she remembered the failed attempts at taking the picture.

A photo album downstairs held some pictures of her dad's behind, as he had dashed back to Lex and her mum, but not quite making it in time before the camera went off.

She held the picture up to show Sam, but noticed writing on the back. It was her dad's handwriting, but it looked hurried and shaky, not his usual neat style.

Alexis, we're sorry. Remember that we love you and always accepted you for who you are. Stay strong xxx

She gasped, "They must have known," Her eyes flood with tears again, but her mouth transforms into a watery smile. "Can you leave me here for a few minutes, please?"

He nodded and stepped out of the room, "Take all the time you need," he said as he quietly pulled the door closed behind him.

Twenty-One

Fuck, fuck, fuck. This is a bad idea.

A very fucking bad idea. There are hundreds of those things. Heading towards me. All I am protected by is a hunk of tin and some windows. The glass kind. The kind that breaks.

I take a deep breath as I quickly rearrange the seat so I can reach the pedals. I briefly consider reversing into the pack that is coming towards me, but dismiss the thought instantly. I can get more momentum going forwards. So I need to turn around. Looking up at the house, I can see Sam and Sally watching me from an upstairs window, staring down at me. I can't make out their features, but I'll bet they're worried. If this plan fails I will die, but so will they. My death will just come a little sooner.

I spin the car around. Fortunately, the cul-de-sac has a nice wide space to turn, so I don't make a mess of the three point turn I perform. Now facing the zombies heading towards me, grateful for my forethought to take the more solid Audi with its four-wheel drive, I reconsider my options. I could plough straight through them, but I don't think the car, big as it is, will be able to knock them all down, and I could get stuck. The left side of the pack is a little thinner, but a car is parked on the edge of a driveway, which will force me back into the group. I'll have to try to pass them on the right.

This is a really stupid idea.

I speed up as I drive towards them, taking care to stay in the centre of the road. I don't want to draw any more of them over to the right-hand side.

When I'm inches away from impact, I swerve to the right and mount the kerb.

I feel the car clip one of them, presumably with the wing mirror, and seconds later there is a thud as I run one over. I probably should open my eyes now.

I open my eyes.

Shit.

There are so many.

They are all turned towards me, their inky black eyes open wide, their faces otherwise expressionless. Hands reach towards me, but the momentum of them lunging at the car is knocking some of them off their feet. The ones that fall are then trampled on by others, all too eager to have me for tonight's chef's special. A feeling of claustrophobia starts to grip me and with it, the certainty that my death is imminent.

Well, fuck them. If I'm going to die it will be on another street. Not this one. I need to get them away from here.

I stamp my foot harder on the accelerator and scream, "Fuck you," as I weave in and out, trying to avoid as many as possible. I don't count how many of them I hit with the car, but within a couple of minutes, I'm through.

There are still some stragglers in front. Some late to the party, others so injured that they're either hobbling slowly on broken legs or crawling towards me.

A look in the rear-view mirror confirms that the pack are still heading towards me. Good. I slow down so they can catch up. I purposefully drive over the crawlers, destroying what is left of their bodies. The end of the street is just metres away, so I beep my horn to let the others know that I have made it out.

Now I need to decide which way to go. Shit. Should have discussed this with Sam. There's no point leading them in the direction that Sam will take the girls, because that means that they'll bump into them eventually. What if Sam and the girls think I would have gone that way, so they go in the other direction.

Right, if we make it to George's house we are going to get much better at planning. Weighing up the two options, I decide it is better to head away from George's and hope the others come to the conclusion that this is the way I've gone. When I'm far enough away I'll speed up, lose the zombies chasing me and I can be on my merry way.

~

God, this is slow going. I've been driving for about an hour, but the car is telling me that I've only gone a little over four miles.

I've been driving slowly, and every now and then I've stopped to let the zombies catch up. I found that beeping the horn excites them, and they do speed up a little, but they are still painfully slow, at least in comparison to the car.

I'm on a country road, surrounded by thickets. I'm sure the sound of the car horn is travelling for miles across the still and silent ground, therefore attracting more to join this horde.

I'm confident that they will not be able to come at me from the sides, the bushes are just too thick. Hopefully, I'll be away from this narrow lane before any get on to this road facing towards me.

I carry on my Pied Piper of Oxfordshire routine until I reach a crossroad. Going right will take me towards George's, left will take me further away. The car is now telling me that I've nearly gone six miles. I think it's time to lose my groupies.

I take the right turn and then speed away, reaching the first bend that will hide me from sight.

My body relaxes, and I allow myself a small smile. The plan was crazy and stupid. So much could have gone wrong. But I am away and free. I can get to George's in less than an hour from there.

The smile evaporates as I hear a massive bang, and the car skids to the right. I fight the steering wheel to try and control the skid, but it's a losing battle and the car ends up head first in a small ditch.

My head is thrown forward, but the airbag doesn't go off. Shaking slightly, I get out of the car. The front tyre has been destroyed, it must have been damaged when I was running over the infected, and the sudden change of speed and the sharp corner I had just taken must have caused it to blow.

Great. I'm in the middle of nowhere, no food, no water, and just a table leg for protection. Awesome. Well done on the planning. Truly this was a splendid idea. Oh, and let's not forget the massive crowd of zombies that are behind me. Any hopes I had of losing them at the crossroads have gone, the sound of the tyre blowing out, combined with the noise of the car crashing, will tell them exactly where I am.

Even if I had any idea how to change a tyre, I don't think I could get the car out of the ditch on my own, so my only option is to walk until I find another car. No point bitching about it.

I set off, the road is still narrow and stretches out ahead of me. Ten minutes of walking and the end of the road doesn't seem to have got any closer. I trudge on. While I know I have no option but to carry on, it doesn't mean I am happy about it. What I wouldn't give for my MP3 player right now.

Even if my phone had any charge left, I don't have any headphones. Blaring out music right now would just be another bad idea to add to the growing list of today's bad ideas.

A glance behind me shows that the zombies are still on my trail. They don't seem to be gaining on me, but equally, I am not losing them. It's okay for the moment, but I don't know how far I'm going to have to walk, and I will eventually get tired and slow down, but will they? I don't think so.

The thought of a horde of bloodthirsty zombies catching up with me and tearing me limb from limb is enough to spur me on. I speed up until I'm almost jogging.

I get out of breath quickly, such is my poor level of fitness, so I slow down to a fast walk. The pounding of tarmac on my feet is already making them feel sore, and I don't think I've walked a mile yet. I really hope I find a town or a village or even an abandoned car soon.

I plod on for an hour, my feet growing steadily more painful with each step. The heels and balls of my feet are starting to burn, and I suspect blisters are already forming. I don't have time to stop, because it looks like some of the faster zombies are catching up with me. My pace has definitely slowed. What I wouldn't give for my walking boots right now.

Ah crap, now I have a song in my head, I only know one line, and it's spinning round and round in my mind.

Oh well, might as well join in, *"These Boots Were Made For Walking,"* I sing quietly to myself. Replacing the words I don't know with, "dum, de da da dum,"

Strange as it is, it does help a bit. It lets me think about something else instead of the long road ahead.

That gets me thinking about other walking songs, and I move on to *"Break My Stride,"* then realise I only know one line of that song as well.

Next up is *"Ain't No Mountain High Enough,"* I remember much more of this one, but once I get to the chorus, I let the song trail off. Not because I've forgotten it, but because it reminds me of Steve. It had come on the radio when we were driving somewhere a few months ago. I'd sung it at the top of my lungs to Steve, who was driving at the time and trying not to laugh at my woefully inadequate singing voice. In the end, he had given in and joined in with me, and by the end of the song we were both in fits of giggles. Every time it has come on since, we both start singing loudly, and purposefully even more out of tune.

I push Steve to the back of my mind, I can't think about him right now. Instead, I rack my brains for other walking songs and struggle to come up with any, until, ah ha … *"I Would Walk 500 Miles,"* How very apt, it feels like I've already covered half that distance. "Dah dah, dah, dah, Bud, da dum, diddy dum, diddy dum …"

I start shouting the chorus out, throwing my arms, including the table leg up in the air. Giggling to myself, I forget that I'm fleeing from a horde of zombies and shout out the words to rest of the song.

A groan behind me brings me back to reality quickly.

Shit.

I turn around and see the horde are close and I mean really close. If I stop walking, they would be on me within minutes. I must have slowed my pace as I sang. Or perhaps they speeded up, not only wanting to kill me for dinner, but also to get me to stop sounding like a cat being strangled.

I stop singing and start running as fast as I can. I am soon panting, but the sheer terror of how close they are means I carry on, despite the pain in my feet and lungs. I'm suddenly grateful that I'm not wearing my walking boots. At least my trainers are light enough to run in.

I run flat out for about ten minutes before my body physically will not let me carry on anymore. I come to a stop, my head dropped as I pant, trying to get the air back in my lungs.

I've made some distance away from those things, but they are still too close for comfort. I know I can't sustain a running pace, but I do need to move quickly. I start walking again, as fast as I possibly can without actually running.

I watch the road ahead of me, neither looking up or back. After half an hour, I decide that I must have put some good distance between myself and the infected, so I turn around.

They're still coming, but it will take them a long time to catch back up to me, as long as I keep this pace going. Turning back around, I look up and see a sight so joyous that I whoop with happiness.

A house. Usually a sign that a town or village is nearby. Although there are bound to be more zombies, but hopefully they won't all be gathered in one place like my horde is.

My horde… the horde that has been relentless in chasing me, as I've led them away from Sam and the girls. Led them away and straight into another town or village. A town or a village where there are likely to be survivors. A town or a village that will very shortly be overrun.

I quicken my pace to a slow jog, because I need to get as far ahead of the horde as possible so I can warn anyone I see. Within minutes I see more houses. I slow down again, looking for signs of survivors. I do not see anyone.

It's only a small village, with few amenities, a garage, a shop and a church. There are probably fewer than fifty houses here. I head towards the shop, realising how hungry and thirsty I am.

There's a sign hanging on the door, saying that it's closed. It has one of those plastic clocks, on which the hands point to two 'o' clock. I try the handle and the door swings open. If it was closed when this all kicked off, then how come the door is unlocked?

The answer greets me as soon as I step inside. The place has been looted, the shelves mostly bare. The only food left is a few packs of chewing gum and Marmite.

I guess this village sits on the hate side of the Marmite fence. Not me, I love it, but I don't think I could stomach it without bread or crackers.

A couple of bottles of energy drink are still in the chiller cabinets. I take one and drink it down quickly.

The sickly-sweet syrup quenches my thirst and gives me an instant boost of energy, but it's not enough to appease the growing hunger that is gnawing at my stomach.

I walk around behind the tills and check for any food hidden on the shelves that sit hidden behind the counter. There isn't any, but there's a door leading out back that is closed. It has a sign saying Private: Staff Only. Maybe it leads to a stock room.

I try the handle. Locked. It doesn't look or feel like a heavy door, so I give the bottom a little kick to see if it gives. It moves a little, so I figure it only has the one central lock on the handle. I step back and give a harder kick to the middle. The door wobbles a little but stays closed.

I step back a few paces, figuring momentum might help. I run up and launch myself at the door. It opens. Not because I am strong enough to kick through the lock but because there is someone on the other side.

I do not stop myself in time, and I accidentally kick an old woman in the stomach. She crumples in two and falls to the floor.

"Oh, my God, I'm sorry," I say as I rush over to check to see if she is okay. 'I didn't realise anyone was here.'

"So you decided to kick the door down rather than knock?" She asks pointedly, taking the hand I offer to pull her back to her feet.

"I'm sorry, I just figured that it was empty, you know with the shop being looted …" I trail off, realising my excuse was rather poor.

"Looted?" she asks, moving me to one side and peering over my shoulder. Then laughs. "My shop has not been looted, dear."

"It hasn't?" I too look back into the shop. It certainly looks like someone has helped themselves to everything.

"No, as soon as I heard about this nasty bug, I decided to move all of the stock into my house. I didn't want those young thugs coming here and using a bad flu as an excuse to damage my shop." She chuckles.

"I even left a few things lying around, so it looked like it had been looted."

"So basically, you looted your own shop?" I ask incredulously.

"Haha, yes, I suppose when you look at it like that, I guess I did. I even left the front door open on purpose, just to add to the effect." She beams up at me with pride.

"Erm, well it worked," I say, "Is your stomach okay?"

"It's fine. I might look old and frail, but I've taken harder kicks than that, dear. You just caught me off guard, that's all." She smiles at me reassuringly.

Harder kicks that that, who goes around kicking old women? Other than me of course. "What do you mean you've taken harder kicks that that?" I ask her, confused.

"In Taekwondo, I go on a Wednesday night, and I can tell you that Doris, from number ten, gives an almighty good kick. Knocked my dentures out once, she did."

"You go to Taekwondo classes?" I am beginning to think that this little old lady might be a touch senile.

"Oh, yes dear, they do them at the village hall every week. Henry never wanted me to go, but when he passed last year, I said to myself, Edna, you can't sit around moping, you need to try new things.' So I signed up for Taekwondo and Zumba."

"Zumba?" Have I stepped into a parallel universe? The thought of this little old lady shaking her assets in time to music makes me laugh old loud.

"Something funny dear?" she asks, glaring at me.

"No… No, sorry, it's just I didn't realise they did classes for… er… well." I realise that I'm about to call her old, which she clearly is but it is still a bit rude and disrespectful.

"Old fogies?" she prompts, "Cotton heads?"

"No… erm… Seniors," I say, relieved the word has come to me.

"It's okay, dear. I know what I am. But they do say, life begins at eighty!"

Do they? I wonder, then realise what she has just said, "You're eighty?" I ask, shocked. I thought she was old, but not quite that old.

"Eighty-two last week," she beams at me.

"Wow, you look amazing. I wouldn't have put you a day over seventy," I tell her.

Her smile grows wider, "Would you like a cup of tea, dear?" she offers, moving back into the room that I thought was a store cupboard.

It's actually the entrance hall to her house.

"Oh God, yes, a cuppa would be great," I say, before realising where I am. "No wait, hang on, we can't stay here."

"Why ever not?" She asks.

"There is a massive horde of zombies heading this way, we should leave, find somewhere safe." The panic rises in my voice.

"Safe?" she questions calmly. "I've lived in this house for sixty-one years. Ever since I married Henry, and I'll be damned if a couple of people with the flu are going to scare me away from it now."

"A couple of people? Flu?" What is she talking about? "Edna," I say in a calmer tone than I am feeling. "Do you know how bad it is out there? The people that caught the flu are rising from the dead and eating each other. Hundreds of them have just chased me from Botley."

"Poppycock." she replies smartly, "You young people, you'll believe anything they tell you. That's why I don't pay any attention to the papers."

The feeling that maybe Edna is a little bit senile is getting stronger, but regardless, we are in danger here.

"Edna, please, believe me, I've seen them eat people."

"Have you?" she asks, still apparently unconcerned.

I think back over the last few days, "Well, no, only on TV, but they have chased me, and well they look… erm… hungry," I finish weakly.

"Okay, dear," she pats me soothingly on the arm, as though I am the one that is senile.

Taking my elbow, she guides me through the hallway into a cosy lounge and points me towards the sofa. "You stay here, dear, I'll go and make a nice cup of tea, and you can tell me all about it."

I sit down dumbly. I've not actually seen anyone being eaten. I can't remember Sally telling me she had either. Could it be that these aren't zombies, that they are just ill? Oh, my God, I've killed some of them, what if they are just innocent people who just have the flu?

Sitting here in this cosy lounge, the walls adorned with pink flowery wallpaper, the two-seater sofa a dark green that complements the curtains. The open fire, stacked with logs ready for winter. Everything feels so normal. So safe.

Edna walks back into the room holding a tray which she places gently down on the table in front of me. The tray holds a teapot, milk jug and matching cups and saucers. It also has a plate of delicious looking biscuits, and my stomach growls at the sight.

"Are you hungry, dear?" she asks, smiling down at me.

"I'm starving," I confess, "I haven't eaten since this morning and … well, it's been a long day."

"Help yourself to the biscuits," she says, still smiling as she pours the tea into the two cups and hands me one of them. I take it and add milk, placing two chocolate digestives on the saucer. I devour them and look longingly at the remaining biscuits. I don't want to appear greedy, but I am so hungry, so I take two bourbon creams.

"So, tell me about your zombies," Edna says. I have a mouthful of biscuit and chew quickly before swallowing.

"It started on Monday …" I begin, then I explain everything that has happened since then, Steve leaving, the woman at the supermarket. When I get to the fight at the airport this morning, Edna gasps. When I finish, she stares at me, seemingly lost for words.

"So there is a horde of zombies heading towards here?" She eventually asks.

"Mmm,' I nod, my mouth full of tea.

"But we don't know if these so-called zombies actually hurt anyone or if they are just very sick?"

"Only what I've seen in the news," I say, 'Edna, I know this seems farfetched, but the way they lunge at people …" A memory of the conversation I had with Sally at the airport flits into my mind. "Paige," I exclaim, as though the name solves everything.

"What page?" Edna is looking at me as though I am insane.

"Not what, who," I explain, "Paige is a friend of Sally's, or rather she was, she was in the quarantine camp at Heathrow. Someone in there turned into one of those things and bit her."

"Did you see it happen?" Edna asks.

"Well, no, Sally told me last night," I reply.

"Was Sally there at the time?" Edna presses.

"No, her friends Claire and Lex were though. They saw it happen," I say.

"I see," Edna nods slowly, and I get the sense that she still doesn't believe me. A knot of anger starts to bubble away in me. I know what I have seen, but I just can't bring myself to shout at a little old lady.

Taking a deep breath, I say more calmly than I am feeling, "Edna, regardless of whether these things want to bite people or not, there are hundreds of them heading this way and your front door is unlocked."

"Hmm, yes, I can see why that would be a problem," she nods slowly and takes another sip of her tea. She doesn't make any attempt to move.

I put my teacup back on the table and stand up. "Shall I go and lock the door?" I ask, not waiting for an answer I head back out to the shop and to the front door.

I look out at the road, it is full of those things, but they are all facing forwards, continuing their steady trudge up the road.

Trying to keep to the shadows I flick the latch on the door and wince at the noise it makes in the quiet room. Looking back outside, the horde does not seem to have noticed. I quietly creep back to the house, shutting and turning the key to lock the door behind me. Returning to the living room, I see that Edna has poured me another cup of tea.

"Is it okay out there?" she asks.

"They are out there, but they're carrying on straight up the road. We should be fine. As soon as they've gone, I'll leave you in peace," I say, picking the tea cup back up.

"You can stay here for as long as you want, dear." Edna offers, and I am touched by the generosity of this stranger. Especially considering I've kicked her, knocked her over and then acted like I should be locked up in an institute.

"Thank you, that's very kind," I say, then yawn. "Sorry, it's been a long day."

"That's okay, I expect you will be exhausted, walking all that way."

"Yep," I nod. Then changing the subject, I ask her if she has any family that she is worried about.

"No," she states bluntly, "I have a daughter, Kate, but she moved to Australia. We don't talk anymore."

"Oh," I reply, feeling uncomfortable. "That's a shame," I cringe, regretting starting the topic.

Edna looks at me, sadness flickers across her face, "Yes, an unfortunate sequence of events…"

As she talks, I make the requisite noises to show I am listening, but I feel my head begin to nod. Here in the relative safety and comfort, I feel more relaxed that I have in days, and the soothing tones of her voice are acting like a lullaby.

"Are you okay, dear?" Edna asks, startling me.

"Oh gosh, I'm so sorry. I'm just so tired."

"I have a guest room upstairs if you want to take a little nap."

I consider her offer. I need to leave and find the others. I also need to be alert. It is dangerous out there. Being delayed compared to being dead makes the decision very easy.

"Thank you, if that's okay with you, I'd really like that."

She nods happily, "I'll show you the way, dear."

I follow her back into the hallway, my hips bump a small side table as I pass. A vase full of wilting roses wobbles precariously, and I grab it to stop it from falling.

"Sorry."

She carries on slowly up the stairs, "Don't worry dear, that table is wonky, I've been meaning to get it fixed."

I place the vase back on the table and hurry up behind her. She leads me through a door to a small room. The only furniture is a single bed and a small side table.

"Take as long as you need, dear," Edna says and backs out of the room, leaving me alone. The bed looks old, but it's stacked with cushions and is covered by a thick duvet. It looks so comfortable and inviting. I undress, and within moments of lying down, I am asleep.

~

The room is dark when I wake. Noises downstairs have pulled me out of a deep sleep. Disorientated, I wonder where I am and where all the commotion is coming from. I sit bolt upright. Edna. I can hear muffled shouts and something else that my sleep-befuddled mind has yet to recognise.

I step closer to the door and open it slightly. That other sound becomes clearer and sends a chill down my spine. Groans. Those oh so familiar groans that can only come from a bunch of bloodthirsty zombies.

I can make out Edna's voice above the noise of the undead. She seems to be pleading with someone, Doris. Begging her to stop. Then I hear her yell.

"Chloe, if you can hear me, don't come down. Don't say a word." I hear a thud of a body hitting the floor, which I assume to be Edna, but then she continues. "Doris has gone mad. I think she might have that flu." Another thud and then the smashing of glass.

I open the door wider and quietly creep across the landing to the top of the stairs. My view is restricted, and I can't see Edna, but I can see that the hallway is crowded with people.

Not people. Zombies.

Hopefully, Edna gets into one of the downstairs rooms, then she can block herself in until they get distracted.

A scream interrupts my thoughts, and I instinctively take a step back from the top of the stairs. I want to go to her, to help. But the pain contained within a shrill cry tells me that it's too late. I swallow a sob and return quickly to the guest room and shut the door. Sinking to the floor, I lean my back against the door and hold my head in my hands. Trying to block the noise from downstairs. It doesn't work, but Edna's scream suddenly cuts off, and all I'm left with is that damned inhuman moan.

My body is tense, and I push my weight against the door. I don't think they saw me when I was at the top of the stairs, but did they hear me close the door? Can they smell me?

It's so dark in this room, I can barely see a thing. I'm not scared of the dark, but it does seem to amplify sound, and knowing that those things are so close terrifies me. The tears flow freely, and a feeling of hysteria envelops me. I need to calm myself down. To stop myself from crying out loud.

I try to go to my happy place. My memories of Steve and me, our first date where we went bowling, and he tried to cover up his frustration at losing to me. Our first holiday together in the sun. The memories serve to calm me, but my thoughts soon turn to the day he left. and everything that has happened since. The hysteria turns to self-pity, and for hours I wallow in my own personal hell until eventually, sleep, once again claims me.

Twenty-Two

She watched unseen from the doorway, taking in the scene before her. They sat at the kitchen table, chatting amiably. Sally and Claire were laughing quietly at something Sam had said. They drank coffee. Chocolate bar wrappers lay discarded on the table. They looked relaxed. Happy. The sight created a knot of anger deep within her.

The chair that had contained her father's body sat empty. They'd moved his body. She scanned the room, searching. Her eyes fell upon carrier bags that were full to the brim. She guessed that they'd gone through the cupboards, taking anything that might be useful. To do so without permission in normal circumstances was just plain rude. To do so when her parents' bodies lay within the house was something else entirely. Her stomach tightened. The anger increased.

The events of the last few days had drained her. The death of her parents had angered her. She felt an overwhelming sense of tiredness, which is why it took her so long to notice that someone was missing.

"Where's Chloe?" she demanded harshly.

The three at the table started at her words. Claire immediately got to her feet and rushed to embrace her friend. "How are you doing?" she asked softly.

"How do you think?" Lex replied curtly. She manoeuvred herself out of Claire's embrace and ignoring the hurt look on her friend's face, she asked again. "Where's Chloe?"

"She … well, she's gone," Sam said, "there were loads of zombies outside, and she led them away."

"She did what?" Lex gasped. "Why?"

"There was no other choice," Sam said, "they would have got in. Besides, I'm sure she'll be fine, and we're going to meet her at Sally's house."

"How long?"

"Eh?" Sam asked, confused.

"How. Long. Ago. Did. Chloe. Leave?" she said, pronouncing each word slowly as though addressing an infant.

Sam, Sally and Claire looked at each other awkwardly.

"Well …" Sally broke the silence. "About four hours ago."

"What?" Lex said. Her cheeks coloured in to an angry red flush, almost the same colour as her hair. "I've been upstairs that long? Why didn't you come and get me?"

An uncomfortable silence fell over the room. None of them had wanted to disturb her. They simply didn't know what to say to her. So they'd left her until she was ready. It had felt like the right thing to do. Apparently, they were wrong.

"Sorry," Claire mumbled eventually. "We thought you wanted to be alone."

"That's not the point, Claire," Lex said, her lips curled up into a snarl. "How could you let Chloe go out alone? What were you thinking?" Even as she said the words, she knew she was being unreasonable, but she couldn't help it. She wanted to shout and scream. To release the pent-up emotion. To make someone else feel the pain that she did.

"I …" Claire began.

"Whatever. Forget it. Let's just go." She turned away from a stunned Claire and stormed towards the front door.

The others exchanged nervous glances.

"She seems angry," Sam whispered.

"Jesus, Sam, her parents just died. Did you expect her to be happy?" Sally said, also in a whisper.

"Are you coming?" an angry shout came from the next room, interrupting Sam's response.

They hurried out of the kitchen, Sam snatching the carrier bags on the way.

Lex glared at them from the door. When the others arrived, she pulled the door open and stepped out. The scene before her was shocking. For a moment, she forgot her anger. Bodies were strewn across the road. Destroyed by the large car Chloe had been driving. She could make out some movement amongst the corpses. Broken bodies, somehow still alive, and responding to the sound of the door opening.

For the briefest of moments, she considered running up to one of the crawlers. Letting it bite her. Kill her. So she could join her parents in death. She shook the thought away almost as quickly as it came. Her parents would not want that.

"We need to leave. Now," she said to the others. Her tone left no room for debate.

"Er, yeah," Sam said as he surveyed the road before them.

They jogged the few metres to the car. Sam stopped at the rear to put the shopping bags in the boot.

"Shit. Sorry. I left the keys in the house." He said, flustered. Dumping the bags on the road, he dashed back to the house. Picked up the keys and ran back to the car. "Got them." He said, dangling the keys from his hand.

"Sam. Unlock the bloody car." Lex hissed, hopping away from a crawler that was lunging for her legs.

He clicked the button for the central locking, and the four of them jumped in.

"Shit," Sam said again. I forgot the bags."

"I'll get them. You get the car started," Claire said, jumping out of the car.

Sam adjusted the seat and started the engine just as the boot slammed shut.

"Okay, we're ready to go," Claire said breathlessly as she slid back into the seat.

Sally sat in the front passenger seat watching the scene from the windows. Sam concentrated on safely navigating past the bodies. Lex sat behind Sally, also staring out of the window, lost in thought and paying no heed to the surroundings. None of them noticed as Claire reached down to touch her ankle. Nor when she discreetly wiped the blood from her fingers on the inside of her sleeve.

At the end of the street, the car came to a stop.

"What way?" Sam asked.

"Left," Sally said.

"Right," Lex said.

"But it's left to my house," Sally said, turning to look at Lex, still sullenly staring out the window.

"Which means Chloe would have gone right," Lex said. "We are going after her, aren't we?" The tone in which she spoke implied it was a command and not a question.

Sam glanced at Sally, who gave a curt nod of her head. Sam turned left.

They drove in silence for a few miles until they reached a junction. Again, Sam stopped.

"Now where?"

"Lex?" Sally asks.

"How far have we gone?"

"Dunno, five or six miles maybe," Sam replied.

"Try right. Maybe Chloe would have figured that she'd led them far enough away."

"Okay. Right it is," Sam said pulling away.

They had only been moving a few minutes when Sam slammed on the brakes.

"Oh shit."

He hadn't even finished the words when Lex jumped out of the car and ran towards the abandoned Audi.

"She's not here," the relief evident in her words. "No blood either."

"Look," Sam said, joining her next to the car. He pointed at the destroyed tyre. "Tyre's blown," she must have gone on foot from here.

"Must have," Lex nodded in agreement, turned on her heel, and got back in the car without another word to Sam.

Sam dutifully followed.

They drove on through a couple of villages, but saw no sign of Chloe. They did come upon a massive horde of zombies, and there was no way around them. Once more Sam stopped the car and turned around to face Lex.

"I reckon that lot are following Chloe. We can't go through and it's too risky to follow them. What do you want to do?"

"Since when did I become the decision maker?" Lex snapped in response, "Why don't you ask Sally or Claire?"

Sam swallowed the response he wanted to give, "Er … okay … Claire, what do you want to do?"

Claire looked up sharply, "Let's just go to Sally. Chloe will meet us there. I'm sure she's fine," She spoke quickly and quietly.

Lex tutted, but said nothing, instead, choosing to stare unseeing on to the road.

"Right, Sally, which way?" Sam asked. Ignoring the tut coming from Lex's direction.

"Take the next left. I'll direct you from there," Sally said, taking care to hide the sense of relief that she was finally going home.

~

The drive was uneventful, the roads deserted. Sam and Sally chatted inanely. The muted conversation served to distract them from the uncomfortable silence in the back seats. Lex remained sullen. Glaring out of the window as if the landscape had offended her. Claire sat quietly, lost in thought. A sheen of sweat glistened on her pale cheeks.

"Take this right," Sally pointed, interrupting Sam's lengthy description of a film he had seen before going to Spain.

Sam obeyed and drove past the wrought iron gates that led onto a long driveway. It reminded Sam of the entrance to a safari park he had visited when he was younger. A large house stood in the distance. As they approached, Sam searched for a way past the house, but the road seemed to stop with the house.

"Are you sure?" he asked Sally, "looks like a dead end," he turned to her and saw the large smile on her face.

"Yes, I'm sure," She laughed. "This is where I live."

Sam turned from staring at the house to Sally and then back to the house again, "What?" he exclaimed, "Well … shit the bed," he took in the impressive building.

The driveway came to an end in a large circle with a fountain in the middle. Water no longer cascaded from the flute held aloft by the statue of a child.

Steps led up to the large double doors that stood proudly between two white pillars. He left out a low whistle, "You must be fucking loaded."

"I guess we're well off," Sally said, suddenly nervous that Sam would judge her because her family had money. Then a thought occurred to her, "Doesn't matter anymore, though, does it?"

Sam considered her words. "No, I guess not. Money doesn't buy much in a zombie apocalypse, does it?"

The doors opened, and a middle-aged balding man came running down the steps towards the approaching car.

"Dad," Sally shrieked and jumped out of the car as soon as it came to a stop. She flung herself into her father's waiting arms. Not ordinarily affectionate, the relief at seeing his daughter was palpable. He held her tightly.

The others got out of the car. George greeted Lex and Claire with a friendly nod.

Sam stood off to one side. Awkwardly shuffling from one foot to the other. Waiting for the older man to notice him.

George looked around, "Where are Chloe and Paige?" he asked, his tone one of polite enquiry, no sense of worry at the response. "And who is this?" he added, finally noticing Sam.

"Dad, this is Sam. My … erm … that's our friend. He helped us get away from the airport. Sam, this is my Dad. George." George didn't notice the nervousness in her voice.

"Sir," Sam said, proffering a hand to shake. Cringing inwardly. He hasn't called anyone Sir since he'd been a school. Was he sucking up to Sally's dad?

"Sam," George responded with a firm handshake. Then immediately turned back to Sally, "Chloe, Paige?"

"Shall we get inside and I'll tell you everything?" Sally said and tucked her arm into her father's. She led him up the steps to the front door.

"I'll get the bags," Claire called to their retreating backs.

"I'll help," Sam added.

The pair returned to the car and opened the boot. Sam took out the lightest bags and handed them to Claire. She took them wordlessly. "Are you okay?" Sam asked. "Still upset with Lex?"

"What? I'm not upset with Lex?"

"So why have you been so… erm..." he paused searching for the right word. "Stroppy," he said, then winced as her head dropped and she fell silent. Sam waited patiently for a response, and eventually she sighed, looked back up and stared at a spot behind Sam's right shoulder. "It's nothing. I'm just tired. It's been a long day."

"Okay," Sam replied, accepting her answer. He picked up the last of the bags from the car, shut the boot and turned towards the house, "Shall we?"

Claire dropped the bags as soon as they got through the front door.

"I'm going to the bathroom," she said.

"Er, where?" Sam looked around him at the large entrance way, unsure of where to go.

"They're probably in the kitchen. Second door on the right," Claire cut him off, anticipating the question.

"Cheers."

Picking up the carrier bags that Claire had discarded, he shuffled in the direction she'd indicated. The inside of the house was even more intimidating than the outside. He felt uncomfortable in such surroundings. He didn't belong here. It felt like a museum, not a home.

He stood awkwardly at the entrance to the large kitchen, watching as Sally talked animatedly with her father, Lex busying herself making coffee. Water was already boiling in a pan on the large range cooker.

He coughed quietly at first, then louder. All in the room ignored him. The feeling of unease grew.

"Um … where shall I put these?" he eventually asked.

George waved a hand idly and pointed in the general direction of the worktop under the window. He didn't look at Sam. Already considering him someone not important. Not worth knowing.

Under the weight of the various bags, Sam trudged over and heaved them onto the marble work surface. He cringed as a tin of tomatoes rolled out of the bag and fell to the floor, hitting the cream tiles with a thud.

"Shit, sorry," he said, then realising he'd just sworn in front of Sally's Dad, blurted out, "Shit, didn't mean to swear. Oh crap … sorry," he felt a flush grow up his cheeks and turned sheepishly to Sally and shrugged his shoulders apologetically. Sally glanced at him with a reassuring smile, then continued her conversation with George.

Reluctant to take a seat at the table without an invitation, he stared out of the window. The garden before him was breathtaking. He had grown up in narrow streets of terraced houses. Small back yards, usually covered in dog shit and discarded furniture. This back garden, if you could call it that, seemed to go on forever. A neat and clean patio area held more furniture than Sam had in his entire flat. It led on to a lush green, perfectly manicured lawn, which was bordered by stylish flower beds.

Stepping stones wound through the grass, leading up to a small bridge over a stream. A woodland area stood in the distance, which seemed to stretch on for miles.

He considered the location. The long driveway protected by large gates. The solid front door. The large garden.

It seemed like a perfect place to hole up until things got sorted out. Then the emotional side of him took over.

He didn't like it here. Sally's dad was already coming across as a bit of an arse. He wasn't comfortable. How long could he stay here? Then a sudden thought struck him. Would he be allowed to stay? Surely, they wouldn't kick him out now that he had helped them get here. Shit. What if Sally told her dad what they had done in Alicante? How he had treated her afterwards? He'd be kicked out for sure.

He stared out of the window, lost in panicked thoughts, his mind conflicted between the intimidation he felt here and the yearning to stay with other people. People that he was beginning to like and consider friends. Then there was Sally. He didn't want to leave Sally. Shit. The more he thought about it, the more anxious he grew. When did that happen? When did he start having feelings for her? Shit.

Lex placed a mug of steaming coffee in front of him. A blush crept up his cheeks as she looked at him with sympathy.

Why was she looking at him like that? Could she tell what he had been thinking? Had she come over to tell him he needed to leave now? Or maybe just to shout at him again.

"Hi," he said, "erm, sorry, I meant cheers." He lifted the mug to show that he was thanking her for the drink.

"Don't worry," she whispered, "you soon get used to it."

"What?"

"The house. It's intimidating at first but you'll get over it."

"Oh, yeah, right. The house."

"I just assumed that was what you were thinking about. You looked so lost in thought and worried."

"Yeah, yeah. The house. It's er..."

"Big?" Lex suggested helpfully, "Pretentious? Ostentatious?"

Sam laughed, "I don't know what those last two mean, but they seem about right."

"Shall we?" Lex gestured to the table.

Sam nodded, "Okay," he felt nervous. Admitting to himself that he liked Sally was scary. He didn't like girls. Sure, he liked sex, but he did not build bonds. Small talk was used to get them into bed. Not to get to know them. Once they'd had sex, he would ignore them. Not even bothering to pretend that he would call or text them. He'd never had a girlfriend. Never thought he would. Now he was about to join the first girl he liked, at a table with her dad.

"Sam," Lex nudged him, "Come on."

They walked over to the table. Lex took a seat next to George. Sam chose the seat next to Sally. He put his coffee on the table and pulled the chair out. It scraped loudly across the floor.

"Sorry."

George looked at Sam with distaste. Then spotting the coffee, he made a point of lifting it up and putting it on a coaster.

"Shit … er, I mean sorry. Again. Ya know, for the chair and the coffee. Yeah, sorry." he stammered.

"Don't worry, Sam,' Sally smiled kindly at him, then turned to George, "Dad. Be nice. Remember I wouldn't be here if it weren't for Sam."

"Nah, you'd have been fine," Sam protested, "Stealing a bus, getting to the airport alone, shooting that guy. Ow." He looked over at Sally who had kicked him under the table. She was frowning.

"What," George's voice boomed around the room, "You seem to have left that bit out of the story, Sally."

'Haha, Sam's just joking, Dad," she turned to Sam and kicked him under the table. "Aren't you?"

"Er, haha, yeah. Just joking."

"You have a very strange sense of humour, young man," George chastised. "It is not amusing to joke about stealing and shooting people."

"No, Sir … er sorry, Sir. I won't do it again," Sam said, relieved when he felt Sally's hand squeeze his knee.

"Please don't call me Sir. I'm not a teacher. You can call me Mr Carlton."

"Er … cheers … Mr er Carlton."

George nodded curtly at him. "Where is Claire? We need to decide what to do next." He said, turning back to face Sally.

"She went to the bog, er… Mr Carlton," Sam said. "Although that was ages ago. Ha. She must be having a …" He let the words trail off, "that is, she might have decided to have a sleep or summat. She said she was tired. Ya know, when we were unloading the car."

"Sally. Go and find Claire," George instructed. "I'd like you all to be here, so I only need to tell you my plans once."

Sally scurried off, keen to hear what her Dad was planning. She felt a sense of relief. She didn't understand what her father did for a living, but she was aware that he knew important people.

Maybe there was a safe place that they had put the Prime Minister and other influential people, that they could go.

Sam noted that very quickly, George had gone from suggesting a discussion about what to do next, to having definite plans he wanted to tell them. This man was intimidating and if Sam was honest, a bit of a dick.

"Plans?" Lex said, her voice light, but Sam saw the familiar hard look in her eyes. Evidently, she had also noticed the quick change from discussion to telling.

"Yes, Alexis. I have an idea, but I don't like repeating myself. Therefore, we will wait until Claire and Sally are here."

Lex did not respond, and the room fell into silence. Sam played with his now empty mug. Ignoring the impatient tapping of George's fingers against the table.

Moments later, Sally returned to the kitchen, followed by Claire. Claire's eyes were red and swollen. Her face blotchy and she walked with a noticeable limp.

"Are you alright?" Lex asked Claire. It was clear that she had been crying.

"I'm just tired,' Claire said, "Oh and I twisted my ankle getting out of the car," she added. Sam looked over at her as she hobbled to the table. She hadn't mentioned that she'd hurt her ankle when they were unloading the bags.

Oblivious to Sam staring at Claire suspiciously, and the silent conversation between Lex and Sally, that consisted of glances and shrugs. George began to address them. "Now that we are all here. I have been made aware of safe zones that have been set up around the country." He puffed his chest out, giving an air of self-importance.

"By whom?"

"Where?"

"How d'you know?"

"One at a time. One of my political contacts has informed me of the existence of these zones. They have been set up by the military. While my contact had no information on the actual locations, I did receive a text this morning suggesting that I head to Linthem."

"A text?" Sally asked, "who from?"

"The number wasn't familiar to me. I did try to call, but by the time I saw the message, I had no signal. However, I do have many acquaintances that would know about such matters, and therefore we can consider the source reliable." He paused. He expected at least one of the young people to challenge him. He was unconcerned as to why someone he didn't know would reach out and offer a safe haven. He was George Carlton. In circumstances such as these, it was to be expected that people would be falling over themselves to try and help.

He looked around at the four faces. They seemed to accept this decision without question, "Right then. We shall leave at first light. It is getting dark now. I would suggest we avoid the roads at night."

"You mean, at first light if Chloe is here by then?" Lex asked.

George looked over at Lex, "It would be ideal if Chloe is here by then. However, if she is not, we must leave regardless."

"No," said Lex.

"Pardon?" George replied, not used to being questioned. Especially by a teenage girl.

"I'm sorry, perhaps I wasn't clear enough," Lex said caustically, "I said no. We are not leaving without Chloe."

"I'm afraid the matter is not up for debate, Alexis."

'Firstly, my name is Lex. Only my parents call me Alexis. Secondly, this is not a dictatorship.

You are not in charge. Thirdly …" her words were cut off by George, whose face was getting progressively redder.

"Listen to me, young lady …"

Lex slammed her fist on the table, knocking her mug over, coffee spilling across the pristine surface. "No. I will not listen to you," She erupted with fury. "Chloe put her life at risk to save your daughter, and this is the thanks she gets? You should have gone to Heathrow yourself. Then Chloe would be safe." Lex rose to her feet and stood over George, looking down at him with obvious disdain. "You, Mr Carlton, are a selfish coward and I... I am not losing anyone else."

Claire let out a loud sob, jumped out of her chair and fled from the room.

George sat in shock. His mouth opening and closing like a fish. He turned to his daughter, "Sally, please talk to your friend. We need to leave as soon as possible."

"No, Dad," Sally replied gently, "Lex is right. Chloe saved us, and we can't leave her behind. It wouldn't be right. Would it Sam?"

Sam had watched the scene in silent amusement. Fair play to Lex for standing up to that man. She was right. He was a coward. Sending his PA to get his daughter. What a prick. "Sorry Mr Carlton, but I agree with Sally and Lex."

"Fine," George replied sulkily. "We will wait for Chloe. If, however, she is not here in two days then we will leave. Is that okay Al … Lex?"

"Fine," She said, the anger and rage indicated by the scowl on her face and by her clenched fists. "I'm going to go and check on Claire. Then I'm going to bed." She got up and stalked out of the room.

The only sound in the kitchen was that of a constant drip from the spilt coffee as it fell slowly from the table onto the tiled floor.

George sat, mouth open, wondering what had just happened. Sally intently studied her fingernails. Sam looked back and forth between the two, feeling more awkward than he had ever felt before.

"I'll clean this up, shall I?" Sam jumped up, without waiting for a response. He took a cloth from the sink and returned to the table, bending down to clean up the mess. He took his time. Anything to avoid the awkwardness within the room.

When he finished, he stood up and made a show of stretching and yawning, "Um, I wouldn't mind going to bed too. Is there somewhere I can sleep? Er please."

Sally jumped up, relieved to have something to do. "Dad, I'll show Sam to the guest room. Then I am going to bed. We'll talk in the morning okay?" She leant down and kissed her father on the cheek. He grunted in response.

Sam followed Sally back into the large hallway and up the sweeping staircase.

"Jesus," Sam exclaimed when he saw the long corridor with dozens of doors. "How many bedrooms do you have?"

"Seven," Sally replied, and pushed open a door at the far right of the landing. "You can use this one. Claire and Lex will be next door, and my room is that one." She pointed to the door opposite. They both stepped into the bedroom, and stared awkwardly at the bed.

"Um … Cheers," Sam said and sat down on the bed. He bounced up and down a few times. "It's comfy."

"Is it? I've never actually slept on it." She sat down next to him. "It is," she agreed. "Although not as comfortable as mine," She cringed as she said the words. That sounded a lot like an invitation. Sam pretended not to notice, and they fell silent. Both conscious of the awkwardness of the situation, but neither willing to say goodnight just yet.

"So, um … nice house."

"Thank you for today."

They both spoke at the same time, releasing the tension in the room and they both chuckled.

"You go first," offered Sam.

"I just wanted to say thank you. You've been a massive help today and despite everything, it's been good having you with us."

"Honestly, Sal, I'm really glad I'm here. If you guys hadn't taken me with you, I don't know what I would have done."

Sally felt a warmth rush through her at the shortening of her name. It sounded affectionate. A term of endearment. "So … we've helped each other then?" she suggesed, he nodded in agreement and they fell silent once more. Begrudgingly, she got to her feet. "Right, well, I guess I better go to bed."

"Yep," he nodded again and stood up, facing her.

"So, um … goodnight."

"Yeah. Goodnight."

Neither moved. They remained standing, facing each other. Tension crackled between them. Sally broke first, unable to endure the knot in her stomach, the lump in her throat. She leant forward and planted a soft kiss on Sam's cheek. She stepped back, measuring his reaction.

Sam had never had a problem picking up girls. He could chat and flirt with ease and confidence. In any other situation, his moves would have been instinctive and automatic. Now he was unsure. Lost. He didn't know what to do or how to respond. So, he just stared back at her big brown eyes, that looked to him in uncertainty.

The vulnerability he saw in them dictated his next move. He leaned forward and kissed her gently on the lips. She responded, her lips parting to encourage the kiss. He placed his hands on her hips and pulled her towards him. He wanted to hold her. To protect her. To never let her go.

To have affection for another person was a new experience for Sam, and he savoured the moment. He breathed in her scent. Enjoying the warmth of her body as it pressed into his. This felt different. It felt real. A moment of bliss shared. Of affection exchanged between two young people in the middle of a nightmare, the thought of sex far from his mind. It is Sally that manoeuvred them towards the bed.

Throughout the night, they shared kisses and held each other tightly. They chatted and laughed quietly. For both, it was a night like no other. Eventually, they fell asleep, wrapped in each other's arms.

That was how Lex found them when she burst into the room the next morning. She showed no reaction to finding the two, still fully clothed, together on the bed. Her panic and fear outweighed any surprise at this situation.

"Get up. It's Claire. She's gone."

Twenty-Three

Friday 20th September

Chloe,

Jonesy is dead. He was bitten. It was stupid, and it shouldn't have happened. But there were so many of them. So many. Swarming us like locusts. We were winning. I just don't understand how it could have gone so horribly wrong.

The plan was conceptually simple, yet a logistical nightmare. It was stupid, but it went unchallenged. Work together to extend the perimeter. The infantry squadrons joined together to lead the assault. Imagine it, Clo, two parallel rows of soldiers stretching as far as the eye could see. You've been to Linthem and seen the guard house. That's where we started. Two rows, so when we had contact, the front line would open fire. Then they would fall back for the second line to provide cover as they reloaded.

Behind us were the guys responsible for clean-up. They'd quickly grab downed bodies, pile them up, then return for the next one. They kept the area clear for the Royal Engineers. Their job was to erect a moving perimeter. Literally a fucking moving fence. They had to carry the damned thing, ready to fix in place when we had reached the five-mile target. It was so heavy they had to be supported by civilians.

There just wasn't enough of them to support the size of the fence they had to move.

Finally, bringing up the rear were the other squadrons, civilians, basically anyone physically capable of moving. These guys were in trucks that carried all the necessary materials for the fencing, as well as medical supplies and ammo. Runners were allocated to go between all three groups to resupply when needed.

Picture it, the engineers were set up in a three-sided rectangular shape. The fourth side of the rectangle was the original camp.

So, as the longest side of the rectangle pushed forward with the moving perimeter fence, the two shorter sides would put static permanent fencing in place. Initially, the static fencing was barbed wire supported by hastily erected posts. Just enough to stop the zebs getting through. Further squadrons of Engineers would then fix more permanent, secure fencing in place. This was to go on for five miles, then the infantry and clean-up crews would fall back. The engineers would finish securing the perimeter, and we would have extended the camp. Simple, right?

There were so many flaws in this plan. I guess testament to how hastily it was put together. The first was the buildings. We would bunch up and provide cover while the Engineers would erect the side perimeters through back gardens.

When that wasn't possible, we'd have to wait while they put the barbed wire around the outside of the house and extend it back the width of the line.

This meant that the guys holding the moving perimeter would also need to bunch up to navigate around the buildings. So, while this was happening, the nice orderly rows fell into disarray, and it took too long to regroup.

Next was the zebs. Someone had severely underestimated the sheer number of zebs we would face. At first, things were going well. Small numbers, which we took out easily. I didn't even open fire for the first mile or so. But the sound of gunfire can echo over open land, drawing in zebs from miles around. By the time we reached The Plain, the numbers of zebs had increased significantly.

Then there was the communication. Or more accurately the complete lack of communication. No one had thought to give us radios to allow us to talk to the other end of the lines. While we started out in a perfect formation, the line soon began to curve in places, break in others.

Then because of the number of zebs, the clean-up crews weren't fast enough to remove the bodies for the engineers to progress the perimeter. So behind us, they were slowing down, but we didn't know.

Without radios, no one could tell us, little point in shouting over the deafening sound of gunfire.

We kept on pushing forward. As the gap grew, it created space for the zebs to breach the sides.

Zebs started coming in from the sides. Some of the clean-up crew were bitten. Their screams pierced the air, and finally, we knew something had gone wrong. But we couldn't stop firing, we were doing everything we could to stop the masses coming in from the front. We could, however, stop moving forward. Which we did. We didn't wait for instructions. We held the frontline.

The Engineers had to abandon the mobile perimeter and take up arms. I tell you, Clo, those Engineers are tough bastards. They cleared the zebs behind us within minutes. Their aim must have been superb.

As far as I know, they didn't hit anyone on the frontline with a stray bullet. Nor was anyone attacked by a zeb. Damn impressive, given the situation. Imagine holding a rifle and shooting accurately, having, just seconds before, been holding bloody massive perimeter fencing.

We didn't know it at the time, but the clean-up crew were ordered to fall back. That was the first thing that made sense all day, the bodies could be cleared after without unnecessary risk. But it did make the Engineer's job harder because they had to step over dead bodies while keeping hold of an awkward and heavy fence.

We had taken out so many in front of us. Yet more were coming. There was blood everywhere.

Flowing like a river. Runners were sent to tell us to carry on moving. The ground became slippery, which slowed us down. Navigating the bodies became almost impossible. Zebs relentlessly lunging at us. Bodies blocking our route. The road slick with blood. People fell, tripping over limbs, then slipping on blood.

I saw as Jonesy went down. He was grinning. He knew that if he made a fuss, we'd all take the piss later. He fell, he laughed, he went to get back up. But he was grabbed on the ankle by a zeb. One of those fucking crawlers. Someone had missed the head. The shot had knocked it off its feet, and the slickness of the road had stopped it from being able to get back up. Undeterred, it had just crawled toward us.

Before anyone could shoot the fucker, he had bitten Jonesy. I watched as his grin turned to into an expression of terror. Over the immense noise, I heard his scream as the dirty motherfucker bit into his calf. I shot it in the face. The head exploded, but it was too late. We could all see the blood on Jonesy's leg. We all knew what that meant. Our part of the line stopped. The row behind us gave us cover fire while we stood on in stunned silence.

Jonesy stopped screaming. All colour drained from his face, and a look of resignation settled on him. He knew what this meant.

He looked me in the eyes. I nodded at him. I know what he was asking. I told him to close his eyes, and as a solitary tear slid down his face, I pressed the trigger.

Not long after that, we were ordered to retreat. We had drills for this. The Engineers created gaps in the fence and the back row of infantry fell back first, then gave the front row cover fire so we could get through the gaps. Then while the Engineers secured the fencing, we took out as many as them fuckers as we could.

I'm told that we lost over five hundred men and women today. Military and civilian. And our reward? Not even two miles of ground gained.

I don't know if we can win this thing.

I'm sorry, I can't go on writing tonight. I need to time to digest what has happened.

I love you.

Steve xxx

Twenty-Four

It is the dawn sun shining through the window that wakes me. My back and neck are aching from the uncomfortable position in which I've slept. I'm still upright against the bedroom door.

I guess I was lucky. The zombies must have been distracted by something else. If they had found me, I wouldn't have been able to hold the door.

It hasn't been a restful sleep, I've dreamed of Sally. Of my arrival at George's, of her throwing her arms around me, sobbing while thanking me for saving them. But then while in my embrace, she changed, she grew taller, her hair shortened and changed from strawberry blonde to dark brown. She became Steve. He pushed me to the floor and walked away. I chased him and grabbed his arm. He turned to face me, only his eyes were black. He was infected.

I shudder as I remember the dream. I'm not superstitious. I don't believe in fortune tellers or fate. I certainly don't believe in dreams being a premonition of the future. But then a few days ago I hadn't believed in zombies either.

There's absolutely nothing I can do about Steve, but I can get back to Sally. I think I'm about fifteen miles away. Sod walking. I probably didn't walk more than four miles yesterday, and my hips are aching this morning.

Right, so, number one priority is a car. As if in protest, my stomach lets out a growl.

Okay. Food. Car. Drive. Get there. Chill out.

Worry about surviving the zombie apocalypse tomorrow.

Plan formed. I get to my feet and quietly open the bedroom door. The little house is silent. I tiptoe across the landing, and at the top of the stairs, I pause, listening for signs of life downstairs.

Nothing. I creep down the stairs with exaggerated movements. If anyone could see me, I'm sure they'd be singing the Pink Panther theme tune. A step creaks and I freeze mid-stride. I wait for a few moments with my eyes closed. I listen intently. Nothing but silence. I resume my Pink Panther routine.

The first thing I see at the bottom of the stairs is that the door to the shop is open. Then I see the blood splattered on the walls and the floors. The vase that I nearly knocked over last night lies shattered on the carpet, the roses scattered around it. The sight of the discarded and blood-soaked flowers makes me shudder. It feels like an omen. A symbol of romance, now destroyed.

I use my foot to nudge the glass and the flowers out of the way. Then continue to look around. There is not as much blood as I would have thought. Shut in the room in the darkness last night, it sounded like Edna's entire body was being torn apart.

My fear must have played tricks on my mind. I'm no pathologist, but I would have thought a body ripped apart would have bled more. Come to think of it, even with my lack of medical training, I would have thought a body ripped apart might have... well... left a body.

Edna is not here.

I consider the implications of this. Zombie bites human. Human turns zombie. But, everything I watched on the news implies that it would take at least twelve hours for the bitten person to change. It's only been five or six since Edna was attacked. I think back, did the news say that twelve hours was for people infected by the initial terrorist attack, or was it for someone that was bitten?

I really miss Google. With search engines and the internet, retention of facts is now redundant. Has memory now become defunct? Would evolution eventually remove it as a core function of the human brain?

I realise that, not only am I digressing, but that it is now a moot point. From all I've witnessed over the past couple of days, I think it's safe to say that it will be a while before smart phones and search engines start working again.

Back to Edna, if it takes a minimum of 12 hours to turn, she should still be alive somewhere. Although, given the number of those things outside last night, she would probably be severely hurt. So, she's probably somewhere in the house.

I take a quick peek around the door to the shop. It is empty. Closing the door to give me some protection from the outside, I look around the rest of the downstairs. It doesn't take long, because it's a small house. I head back upstairs.

There's only a bathroom and bedroom up here. Other than the guest room, but I'm fairly certain I'd have noticed if she'd come in the bedroom last night.

I check the remaining rooms. Nothing. Not even a single spot of blood. Ah ha, blood! I can follow the trail of blood. I run back down the stairs and look at the floor. The blood is more concentrated in one spot. This is likely to be where Edna fell. I think back to every episode of Dexter I've ever watched. Dexter was a blood spatter expert that worked on crime scenes with the police to help catch the murderer. He was also a serial killer, but that's neither here nor there.

Right, so, blood spatter patterns. What do they tell me?

Absolutely sod all.

While there isn't a lot of blood, there are drops all over the walls and carpets. The best I can tell is that someone got attacked here. A fact I already knew.

Okay, so, Edna was bitten. Edna will be infected. If she was hurt, would she have played dead until the zombies left?

If so, why would she have left the house? Did she fight back and escape the building, knowing that she was leading them away from me?

No.

I heard her screams. I also heard them stop. Not fade or grow weaker. They stopped, as though cut off. Cut off. Dead. Edna died during the attack, and she's not here. Dead people don't walk.

Unless Edna is a zombie.

Despite the amount of news that I watched during the initial breakout, I can't recall any mention of someone dying straightaway. The chain of events was always consistently described. Get bitten. Go home. See family. Maybe infect others by sharing bodily fluids. Die. Wake up a zombie. Eat the family.

It was talked about so much. If people turned straight away, then it would be easier to contain. Less risk of it spreading.

But Edna was old. Very old. Maybe her heart gave out. Maybe her body couldn't stand the pain. She was infected when she died. The fact it wasn't the infection that ultimately killed her is irrelevant. She still turned into a zombie

Poor Edna. She died bravely. She could have begged for help, but instead, she warned me to stay away.

I will not let her sacrifice be in vain. I will get out of here. I can mourn her death later. For now, I need to resume the plan and get out of here. Food first.

Edna wasn't kidding about looting her own shop. The kitchen is piled high with tins, bottles, chocolate bars and crisps. There are even stacks of magazines on the kitchen table. I can't leave this food to rot. It would be a huge waste. Change of plan. Food. Car. Stock up. Drive.

I pick up a tin of beans and sausages, but one look at the cooker tells me it's electric. Mmm, yummy, cold beans it is. I tuck in.

Despite my earlier resolve, my thoughts turn to Edna as I eat. I'm in her kitchen, eating her food. I'm sure if she had any conscious thought, she would be more than happy for me to help myself. She did seem to like me. Besides, it's not as if she would want it. As far as I know, zombies don't eat per se. They just bite. Blimey, I hope she had her dentures fixed in nice and tight. She'll make a pretty crap zombie otherwise.

Shit. I can't believe I just thought that.

I'm ashamed of myself. Not ashamed enough to stop eating, though. I am only human.

Unlike Edna. The toothless zombie.

What the hell is wrong with me?

To distract myself, I pick up a magazine from the table. It's porn, the sort you would find on the top shelf.

I put it down quickly and root through the pile until I find a Woman's Weekly, full of sob stories and knitting patterns.

Not my sort of thing, but better than porn. I flick through it mindlessly. Anything to take my mind off Edna, specifically off making jokes about her.

Hunger sated, I throw the empty tin in the bin and move on to part two of the plan. Find a car.

I make my way back through the shop. The putrid stench of the warm, still air hits me as I step outside. I've read enough books and seen enough films to know that decomposing bodies smell bad. I just hadn't appreciated just how bad it is. Even Lex's house had not smelt so bad, but then that was two bodies. There must be hundreds of corpses decomposing in the sunlight.

I wonder about this. You get bitten, and eventually, you die and come back as a zombie. So there probably aren't piles of dead bodies anywhere.

So are the zombie's bodies decomposing, even though they are still moving? Is that what's causing this foul, evil smell? Does that mean they'll all eventually rot away and die properly? Or were people bitten and took their own lives to avoid becoming one of those things? No, if you die while infected you come back. I think back to the scene in Lex's kitchen yesterday. Her father was bitten and then killed himself. He stabbed himself through the eye, which would probably have penetrated the brain. He didn't come back.

Okay, so it is possible to be bitten, take your own life and not return as a harbinger of hell, as long as you damage the brain. Right. Good to know. Although that still doesn't answer my question about the source of this damn smell. Is it rotting zombies or rotting corpses? Is it both?

Actually. On reflection, I really don't want to know. Sometimes ignorance is bliss. Well, as opposed to the alternative, which is either coming upon a giant horde of zombies or a giant pile of corpses.

I pull my thoughts back to the task at hand, and realise that, as I've not been paying attention, I've already walked past a few cars. Shit, I need to be more aware of my surroundings.

Unfortunately, seeing a car is a lot easier than acquiring a car. I try the handles of a few. All are locked, I change tactics and instead look for houses that are open. There are several benefits to this.

Firstly, it saves me breaking into someone's house. Breaking and entering is not a skill I've acquired over my years of being a personal assistant.

Secondly, if the door is open, it means that any resident zombies would have been able to leave, so less likely they're inside waiting for me to turn up for breakfast. Lastly, it probably also means the resident has left, either the house or human existence. Either way, it won't feel quite so wrong stealing their car.

Surprisingly, there are quite a few houses with the doors wide open, although it takes some searching to find one which has a car parked outside. I approach it but stop abruptly. There is a dog in the threshold, lying half inside and half outside of the house. It has its head on his paws, but lifts it and cocks its ears as it sees me approach. As I assess the situation, it rises to its feet. It is big, easily waist height. Its fur is a mixture of brown and gold colours. I am not good with dog breeds, so I have no idea if it is the sort of dog that might like to attack or one that just wants a cuddle.

It doesn't look menacing, like it's going to rip my throat out for having the audacity to breathe. However, the absence of a wagging tail implies that it's not feeling particularly friendly either. It has a tail. It's just not wagging. I don't fancy my chances against a dog that probably hadn't has his Pedigree Chum this morning. It watches me as I slowly back away, but does not move to follow.

Eventually, I come across a house that has an open door, a car parked in the driveway and this time, no dog in view. I want to find the owner and kiss them. Right inside the door is a telephone table. On top a set of keys. Car keys. I pick them up and run over to the Black Ford Ka. I press the clicker, and the car unlocks. I'm about to open the door when it occurs to me that the owner might be in the house. What if they are alive and well and just about to pop out. Only to find that someone has nicked their car.

Cursing I run back over to the house. "Hello," I call into the empty hallway. "Is anyone home. I'm er… just going to borrow your car. But if you're alive then... er well… I won't. Obviously." I realise that I sound like a moron, but I want to be sure I give them fair warning.

A thump on the closed door to my right makes me jump. It is followed by an inhuman groan that is becoming far too familiar. The owner is a zombie. I guess they won't mind me borrowing their car then. I've also changed my mind about kissing them.

I'm relieved to see that the car has an almost full tank of petrol. More than I need. Scratch that, more than I should need, if everything goes to plan. Yeah right. Even so, when things do go pear shaped, as they will inevitably will, I should still have plenty of fuel.

Part three of the plan. Stop at Edna's to stock up on food. It dawns on me that having a plan is quite calming. Having a plan broken down into small steps even more so. I'm feeling confident, smug even.

Then I pull up outside the shop and notice the door is open.

When I left, less than an hour ago, I was distracted by the stench of the dead. Now thinking back, I cannot remember if I closed the door behind me. It would have been the sensible thing to do. Leave building, close door. Something I've done multiple times a day for my entire life. An act borne out of habit. Was the mere act of closing a door so insignificant that my mind chose to wipe it from memory? Or did I leave it open?

Regardless. The fact remains that the door of the shop is open. Someone or something could be inside.

When I was younger, I was a smoker. I tried quitting so many times but always struggled to go longer than a day or two. I used to imagine that I had an angel on one shoulder and a devil on the other. The angel would be telling me that I didn't need to smoke. It would ply me with benefits of why I should stop. The devil, however, the little bastard, shouted louder than the angel. He would fill my mind with images of warm days and pub gardens, cold beer in one hand, cigarette in the other. He would tell me, one more wouldn't hurt, I could stop again tomorrow. For years, the devil won, until one day I told him to fuck off.

He did, and I finally quit.

Today, sitting outside a building full of food, the little wanker is back.

The angel is also here, telling me not to take the chance. We aren't in desperate need for food. We can find some elsewhere when we run out.

The devil is showing me images of Edna's kitchen. Stacked full of goodies. He is reminding me that I don't know where my next meal will come from. Reassuring me, don't worry, it'll be perfectly safe.

My body moves, almost against my will. I climb out of the car and step through the open door into the shop. I can hear that little arsehole devil cheering, while the angel is silent. Obviously having a strop.

I walk through the shop back into the house. Nothing looks to have been disturbed, but I stay quiet, just in case. When I reach the kitchen, I see a man at the table. Unless zombies have started reading porn, it's safe to say he is not infected. He is, however, eating from a tin of spaghetti hoops. Shovelling the food so fast into his mouth that he doesn't seem to notice that tomato sauce is falling off the spoon onto his t-shirt. He is also so absorbed in the porn and the food that he doesn't see me stood in the kitchen doorway.

"You really should check out July's edition. It's a stars and stripes special." I have no idea what is in the July edition, but my words have the desired effect. He jumps up and turns to me.

"Oh, my. I'm ever so sorry. I thought this house had been abandoned," he replies. Then notices the magazine still in his hand. "I was … just flicking through … erm to pass the time."

"Sure," I reply in a tone that implies I know he is lying. The evil part of me is enjoying his discomfort. Then I notice his eyes flick to the pile of porn on the table.

He grins, "So is this your house then?" he asks.

Crap. I either tell him it's my house and accept the fact that it makes me look like a sex addict or admit I had just come back for food.

"Um … no, well that is … not exactly," I stumble over my words.

"The lady that lives here, sorry, lived here, took me in last night. I'm heading out now, but I thought I'd just come back and ... well ... get some of this food."

"Right," He says, drawing out the word and nodding slowly. "So ... it's not your house. Not your food." He smiles evilly, "Not your magazines."

I am standing up, he is sitting down. His top covered in spaghetti sauce, he is holding a porn magazine. Everything about this situation suggests that I should be dominant. So why does it feel like he has the upper hand and I am being told off for lying?

I lean against the doorframe, an intentional move to show that he is not intimidating me, "No. It's Edna's house."

"Who is Edna?"

"The old lady that lived here and ran the shop."

"Lived? Is she dead or is she one of those things?"

"I don't know," I confess. "The zombies came last night, and I think she was bitten. But I don't know what happened to her."

"How did you escape?"

"What?"

"How did you escape the zombies that came here last night?"

"I was upstairs, sleeping. The noise woke me up."

"You didn't help her?"

"Who? Edna? No, she told me not to."

"Sure," he replies in the exact same tone I used earlier.

I'm getting angry now, the casual door frame lean did not work, so I pull myself up to my full height and cross my arms, "No. Look. She told me to stay upstairs. I guess she knew it was hopeless."

"And you listened. You let an old woman get attacked by zombies while you stood and did nothing." His tone is accusatory, but there is a gleam in his eyes. The bastard is enjoying this.

"And you broke into an old woman's house, took her food and started reading her porn," I snap back at him.

"I didn't break in. The door was open."

Crap.

"Yes... well, not the point. Look, I feel bad enough about Edna, I don't really need to some perverted stranger telling me I did the wrong thing."

He lifts one eyebrow, "Perverted?"

"Well, you are holding a porn mag."

He puts the magazine back on top of the pile. "Fair point. Listen, I think we got off on the wrong foot. I'm Brian." He extends his hand out to me.

I note that he does not make any attempt to stand, but I step forward anyway and shake it. "I'm Chloe. So, Brian, how did you end up here?"

"I have a house down the road. I just use it at weekends, and when this all happened I should have been in London working.

Fortunately, I had a long weekend, so I was here instead. The problem is I don't keep a lot of food in the house, and I've run out. I did try to go and get some yesterday. But there were hundreds of zombies here."

I shift uncomfortably and break eye contact to stare down at the floor, "Ah, sorry about that." I say, "I kind of led them here."

"Why on earth would you do that?" he asks, as though I am an idiot.

I pull my eyes up from staring at the floor, and hold my head up in defiance, "Oh you know, yesterday I was bored, so thought I would go out and play hide and seek with a zombie horde."

"No need to get testy, Chloe." This guy is really beginning to piss me off.

"Sorry, Brian." I reply caustically. "My friends and I were trapped in a house. I created a diversion so my friends could get out. But my tyre blew, so I had to walk. This was the first village I found. I came to this shop looking for food and somewhere to hide."

"Oh, well, I see. That's very brave. Well done." I can't decide if he is being intentionally patronising.

"Thank you. Anyway, I need to go and find my friends. So, I'll just take this food ..."

"Hang on," he cuts me off. "Why do you get to have the food?"

He has a fair point, I can't claim ownership any more than he can.

I resort to the only thing I can think of, a line of reasoning that has spun through the ages. "I was here first."

He raises one eyebrow again, "So you say."

"What? I was."

"Yes, so you say. However, when I got here ten minutes ago, there was no one here. So how do I know you were really here first?"

This is becoming too much like hard work, but my stubbornness refuses to let me leave empty handed. "Right how about we split the food fifty-fifty?"

He considers this for a moment. "Hmm, that seems agreeable." He nods, gets to his feet and begins to arrange the food into equal piles. I join him to help, and it's not long before we have divided the food and packed it in carrier bags that I found under the sink.

"Right then … I'll be off. Erm, good luck I guess," I say, picking up my share of the bags.

"Yes, good luck to you too, Chloe." He responds, "It's been a pleasure talking to you."

"Er…yes… you too," I'm at the door that separates the house from the shop when I turn back. "Oh, and Brian," I call out.

"Yes," his head pops back into view.

"You can keep the porn." I turn on my heel and walk out. Pleased that I got the last word.

I dump the bags in the boot and get back in the car. On to the final part of the plan. Drive.

Reason dictates that the horde that followed me yesterday would probably have kept on going in the same direction. There's no logical reason that they would have turned around and gone back the way they came, although they might have been distracted by other survivors. But it feels safer to retrace my steps, than follow in the direction they would have been likely to go.

I visualise the route ahead of me. There are no major towns on the way, although I will pass a couple of small villages.

They shouldn't pose too much of a threat.

It's not long before I come across the Audi I was driving yesterday. I pull up alongside it. I can't remember if I put my bag in the car I drove from the airport, or if Sam had put in it the Honda. I glance around to make sure I'm not about to get eaten and quickly check the boot. I breathe a sigh of relief when I see the rucksack.

It holds the picture of Steve and me that I took from home. I would have been devastated to have lost it. As though to reassure myself I pull the picture from the inside pocket and stare at it.

Tears prick my eyes. God, I miss him. Suddenly the thought of not seeing him again is too much to bear. My mind fills with images of the dream last night, then of the blood-soaked roses this morning. I need to know that he is safe. The world has changed so much since Monday.

Sitting at George's, waiting for him to turn up no longer seems acceptable. I adapt my plan one last time. Drive back to Sally. Let them know I'm safe. Then find Steve.

My mind made up, I get back in the car and drive as fast as is safe, keen to put my plan into action.

As I drive, I think through the options of where Steve could be. Unless they've moved him across the country, which doesn't seem likely, he is probably going to be at one of the local army bases. Amesbury is closest. I will try there first.

I'm lost in thought, considering what I'll need to get there. It's probably less than two hours away by car. But I should plan on it taking a few days, judging by what I've seen so far. I'll need food, shelter, weapons. I'm caught up with planning, when a person on the other side of my road catches my eye. I drive on for a few seconds allowing my brain the necessary time to process what it's just seen.

Then I hit the brakes and jump out of the car.

I call out, and the figure turns and runs from me. I give chase and catch up quickly. I grab the shoulder and turn the body towards me.

"Claire? What's happened? Why are you out here? Are the others okay?" I am throwing questions at her, I back down and look at her properly. Her tear stained face looks pale and drawn. She looks up at me, and I see her eyes. Her eyes that show streaks of black snaking through the whiteness towards the pupil.

"Oh," I say.

"Yes," She nods, "I'm infected," She burst into tears and throws herself into my arms.

I will hate myself forever for what I did next. When this young girl, the hands of death grasping at her, reaches out for comfort, I instinctively back away.

Twenty-Five

"What do you mean, gone? Gone where?" Sam asked, as he disentangled
himself from Sally and got out of bed.

"Oh, she's in the kitchen," Lex replied.

"Is she?" Sam asked, confusion apparent on his face.

"No. Of course she's not in the bloody kitchen," Lex replied angrily. "I don't know where she is. Which is why I said she's gone."

Sally placed a hand on Sam's shoulder, the touch suggesting he should not speak. "Do you know how long she's been gone?" Lex softened, "I don't. I woke up about twenty minutes ago, and she wasn't in bed. I've searched around the house, but I can't find her. She could have been gone for hours. Or she might have just left."

"Right, okay," Sally leapt into action. "We need to go and find her."

"Obviously," Lex replied and followed Sally out of the door, leaving Sam alone in the room. He settled back on the bed, smiling at the memory of the night before.

"Sam, are you coming?" Sally yelled from the stairs.

"Oh right, yep," He replied leaping from the bed and running to join the girls.

"Is my Dad up?" Sally asked Lex.

"I don't know, I've not seen him yet."

"Right, I'll go find him, he might have seen her. Can you two go and check out back?"

Sam and Lex headed down the stairs together, through the kitchen, then out to the back garden. No sign of Claire. Sally was coming down the stairs as they returned to the hallway.

"Dad's just getting up, he's going to come and help search. He'll meet us outside."

The trio stepped outside the house. The air was still, the only sound that of birdsong. Of Claire, there was no sign.

Together, they walked down the long driveway, scanning left and right for any indication that Claire had come that way. They had only been walking for a few minutes when the low hum of an engine broke through the tranquil surroundings.

"Chloe?" Sally asked hopefully.

"Hope so," Sam replied. 'If not, I hope they're friendly, because we…" he gestured around them, "are completely exposed."

The car came into view, but the early morning sunlight glared on the windscreen, and obscured the driver.

"We should have brought weapons," Sam said, as the three of them paused to watch the car come to a stop in front of them.

He instinctively stepped in front of the two girls, offering his body as protection. "There are two people in there," he whispered.

The driver's door was pushed open, and Chloe stepped out.

Sally stepped past Sam and broke into a run, launching herself into Chloe's arms.

"I'm so happy to see you," she sobbed. "When you didn't get here yesterday, I thought … and now Claire's gone and …"

"Ssshhh," Chloe comforted the crying girl. "It's okay, I'm here now, and Claire is…"

"I'm here," Claire said, getting out of the car.

"Claire, what the hell?" Lex demanded, relief that her friend was safe manifested as anger, because of the worry she'd caused. "How could you? You can't just go off on your own."

"I… I'm sorry."

"Not good enough, Claire," Lex virtually spat at her. She towered over the trembling girl, face red and body trembling with anger.

Chloe released Sally from her hug, and stepped in front of Lex. "Not now, Lex," her voice carrying a warning tone.

"Chloe, you don't understand. She just us left us."

"No, Lex, you don't understand. She felt she had to go."

"Why? Because I was a bit stroppy yesterday. Pathetic."

"No," Claire spoke out, stepping around Chloe to come face to face with Lex, "To protect you. I'm infected."

Lex stared at her, the anger draining from her, leaving her body to sag, "What? No. That can't be possible." Lex whispered, her voice cracking. The tears began to fall as she pulled her friend into a hug. Sally rushed over to join them, and the three friends held each other as they sobbed.

"Come on, Sam," Chloe whispered, taking the shell-shocked young man's arm. "Let's go inside and give them some time."

Sam nodded dumbly back, his mind frantically searching back over the last few days. "How?" he asked.

"Yesterday, just after you left Lex's house. She was bitten on the ankle."

"No," he whispered, his voice breaking. "It's my fault. I forgot the keys, then I forgot to put the bags in the boot. She offered to do it for me."

"I know, Sam, she told me, but it's not your fault," Chloe put her hand on his back and guided him into the house. "It could have happened to any of you."

"I know," he said, "But it should have been me."

"Sam, you can't think like that. What's done is done, and now we need to work out what to do with her."

He came to a stop, realisation dawning on his face, "Oh no."

"Yep," Chloe nods.

"What is going on?" George asked, standing in the doorway, immaculately dressed in a suit and tie. As though he was attending a meeting, not waiting out the apocalypse.

He gave no acknowledgement that Chloe had arrived. No thanks for rescuing his daughter.

"Nice to see you too, George," Chloe replied.

Ignoring the sarcastic tone, he asked, "What are they doing?" he nodded in the direction of the three girls, who are still huddled together.

"Claire has been bitten. Sally and Lex have just found out, they are all upset," Chloe explained.

"Bitten," he asked, a thoughtful look crossed his face, "I see," he nodded as though coming to a decision, "Wait here."

Sam and Chloe exchanged glances. Not sure why they were being asked to wait. Within moments, George returned, holding the shotgun that Sam had left in the kitchen the night before.

"What the hell are you doing with that?" Chloe demanded.

"Sorting the situation out," George responded.

"Not with that bloody thing you're not."

"Chloe. She is going to turn into one of those things any minute now. We cannot allow that to happen."

"It's barely been twelve hours since she was bitten. It can take up to forty-eight hours for her to turn. Claire should be given a choice about how she dies. Besides, other than a temperature, she isn't displaying any other symptoms yet."

"You can't seriously think she's going to be immune," George sneered, checking to see if the shotgun was loaded.

"No, of course I don't. As far as I know, immunity isn't possible. But you going around waving that thing is going to terrify the poor girl. She's already scared and upset. Can we please just make her last few hours as easy as they can be?"

"Er, guys," Sam attempted to interrupt the argument.

"Fine. I won't shoot her. But she is not coming into my house."

"Guys... Chloe, Mr Carlton," Sam's tone grew more urgent. Yet he continued to be ignored.

"So what? You're going to just leave her out here, while we what, wave from the window?"

"If needs be. My only priority is to protect my daughter."

"And yourself," Chloe challenged. "George, I have worked with you for long enough to know how fucking self-interested you are. Now a young girl is dying, and you want to leave her outside like a stray dog."

"Mr Carlton. Chloe," Sam tried again.

"What, Sam?" Chloe shouted at him, annoyed at being interrupted in her first ever opportunity to lay into George.

"Look," he pointed to the three girls, who now stood just a few feet away, listening as the argument unfolded.

Sally's face was thunderous, her arms folded defensively.

"Dad, either you let Claire into the house, or I will stay out here with her," she said.

"Sally, it's not safe," George pleaded.

"Which is why I left," Claire interjected. "I know I'm a risk to you all."

"How about a compro... er... thingy?" Sam suggested.

George stared witheringly at the young man, "Compromise? What do you have in mind."

"What about we let Claire in but... er... I don't know... tie her up or summat?"

"What?" three female voices chorused.

"I think that's a good idea," Claire said. "I would like to spend my last few hours with my best friends, but I don't want to put them in danger."

"Okay, if you're sure," said Sally, "what do you think, Dad?"

George looked at the five faces staring at him, "Fine. I can agree to that. Sam. There is some rope in the shed out back. Would you get it?"

"Yep," Sam sped off towards the back garden.

"Come on, Claire" Sally linked her arm through her friend's and led her into the house. Lex trailed closely behind.

"Er Chloe… a word please," George called as Chloe moved to follow the girls in the house.

"What?" she snapped at him.

"I do not appreciate being spoken to in that manner. I would like to suggest that when things go back to normal, you seek employment elsewhere."

Chloe stood in stunned silence for a few seconds. Then her mouth broke out into a broad smile, and she let out a deep belly laugh.

"Oh George," she said as she walked past him, she patted him heartily on his back, "back to normal? You really are a clueless prick, aren't you?"

She left him standing alone, fixed to the spot.

His mouth hung open in confusion. For once in his life. George Carlton was speechless.

Chloe found the girls in the living room. They stopped talking the moment she entered. The three girls exchanged guilty glances. She sensed that she had interrupted something important.

"Come on, what've I interrupted?" Chloe asked.

"We were talking about what to do with me," Claire replied, the defiance in her eyes suggesting that she expected to be challenged.

Chloe tried not to let the relief show. She knew that the conversation needed to happen, but really hadn't wanted to be the one to instigate it.

"What have you come up with?"

"I don't want to become one of those things. I would like to die before I do."

"Okay," Chloe nodded slowly, "that's totally understandable."

"I think my best option would be to slit my wrists," a fat tear rolled slowly down Claire's cheek. Sally slipped her arms around her shoulders, offering what little comfort she could.

A pained expression flickers across Chloe's face, unnoticed by the others, "Okay," she said, "Erm Lex, why don't you come and help me make coffee?"

"Coffee? Now?"

"Yes," Chloe's tone left no room for debate. Lex dutifully followed her into the kitchen. They passed Sam in the hallway. He was holding a large spool of rope.

"Will this work?" he asked.

"Should do," Chloe replied without stopping.

When they reached the kitchen, Lex turned on Chloe.

"Are you going to tell me what you needed to talk to me about?"

"Ah, you picked up on that then."

"Well, you weren't exactly subtle. But Chloe, this better be worth it. I've only got a few more hours to spend with one of my best friends."

"I know. I'll be quick. The thing is … when Claire dies, she will come back as a zombie."

"Oh God," Lex collapsed onto the nearest chair. "Isn't there anything we can do?"

"I think the only thing that will either stop it happening, or kill her when she has turned, is to damage the brain."

"My dad …" the realisation dawned on her. "that's why he killed himself, why he stabbed himself in the eye, isn't it? So that he didn't come back as one of them."

"I think so."

"Oh God," she said again. "What are we going to say to Claire?"

"That's why I wanted to talk to you. Do we need to tell her?"

"I don't know. If it were you, wouldn't you want to know?" they paused and considered Lex's words. It was a scenario from a nightmare.

"How long?" Lex suddenly asked. "How long after she dies will she turn?"

"I don't know. It would be quick I'd imagine. Regardless, we'd need to assume it will happen quickly. Otherwise, she could be a danger to us."

"I think we should tell her. She needs to make the decision, knowing all of the facts."

"Okay," Chloe nodded in agreement.

They made the coffee in silence, both reflecting on the conversation. Both dreading the impending conversation. The coffee was made in six identical mugs which Lex arranged onto a tray.

Chloe stared at them for a second.

"Wait," she said and took one of the mugs from the tray. Then with the coffee in hand, she started opening and closing cupboards.

"What are you doing?" Lex asked, confused by the odd behaviour.

"Ah ha," Chloe said and presented an empty mug to Lex. The mug was purple with the words 'World's Best 18-Year-Old' written in a whimsical yellow font.

"What's that for?"

"If we use identical mugs, we could get them mixed up."

"So?"

"I heard on the news that it is possible to pass the infection on by exchanging bodily fluids. If we accidentally mix up the mugs and even a little bit of Claire's saliva is on one that someone else drinks from then…"

"Oh, yeah, we figured that might be the case. If we accidentally drank from the same mug, we could get infected,"

"Yep."

"We need to tell everyone to be really careful around Claire and… Oh no."

"What?"

"If she slits her wrists, there is going to be a lot of blood. We can't risk it."

"Good point. Okay. Let's go and talk to her." Chloe lifted the tray of coffee from the side and followed by Lex, carried it into the living room.

They found Claire tied to an armchair. The rope was around her waist. Leaving her arms and legs free. She looked as comfortable as she could be in the circumstances. Sam and Sally sat together on the couch.

"Dad didn't specify how tightly up she needs to be tied up," Sally said grinning up at Lex and Chloe.

"Where is he?" Chloe asked.

"I think he's in his office. I'll take his coffee out to him, shall I?" Sally offered

"Good idea. I don't suppose he wants to see me right now," Chloe laughed as she handed the coffees out. If anyone noticed that Claire was purposefully given a distinctively different mug from the others, they didn't say anything.

They drank their coffee in silence, now was not the time for idle chit chat. When Sally came back into the lounge, Lex cleared her throat. "I'm so sorry Claire, but we need to talk."

~

The sun was setting as Sam, Sally, Lex and Chloe supported a weary Claire out into the garden. The sky was a deep blue streaked with flashes of pink. The air was warm and still.

The absence of traffic driving through the village, of planes flying overhead allowed nature's song to be clear and beautiful.

The mood was sombre as the five sat on the garden furniture, watching the sun set behind the trees. The lack of conversation did not create an uncomfortable air, nor did it create the need to fill the silence. Instead, they all sat in quiet contemplation, reflecting on the events that led them to be here.

To this time. To this place.

For Sam, the fear of what he must do. The promise he had vowed to keep.

For Chloe, the shame of her rejection when Claire had told her she was infected. That it was because of Chloe's intervention that Claire's final moments would be with her friends, did not absolve her of the guilt.

Lex and Sally sat either side of Claire, each holding one of her cold, clammy hands in theirs, their heads resting on her shoulders. There was no need for words. They allowed the memories of their times together to flood through them. The memories that both provided comfort and an unbearable sense of loss.

Claire felt the changes coursing through her body. Unsure whether she was feeling the effects of the infection or of the large dose of codeine she had taken earlier. She suspected it was both.

She sat with the calmness of someone that has accepted their fate. In her hands, she held the picture that Chloe had taken from Lex's house. The four friends, laughing together. Soon there would be just two of them left. She stared down at it, on to Paige's face. She envied the suddenness in which Paige had lost her life. The reaper's scythe had hung over her head for the last day. It had consumed her every waking thought. But she was no longer afraid. Instead, she was thankful that her friends were near. If Chloe had not found her, she would be alone now.

Earlier, when Lex had explained her options, she had made the decision quickly. She made the others promise that there would be no more tears. She knew they would cry once she had gone, but she could not bear the burden of their pain. She had enough of her own to deal with.

They had spent the rest of their day drinking coffee, telling stories and playing games.

An unspoken agreement to ensure that Claire's last day was as pleasant as possible. A casual onlooker would never have guessed the dark cloud hanging over them.

They had agreed Claire would take the codeine twenty-four hours after she had been bitten. Earlier if she had started to show more symptoms. She didn't mention her headache, and otherwise, she felt fine. When the time had passed unobserved by the others, Claire had remained quiet.

However, when the sun began to sink low in the sky, she told them the time had come.

Observed silently by her four friends, she took the pills.

Now just under an hour later the tiredness was becoming almost too much to bear. With as much grace as she could muster, she rose to her feet.

The others rose with her. Turning to each of them in turn, she hugged them, and said goodbye. Hugging Lex last, she passed her the photograph.

"Remember us," she whispered into her ear.

Lex nodded, the lump in her throat leaving her unable to speak. There was so much to say, but if she spoke, she would cry. She'd promised Claire. Instead, she held her tightly, until Claire backed gently away.

Then, supported by Sam, Claire slowly made her way up the garden towards the tree line.

"I forgot how long this garden was," Claire's joke fell flat, marred by the gasp as she struggled to catch her breath.

"Am I going too fast?" Sam asked.

"A little," she wheezed, "but I don't think we have long."

Without a word, he picked her up in his arms and carried her over the little stream and into the woods.

He found a spot, that was big enough for her to lie down. Placing a rucksack beneath her head, he gently lay her down and crouched next to her.

The shade of the overhanging trees blocked out the dying light of the day. Sam took the torch from his pocket and flicked it on. The soft glow lit Claire's face, her eyes were closed, and her breath was shallow.

"Claire?" Sam whispered.

"Mmm."

He took her hand in his and stroked it gently. "I just wanted to say it's been good to know you. You're a nice person, and I won't forget what you did for me."

Claire smiled softly, "It has been good to know you too, Sam."

They sat in silence, Claire's breathing becoming progressively slower. "Sam?" she whispered.

"Yeah?" He leant closer, barely able to hear her.

"Promise me…" She gasped for air. "You'll… look… after," another gasp, "them."

"I will. I promise."

"Thank… you." She sighed heavily then started to choke. Sam sat her up and rubbed her back as she vomited. Lex had explained that this might happen. It was the reason that Claire had asked Sam to take her away from the others when it was time. She wanted Lex and Sally to remember her as she was. With dignity.

A tear rolled down Sam's cheek as he held her. She no longer had the energy to retch, and the vomit slid back down her throat as she slipped into unconsciousness.

"Claire?"

No response.

"Claire?" His voice grew more frantic. "I'm not ready… please… not yet."

He rocked her gently as she died in his arms.

Lex had advised him to act swiftly once she had gone. None of them knew how quickly she would come back. It had sounded simple at the time. As soon as she was dead, he must do it. A conversation in the light of day, sitting in comfort, and surrounded by friends, was a stark contrast to the situation in which Sam now found himself. He had thought her death would be instantly noticeable. That he would feel her life slip away. He had not realised that it would hurt so much. That he would not, could not, accept that she had gone. For long moments, he continued to rock her. To beg and plead for her to stay with him. It was only the nagging voice in the back of his mind that prompted him to feel for a pulse. A pulse he could not find. Ice ran through his veins as he remembered the look on her face when she had expressed her passionate desire not to turn. He needed to act. He would not break his vow.

He gently turned her over and lay her face down on the ground. He reached into the bag, and by torchlight, he found the bundle he was looking for. The tea towel that protected his hands from the sharp blade contained within.

Placing the knife on one side, he shone the torch on to the back of Claire's head. The torchlight on her golden hair gave the impression of an ethereal being. With a heavy heart, he parted her hair and felt for the spot Lex had shown him earlier on her own head. He found it easily. Through a blinding blur of tears. Sam picked up the knife and plunged it into Claire's brain.

The act complete, the promise kept. A man now changed forever by the acts of today.

Eventually, he lifted her body and turned her over. She looked peaceful, as though she were merely asleep and would wake up at any moment.

He took the last item from the bag, a bed sheet. As gently as he could, he wrapped her body in the sheet. Then he left her alone. Forever.

A lone figure stood in the kitchen, staring out at the large expanse of the garden. She watched as the young man made his way back to the house. His frame was lit by the bright moonlight. She knew instinctively that it was a different Sam that emerged from the woodland. The cocksure gait that was once a natural movement for him, was now replaced by sagging shoulders. He walked as though the weight of the world were on them. His head held low. His movement slow.

In the darkness, Sally continued to watch as Sam neared the house and then disappeared from sight. She heard the back door open, then close.

She wanted to speak, to reach out to him. To offer comfort and to be comforted. Yet she didn't know the words. So, she remained silent and unnoticed as Sam left the kitchen.

Lex lay on the sofa, her head upon Chloe's lap, her heart in shreds from the events of the last week. Her parents and two of her best friends were gone. The feel of Chloe's hand gently stroking her hair gave her assurance that she was not alone. But did not dispel the growing fear that she soon would be. The sound of the kitchen door closing set the tears flowing again. Claire was dead. She buried her head in the older woman's lap and cried as though she would never stop.

Twenty-Six

George Carlton sat in his unnecessarily large chair behind the unnecessarily large desk in his unnecessarily large office. He had been in the same position all day. Staring at the wall. In front of him stood a cold mug of coffee, untouched.

Hours passed, and still, he sat. He was not aware that it was now dark. The events unfolding in the house around him went unnoticed, his mind an unending sea of thoughts. Chloe telling him he was clueless. Lex calling him a coward. They were right.

Twice he sent someone else to get his daughter. Twice he put his own life before hers. Now there is an infected in the house, but he could not act. Once again, he could not protect Sally, but this time because she would not allow him to.

He was a failure.

He was selfish.

He was a coward.

He was insignificant.

All he had done, all he had achieved meant nothing. No one was coming to help him. The world had changed.

He was unimportant.

He was irrelevant.

A life spent putting himself before his family. He did not hear Sally's first words; he was on an important call. He was playing golf when she took her first steps. He made excuses for every school play and parents' evening.

While his wife lay dying of cancer, he worked twelve hour days. The day she had succumbed to the disease, he had been having drinks with a politician.

He would die soon. Of this he was certain.

He was unable to comprehend the wasted life. Unwilling to accept that it had all been for nothing.

He sat, and he stared, and slowly his mind began to fall apart.

Twenty-Seven

Saturday 21st September

Chloe,

We were told last night that we are going out again today, to try again. We've have been reassured that it will be better. That the powers that be have learnt. None of us were convinced. We were wrong.

Right from the start, it felt different. I think that might be our attitudes. Yesterday we were confident. Arrogant. The zebs didn't seem like a threat. They were dumb, slow, unorganised. We were the British Army, the best in the world at what we do. We knew everything, and it would be easy.

Today we were humble. Our attitudes towards the enemy have changed. They are still slow, dumb and unorganised, but they are greater in number. They do not need to stop, to listen to commands. They don't need to eat or drink, to resupply or to communicate.

They have one mission, and that is to kill. To understand that is to survive.

Yesterday we were all in the same place, sure we had a common goal, but you can't have that many people together, civilian and military, actives and reservist all working in perfect synchronicity with each other. In hindsight, we should have known that.

So today we were split up.

I'm going to try to explain what happened. But some of this letter is what others have told me. We had three teams.

Team one's role was simple. Fix the posts in place first. Roll out the razor wire. Then when the perimeter was in, put up the permanent fencing. The Engineers would do the construction. The infantry would provide cover fire. They would be covering the verticals of the rectangle

Team two did the same, but they would be covering the horizontal of the rectangle. They started five miles out from the extension we made yesterday. Instead of carrying massive fencing, they too used razor wire. The more permeant solution could come after.

Team three were the key, though. This was my team. We headed out in a combination of vehicles. We drove to about two miles away from the five-mile mark. Then we stopped and waited for the order to come.

I don't know if you have ever heard the noise that a post rammer makes, but it's loud, and it echoes. In an expanse like The Plain, it can echo for miles. It's that, combined with the gunshots, that drew the zebs to us yesterday. So, our job today was to create the distraction. To draw the zebs in the area to us and away from the base. Our role was risky. We were basically used as bait.

When the order came, we started to make noise. I still can't really believe it, but we had The Royal Artillery Band with us.

A band. On the frontline. It was just insane.

Anyway, all they needed to do was to make lots of noise. We weren't expecting them to play anything.

Just bang drums, blow trumpets. Create a racket. However, when the command came, they started to play Rule Britannia.

I've always been a bit sceptical and maybe a bit judgemental of the role of the band in the military. I get the public relations angle, but I've never seen it as morale boosting, as we are made to believe. However, sitting in the back of the SV, after the events of yesterday, hearing that music was uplifting and got us all fired up. The band were on foot. The Drum Major insisted upon it. They were protected on all sides by SVs, but still, it was a brave decision. They were also in full ceremonial dress. Fair play to them.

The zebs came. We took them down as quickly as we could, and all the while the vehicles rolled slowly, and the band continued to play.

From what I've heard, about twenty minutes after we started, the order was given to teams one and two to begin the fence construction.

The diversion worked. Sure, they had contact. But only a few zebs in comparison to yesterday, so the numbers were easily manageable. They got the razor wire fence up within hours.

When the next order came, the band stopped playing and got back into the Armoured Personnel Carrier.

The zebs were still coming, and our primary objective was to take out as many as we could. When enough of them were gathered together, we threw grenades. Grenades don't kill zebs. At least not all of them. They don't destroy the brain. However, they sure as hell destroy the bodies. Within minutes we had gone from mass hordes moving relentlessly towards us to piles of broken bodies. The GPMGs then took out as many as possible. Those of us with assault rifles finished the rest off.

I guess the noise we had made was still drawing more in, and we could have stayed in a never-ending loop of killing, making noise and inviting more to come.

As soon as the majority within eyesight were destroyed, we drove slowly back to the base. The GPMGs carried on taking down any that we saw between us and the base, but the journey back was straightforward.

It felt like a different camp when we got back. We added five square miles to the perimeter, and not one person died. It's hard to explain on paper, but the morale, the camaraderie, just the general atmosphere…. it was intense. Insane. Wonderful.

We've just come back from the debrief. Tomorrow we're going to be digging a moat around the camp. Same drills as today, with a diversion away from the camp. The original plan to join zones together has been put on hold until the situation is more stable.

In the coming days and months, we'll be creating secure supply routes between us and the closest zones, so we can trade goods, and move personnel around as necessary. That's particularly important, given the other news...

Zone E is going to be led jointly by military and civilian leaders. In a few weeks, there will be a vote for a civilian leader who will work alongside the top brass of the military. Civvy committees will be set up, and they will be responsible for building, farming, catering and basically everything that is needed to create a sustainable community. Once we've fully secured the camp, the role of the military will be protection, law enforcement, supply runs and most importantly of all, we will be going out and actively searching for survivors, That's right! We are going to be allowing survivors in. The cheers that went up around the room when we got told that was deafening.

I'm still buzzing from the events of today, but it feels good. We're moving in the right direction, and we're going to win this war. Life will never be what it once was. But the human race will survive, and that is what matters.

Hopefully I'll see you soon.

I love you.

Steve xxx

Twenty-Eight

The sun neither knows nor cares that the world has ended. It has risen today as it did yesterday. As it will do tomorrow. It does not understand the shroud of pain that covers this house. It does not appreciate that it should hide from view. Be covered by dark, tempestuous clouds. It should not be shining in an already bright blue sky. It should be dull and grey outside. More fitting to match the mood within.

As I comforted Lex last night, I heard Sally follow Sam up the stairs. I wanted to call out to her. To offer her my love and support, but I stayed silent, suspecting that she sought this from Sam. While their blossoming feelings went unmentioned, they did not go unnoticed. I saw the glances between the two of them. The odd touch of their hands. The closeness in which they sat.

A couple of days ago, I would have been unhappy with this turn of events. I am still angry with the way he treated her, but in the grand scheme of things, it no longer matters. Worse things have happened, will likely still happen.

Instead, I am worried. Not for Sally nor Sam, but for Lex. She has lost too much over the past week. If Sally turns to Sam for comfort, who will Lex turn to once I am gone? I wonder whether my worry is because of the burgeoning relationship, or because of the guilt I will feel at leaving them behind.

But I must go. As soon as I found out about Claire yesterday, I put my resolve to leave at the back of my mind. I would stay for as long as they need me. But I dreamt about Steve again last night. He and Edna were sitting in her lounge, silent and unspeaking, just staring at me with cold, black eyes. A wilted red rose, dripping with blood lay between them. I need to know if he is still alive. I need to go.

I eventually encouraged Lex to go to bed. I took her upstairs to the room she had shared with Claire the night before. There I sat with her until she fell asleep. I had considered sleeping in the same bed as Claire had the night before, but it didn't feel right. So I chose another of the rooms for my slumber.

The house is quiet and I think I'm the first to wake. There are no noises anywhere in the house. I've always felt awkward when I stay at someone else's house and am the first up. It feels rude to be the first out of bed. For once you are out of bed, you must do something. It would be strange to sit on a chair and wait, but equally rude to help yourself to a drink or to switch on the television.

Today, I feel none of that social awkwardness. I know this is not my home, but it doesn't feel like someone else's either. It feels like a refuge from the horrors of the streets. I do not feel like I am an intruder.

Plus, I do not have the luxury of time to stay in bed and wait for Sally or George to get up. For today I have plans to make and things to organise.

Which I will do, soon, once I have had coffee.

I long for a shower; it's been days since I've felt clean. The water still appears to be running, but the shower works off electricity. It's not warm enough to stand under a cold shower, so instead, I fill the sink and wash my body with cold water and soap. When I'm clean, I fill the basin again and wash my hair by dipping my head in the sink. It takes too long, and now there is water everywhere. I dress and pull my wet hair up into a ponytail. Then I go downstairs.

I'm drinking my coffee at the kitchen table when Lex enters the room. I start to say good morning, then think better of it. There is nothing good about this morning. So instead I lift my mug up.

"Coffee?"

She nods, "Yes please," she sits down at the table, her head resting on her hand.

I make her a cup and sit down across from her. "How are you feeling?" I ask.

She shrugs, "I don't know really. It doesn't feel real. I keep expecting her to come through the door any minute now."

"Well, if Sam didn't do his job properly, she still might," I say, the words coming out before I can stop them. "Shit. Oh, my God. I'm so sorry, I don't know why I said that."

"It's okay," she reassures me with a weak smile. "Have you seen Sam since…?" Her words trail off, but I know what she is asking.

"No, but I'm sure he did what he needed to do."

She nods, "I can't imagine how he is feeling. To have to watch… then to…" She trails off, unable to say the words.

"No, me neither," I say.

A creak on the stairs indicates someone else is up; I look expectantly towards the door. Sam and Sally enter the kitchen together.

"Coffee?" I offer them.

"Yes please," they reply in unison.

I go back to the stove and the pan of boiling water. As I start to make them coffee, I turn to Sally and ask her if she has seen her dad yet.

"No," She pauses, head tilted as though in thought, "I've not seen him since yesterday morning, in fact… has anyone seen him since then?"

"Last I saw," Said Sam. "he was going into the room next to the lounge."

"That's his office," Sally replied. "I'll go check."

Sally heads out of the room, and I give Sam his coffee.

"How are you feeling, Sam?" I ask.

His shoulders sag, "It was hard, ya know."

"Did she look like she was in pain?" Lex asked quietly.

"Nah." Sam shrugs, "I think she was unconscious when she died."

"And did you…" Lex asks. Sam nods, his eyes filling with tears at the memory. Lex quickly stands and approaches Sam. He turns to her, and Lex embraces him, "Thank you," she whispers quietly, then releases him and returns to her seat.

Sally comes back into the kitchen, a full mug of coffee in her hand, "Dad is in his office, but he doesn't appear to be in a good way," she says, pouring the fluid down the sink.

"Why?" I ask, my tone harsher than I intended.

"I don't know," says Sally "It's hard to explain. I've not seen him like this before. I think he slept there and now he is just muttering stuff. I couldn't really understand him. He was saying things like it's all pointless, meaningless, how it's all gone."

"What? What's gone?" I ask.

"I don't know. It was weird, it was like he didn't really know I was there."

"Sounds like he's gone mental," Sam says. I shoot him a look.

"Chloe… would you mind going to talk to him?" Sally asks. My first reaction is to say no, let him wallow in his own misery, but I see the look on Sally's face and agree.

Out of habit, I knock on the office door. There is no response, so I push the door open.

"George?" He does not respond to me. "Er, George…" I say again.

Not only does he stay silent, but it is also as though he hasn't even acknowledged my presence. I stand in front of him, but he just stares blankly at me. Shit, Sally is right. While I don't like the man, it is strange to see him like this. He's usually so brash and confident, and now he looks, well, broken. He's muttering to himself, the words nonsensical.

"George." I try again and shake him on the shoulder. It seems to stir him from whatever recess of his mind he was lost within. He looks at me, but I don't recognise the man staring at me. His eyes are wild with an almost childlike manner about them.

"Chloe," he says, his voice pleading. "What have I done?"

"Er… I don't know. What, er… have you done?"

"I missed them. All of them." his eyes frantically scan the room, as though looking for something.

"What? Missed who?"

"The plays."

"What plays? George, what are you talking about?"

"And the parents' evenings," he continues as though I hadn't spoken. "I don't even know what her first words were."

A big fat tear rolls down his cheek.

I am beginning to think that Sam was right, I think George has lost it. I have no idea what to do, and no experience in mental health issues. I'm at a loss, and if it weren't for Sally, I would happily close the door and just walk away.

Instead, I choose to lie. "It was dada," I say, "Sally's first words were dada." I have no idea what her first words were, but I don't think a little white lie at this point will hurt. He looks at me with joy in his eyes. He takes my hand in both of his and shakes it vigorously up and down.

"Thank you," he says, "thank you."

I extract my hand from his.

"George, come out with me to the kitchen. Let's get you a coffee. You'll feel better after coffee." Another white lie.

He shakes his head. "I'll stay here. It's safe here." Again, his eyes search the room.

I can see that no amount of cajoling is going to get him to move. "Okay. How about I get you a coffee and bring it to you?" He nods his head with childlike enthusiasm.

I return to the kitchen. Sally is looking at me expectantly, but I shake my head, "I think he's in shock. I 'll take him a coffee, perhaps that will help." Sally seems to accept this as a reasonable solution, but I see Lex looking at me suspiciously. I avoid meeting her eyes and busy myself making yet another cup of coffee.

Once it's made, Sam surprises me by offering to take it out to George. I'm not sure of his motivation, but after a moment's thought, I realise that I don't care. I hand the coffee to him.

Once he's left the room, I turn to Sally, "So…" I say, "Sam?" I grin at the blush that creeps up her cheeks.

She looks at me coyly, "We didn't do anything."

"What, when?" I ask confused.

"For the last two nights. We kissed a bit, but last night… well… last night we just cried together."

I laugh, "Did you think I was asking you about spending the night with him? I wasn't even aware that you had. Other than Alicante of course."

"Oh," she blushes. "What were you asking?"

"I was just wondering what was going on."

"I don't know. I think I like him and I think he likes me." She blushes. "I know he was a bit of a dick early on. But he's changed."

I think on this. She's right; Sam does seem to have matured in the short time I've known him. "If he makes you happy, then go for it. Times have changed."

Lex, who's been observing the conversation with a neutral look on her face, nods, "I suggest taking happiness where you can find it."

Sally nods happily, pleased to have our blessing.

"Actually, there is something else I need to talk to you about," I say. They look at me expectantly, "I need to go and find Steve."

Lex shrugs, "Okay. When shall we leave," she asks.

That was not the response I expected. I thought they would beg me to stay. Not that they would assume I was taking them with me. "We?" I ask. They both nod back at me.

"Yes," Lex was firm in her response. "We need to stick together. There's no way we would let you go alone."

"But you'll be safe here."

"For a time, yes." Lex concedes. "But what happens when we run out of food? If someone gets hurt? This house is a good place to hide out for a few days, but it's only a temporary solution."

"I agree," nods Sally. "From now on we stay together."

"It will be dangerous getting there. I don't want anyone else to get hurt."

"It will be safer together," says Lex, fire burning in her eyes, "Besides. You don't know where 'there' is do you?" Damn, she's smart.

"No," I admit.

"So basically, you want us to let you go out. Alone. To wander the country looking for your boyfriend?" Sally asks. She's smirking, because she knows that they have already won the argument, "Would you let any of us do that?"

I don't answer. I don't need to, because we all know I wouldn't. There we have it, they're coming with me.

"Okay," I finally say. "I want to leave in the next hour or so."

"That's fine, but where are we going to start?" Lex says. There's a glimmer in her eyes, and the innocent tone of voice gives me the impression she's holding something back.

"I was going to try Amesbury first. It's closest. If he is not there, I'll keep going until I find him."

"Mmm," Lex says thoughtfully, "That's a good idea. Or you could just go straight to Linthem."

"What? Why Linthem?"

"Because I think that's where he is."

"Why would you think that?" I look to Sally. Her brow is furrowed, she looks as confused as I feel.

"When we got here the other night, George mentioned that he was told about the military setting up safe zones," Lex explains, "then he told us that he got a text on Friday from a number that wasn't in his contact list. The text said to go to Linthem." She paused and took a sip of coffee.

"So? What's that got to do with Steve?" I ask impatiently.

"I'm getting to that…" she's enjoying this.

"Well let's say things got quite heated after George showed us the message. George wanted to leave straightaway. Without you."

"Wanker," I mutter, then turn to Sally. "Sorry," She shrugs, not offended.

"It didn't occur to me until I was in bed later, that anyone who would possibly have any interest in George's well-being must surely be someone who either owes him a favour or would want something from him."

"Makes sense," I nod and take a sip of my coffee.

"Well, what could George possibly do for anyone now?"

I consider this question. George's influence comes through playing political games. Treating MPs and CEOs, alike, as though they were pawns on a chessboard. There is simply nothing he can offer now.

"Nothing."

Lex smiles, "Exactly, so that leaves someone who owes him a favour. Agreed?"

I nod, eager for her to go on.

"So, if someone owed George anything, I would bet that they would be in his contact list."

"Yes definitely. One of my jobs was to make sure his contact list was up to date, so if he needed to call in a favour he could."

"Right. But the number wasn't in it. So… if we agree it wasn't someone who wanted something, and it wasn't someone that owes him something, what does that mean?"

I stare at her blankly. I have absolutely no idea where she is going with this.

"Um,"

She smiles patiently at me, "It means the text wasn't intended for George. At least not directly. It was for someone that was with George," she sits back in her chair as though the answer is obvious.

"Who was it meant for?"

She groans, "You, obviously."

"But I wasn't with George when he got the message," I say. I have not had another coffee this morning, and it sounds like Lex is talking in riddles.

"No, but you were supposed to be, weren't you?"

Ah, she has a point. Steve told me on Thursday to get to George's. As far as Steve knows, I drove straight here. Still, something doesn't make sense.

"Why wouldn't he text me?"

"When did you last check your phone?"

I think back. My phone ran out of battery on Thursday night when I got to the airport. Steve is practical. He could well have text both me and George, just in case. I know he has George's details, as I gave them to him for emergencies, but I've never put Steve's number in George's phone. I never trusted him not to contact Steve if he couldn't get hold of me.

Lex is right. My heart leaps. Steve could be at Linthem. "Lex, you are a genius."

Her face lights up with the first genuine smile I've seen in the last couple of days.

"So, we're going to Linthem," she states.

"Yep. Sally, is that okay with you?" I ask.

Sally seems distracted, she is staring at the kitchen door. "Sally?"

"What? Yes, of course," she turns back to the door. "Do you think Sam seems to be taking a long time giving my dad his coffee?"

I've been so caught up in the conversation with Lex that I'vee completely forgotten about Sam. She's right, he has been a long time.

"Do you want me to go and find him?" I ask.

She thinks on this before replying. "No. Whatever he's doing in there, let's just leave him to it." Does she think that Sam is buttering up her dad, now that he is forming a relationship with her?

I suppress the smile, as I imagine the how that conversation would go.

"Okay. Right, I'll make another coffee, then let's work out what we need to do in order to leave."

"I'll make them," Lex offers. "Do you want to work out how to get to Linthem?"

"Good idea. Sally do you have any maps or road atlases?"

"Yeah, I think so," she leaves the room, and I hear her bounding up the stairs.

Before Sally returns, Sam comes back into the kitchen.

"George will be here in a minute."

"Don't you mean Mr Carlton?" Lex asks with a grin.

"Nah, we've reached an understanding now." Lex and I turn to look at him. He's grinning and looking rather pleased with himself.

"What did you do?"

"Well… he wasn't making any sense… So I punched him."

"What?" I exclaim. I bet George has never been hit before. The image of this young lad giving him a good wallop is surprisingly pleasing.

"He just kept going on, blabbering away to himself. I watched a film once when someone was in shock. They slapped them, and it seemed to bring them around. I thought I'd give it a go."

"Except you punched him."

"Well yeah," he looks sheepish, "He was in a lot of shock."

Lex and I burst out laughing at this. I don't approve of violence in ordinary circumstances. But this is just too funny. The innocent way in which Sam's mind works is endearing.

"Did it work?" I ask, wiping a tear from my eye.

"Yeah. I mean, he cried for a minute. But when he realised I wasn't going to hit him again, he seemed to come round a bit."

"You made him cry?"

"I didn't mean to," Sam says defensively, "I was just trying to help."

"Don't worry, Sam. I think you did exactly the right thing."

"Yep," says Lex. "Especially after he made us tie Claire up yesterday."

Her comment seems to sober us up, and the laughter dies away. Sally returns to the room, carrying a bundle of books, maps, notepad and pens.

"Is my Dad okay?" she asks Sam.

"Yeah, he'll be here in a minute," Sam says, keeping a straight face.

"Great, thanks, Sam," she beams at him.

I buried my face in the maps, concentrating on stopping the fresh bubble of laughter that's trying to escape.

"Are we going somewhere?" I get the sense that Sam's trying to change the subject. It's not the best move to tell your new girlfriend that you just punched her dad.

Lex gives us the coffee and explains the plan to Sam.

He doesn't offer any objections, so she takes the notepad from me and starts making lists about what we will need. Having a purpose and being busy seems to help her. The colour returns to her cheeks, and she appears more animated than she has been over the last day or two.

The route looks relatively straightforward. The camp should be about fifty miles away. The quickest route in normal circumstances would take us directly through Swindon. I rule out this as an option. Swindon is a big over-populated town.

The A34, however, is longer, but bypasses the towns. I choose this as our primary route, but mark out a few other options. Just in case. Lex sends Sam and Sally to fetch various bits and pieces that we might need on our journey, while she busies herself, emptying the kitchen cupboards.

George skulks into the kitchen. I can't help but grin at the rosy red mark on his cheek.

My opinion of Sam is increasing rapidly. Lex turns on hearing him enter, a look of guilt on her face, because she's just been caught going through his cupboards. He looks at her, but makes no comment as he takes a seat at the kitchen table.

"We're making plans to go to Linthem," I tell him. He looks back at me, but stays silent, "We're just getting supplies." Again, no response. "Would you like to make yourself useful and help Lex?" I ask.

He stays quiet, but gets off the chair and joins Lex at the cupboards. He stands there as though waiting for instruction.

"Um… you could put those tins in a bag for me?" Lex suggests, gesturing at the canned food stacked on the side. Meekly, George collects a carrier bag from under the sink and starts loading food into it.

George Carlton has just taken instruction from a nineteen-year-old girl. I never thought I would see the day.

Okay, I never actually thought about it, but if I had, I would never have said he would take instruction from anyone. But then I never thought I'd see zombies strolling around either. Just goes to show that you can't assume anything.

Sam comes back into the kitchen, holding a jerry can in one hand, a long hosepipe wrapped around his arm, and his other hand holding an axe.

"Will these do?" he directs his question at Lex.

"Perfect. Although… do we need the hose to be that long?"

"Nah. I was going to cut a piece off."

It took me a while to realise that the hose is for syphoning fuel if we need to. Good thinking. I hope it won't come to that, but it's better to be prepared. I hadn't thought about the logistics until now. There are five of us.

We could all fit in one car, particularly as George has a large Range Rover but judging by the amount of food on the sides we are going to have a lot of supplies. Also, doubling up on transport like we did yesterday gives us a backup plan if something goes wrong.

"Sam, can you cut two pieces? That way we can have one in each car."

"Yeah sure. There was another jerry can in the shed as well. I'll grab that in a minute." He measures out the length of hosepipe. "George, do you have any scissors?" I stifle a laugh. George jumps at being addressed by Sam.

He dashes over to a drawer next to the sink, pulls out a pair of kitchen scissors and wordlessly hands them to Sam. That is the fastest I have ever seen him move. I don't know what went on in that office, but it would appear that Sam has put the fear of God in George.

I return to the maps and realise the flaw in the two-car plan.

I only have one map that covers the various routes and with no power, I can't photocopy them or take a picture on a phone. The lead car will have to take the map. The car following will just need to know the general route. A military base the size of Linthem should be signposted from the A34. Assuming we stay on the A34, that is.

Sally is next to enter the kitchen. "I've put everything by the front door, except…"

"Did you pack trousers?" Lex interrupts, without looking at Sally.

"Yep and…"

"Good, and jumpers?"

"Yes."

"Clothes for your dad?"

"Yes."

"Did you...?"

"Lex, I packed underwear, including socks and bras, t-shirts, spare shoes, Tampax, hair brush, hair ties and towels, basically everything you put on the list. I also…"

"Great," Lex says, stretching up to retrieve something from the top shelf of a cupboard, completely oblivious to Sally's indignant tone.

"I also found some rucksacks, which I thought we could put stuff in rather than carrier bags."

Lex turns to look at Sally, "That's a really good idea."

"Thank you," Sally replies with an air of sarcasm in her tone.

We know the route. We have spare clothes and personal items. We have, by the looks of the piles of bags in the kitchen, plenty of food. Sam found an axe, and we have the shotgun. I guess some of the table legs we used to escape the airport are still in the Audi.

It doesn't feel enough. We'll be in cars from almost the moment we leave the house. But not much has gone to plan so far, so it's better to be prepared.

"George, do you have any more shotguns?" I ask. He turns to face me, and seems jumpy, nervous at being addressed. For the first time today, I look at him. Really look at him. His eyes have a wild look to them. He can't hold my gaze, and his eyes flick around. His hands are held together in front of him. He pulls at his fingers, like a scared child that is up to no good.

"George," I soften my tone, "Are you okay?" He nods vigorously and points towards the kitchen door.

"Shotguns. Study," he says, his head still nodding.

"I'll get them," Sally offers and leaves the kitchen straightaway. It seems like everyone is relishing having something to do. A task, however menial, is better than sitting and thinking.

So that's everything then. Food, clothing, weapons. Am I missing anything? There's a feeling in the pit of my stomach. I'm nervous. No, I'm scared. I'm taking four people out there so that I can see my boyfriend. It sounds pathetic. Whatever happens is on me, so I need to give them another chance to back out. The girls and Sam have been out there and know what's at stake. George might be a problem. Even though Sally has left the kitchen, George is still nodding and pointing at the door.

"Er George... um... you can sit down now." Almost like an obedient dog, he takes a seat, then turns to me as though he's expecting another instruction. What the fuck has happened to this man? How could someone break so quickly? His actions this morning are almost childlike. Is it right to take him with us? If he doesn't snap out of it, he could be a danger to himself and to us.

Sally returns to the kitchen, balancing two cases with six or seven small boxes on top. I can only assume they are the shotgun shells. Sam goes to her and takes the cases and the boxes from her. He puts them down on the table and opens one of the black cases. He leans in gently as though cooing over a baby and lovingly picks one of the shotguns up.

It's long and looks awkward to hold. Only George and Sam can shoot, and we have three shotguns. I'm not sure giving one to George is a good idea in his current state.

"Sam, could you show us how to shoot them?" I ask. He nods back enthusiastically. "Yeah, course. They're easy to shoot, but really, they are only any good at close range. They will cause a shitload of damage though so you don't need to worry too much about accuracy."

"Okay. George, can you get the food packed into the rucksacks please? Sally, Lex, we'll go out into the garden with Sam." George dutifully rises from the chair and heads over towards the stove. I know he is probably more experienced than Sam, but I just don't think given him a weapon in his current state is a good idea.

It's warm in the garden. The little breeze that flows through the air makes the leaves in the trees rustle gently. Otherwise, it's silent out here.

"How loud are these things?" I ask Sam.

"Very."

"Maybe just show us the principles of shooting and reloading. It might not be a good idea to make a lot of noise."

Sam looks sharply at me. "No, you need to have a go at firing them. They've got quite a kick, you could hurt yourself if you aren't prepared."

An image of a little foot coming out of the gun and kicking me in the face pops into my mind. Embarrassingly it takes me a few seconds to realise he means the recoil. Thankfully I never spoke, so instead, I nod knowingly, "Mmm, yes, good point."

Sam talks us through the components of the gun, and he calls out the various names of the different parts, then shows us to how to break and reload it. He explains how the shells are made of tiny balls of shot that spread out once fired. He talks for over twenty minutes until we are finally allowed to take turns holding the gun.

I go first. The second I touch the gun, everything Sam has just said is forgotten. I rest the gun on the top of my shoulder. My right hand is on the trigger and my left hand a few inches away, holding it upright. It feels ungainly and uncomfortable.

"This feels awkward," I complain to Sam. To his credit, he doesn't laugh. He just comes over and corrects me. He takes my right hand from the trigger then moves the gun down, so it is nestled into my shoulder. He places my left hand further down the gun.

"Better?" he asks.

"Much," I agree.

"Good." He nods, then his face takes on a serious expression. He turns to Lex and Sally, who are watching. "Never have your finger resting on the trigger until you are ready to shoot."

I feel like I've just been told off.

"Put your weight on your front leg. You'll have better control."

I swing around to face him, "Like this?"

Sam instinctively jumps out of the way of the barrel that is pointing right at him

"Never, ever, point a gun at someone that you are not going to shoot." he says. This time I know I have been told off.

"Oh, sorry. It's not loaded, though."

"No Chloe. I know that it's not loaded because I've checked it. Unless you've checked for yourself, you must always assume it is loaded."

I nod guiltily, turn away from him and practise aiming.

We spend the next hour with the three of us taking turns at quickly getting into a firing position. Then learning how to reload. Sam stands by and observes us. As we become more confident, his comments and corrections become less frequent.

Again, I go first. I reload, then quickly assume the firing position. Sam points out a tree in the distance for me to aim for. I do so, then I gently squeeze the trigger.

Holy shit. That is loud. The boom reverberates in my ears. Although the recoil isn't as bad as I thought it would be, it does make me feel like I've been punched.

"That was good, Chloe, well done." Sam smiles at me. I grin at his praise and then hand the gun over to Lex.

I rub my shoulder as I watch Lex and Sally take their turns. I'm worried about the noise we're making. If those things are attracted to sound, they will be headed over here now. The risk is worth it. I wouldn't want my first shot to be taken in a life or death situation. Now at least I know what to expect.

We head back inside. George is sitting back down at the kitchen table. He's finished loading the rucksacks and they are lined up by the door. There are even four mugs of coffee waiting on the table for us.

"Cheers, George," I say and hold my mug up to him in thanks. He nods back silently.

"I think we are ready," I announce, once everyone is sitting down. "Before we go. I just want to make sure that you are certain that you want to come. It will be dangerous, and we don't even know if Steve will be there. You could all be putting yourselves at risk for no reason."

"We are coming," Lex says firmly. "We know the risks. But from now on we stick together. Okay?" She looks at Sally and Sam, who both nod in agreement. "George?" She turns to the older man. He looks back at her, but doesn't reply.

"Dad?" Sally asks, adopting a gentle tone, as though she were addressing an infant. "You're happy to come, aren't you?" It's a statement, not a question. He continues to stare at her, but does not say a word.

I choose to take this as consent, "Great," I say. "And… I guess… thank you. This means a lot to me and…" My words break off, as I realise how much it does really does mean. Until a few days ago I barely knew Lex, and Sam was a stranger. Now they are throwing away the relative safety that this big house offers, for me. The thought brings a lump to my throat.

"Chloe, for everything that we've been through over the last few days, everyone in this room is like family to me now," Sally says, and reaches across the table to take my hand in hers, "But you… for years you've been like a mother to me. For everything you've done for me, before all of this, and after what you did to come and get us from Heathrow. You didn't even need to ask. I love you, Clo."

The tears threaten as I realise she has just used the exact same words as the last ones that Steve said to me. "Thank you." I reply, "I love you too, Sal."

Never again will I leave those words unsaid.

Twenty-Nine

Sam sat at the table in the large kitchen, enjoying the sense of belonging, the first that he'd felt since his parents had died. The hot cup of coffee warmed his hands, while the conversation surrounding him warmed his heart. It was his blossoming feelings for Sally that made it so easy for him to agree to go with Chloe. Yet her words struck a chord. He hadn't known these people for very long, but what they'd shared in that short time had created a lifelong bond. Despite all that he had lost, and all that this life had become, he wouldn't have wanted to be anywhere else than here right now.

A silence descended over the room as the five of them finished their coffee. They each took this moment. This time of peace and inactivity. It was an opportunity to think, to reflect. The serenity was eventually broken.

Chloe announced that they should get the cars loaded up and begin their journey.

Sam collected the mugs from the table and rinsed them out in the sink. He stacked them up on the draining board and considered whether to bother drying them, but decided against it. Instead, he joined the others in taking the supplies out to the car. Chloe was outside surrounded by bags of supplies. She appeared to be splitting the contents in half.

"Are we taking two cars?" Sam asked, as he looked doubtfully over at the Ford KA, then back over to the piles of bags.

"Yes. George has a Range Rover. We'll take that and the Honda," she replied. She tossed a set of keys to him. "Here, can you drive the Range Rover with Sally and George? Lex and I will go in the Honda."

"Yeah … but … um … where is it?" he asked, looking around as though the car might suddenly appear.

"Garage. Just over there,"

Chloe answered and pointed towards the side of the big house. "The garage keys are on the car keys."

Sam didn't ask why George wasn't going to be driving his own car. He didn't need to. The older man was just standing dumbly next to Chloe, awaiting instruction. He jogged over to the garage, unlocked the door and let out a low whistle. The Range Rover was a beautiful beast of a car. The license plate told him that it was less than twelve months old. It looked robust and reliable. Perfect for the coming journey.

Lost in thoughts of admiration for the car, he didn't hear Sally approach. Without a word, she stepped over to him and pulled him to her. Their lips met, and they shared a tender kiss. After a long moment, Sally pulled away and stared up at him.

"I meant what I said in there," she whispered softly, "I know we've not known each other for very long and, well, things didn't get off to a good start…"

"I was a dick," Sam stated.

"Yes, you were," she agreed with a smile, "but despite all of that, I like you, Sam. I really do, and I… just need you to know that."

"I like you too, Sally," his brown eyes gazed down warmly at hers. "More than I've ever liked anyone." He took in a deep gulp of air, "In fact… I think I'm falling in love with you."

She held his gaze, wordlessly staring up at him. It was too long and the silence became unbearable, the atmosphere strained and awkward. He cursed inwardly at his stupidity. "That is… erm… I know we don't know each other. It's stupid, actually. Forget I just said that." He felt the blush creep up his cheeks. She must think he is a right idiot now.

"Sam," eventually she spoke, "we barely know each other. We only met eight days ago. We have very little in common…" Her words sent daggers to his heart. He hung his head, breaking away from the intensity of her stare, "but I think I'm falling in love with you too."

It was as though a physical change was taking place within his body. His heart expanded and threatened to burst from his chest. A warmth flowed through him, and a huge grin lit up his face. He pulled her to him in an embrace so passionate, yet already so familiar, and the kiss they shared was pure perfection.

They broke apart quickly when they heard footsteps heading towards them. They looked shamefaced as Lex entered the garage.

She absorbed the situation and guessed what she had just interrupted.

"Thought you'd got lost," she admonished with a smile. "But I can see you were just busy."

"We're ready now," Sam said, unable to remove the grin. "I'll bring the car out."

Sally and Lex headed back outside, and he could see they were talking rapidly. No doubt Sally was relaying the words that had just been spoken. He didn't mind. In fact, it just solidified the moment they had just shared. His happiness was all consuming.

Regaining composure, he got in the car. After arranging the seat to suit his long frame, he inserted held the key, perplexed as he found nowhere to put it, and took a gamble on the button labelled "Start" high on the dash.

Nothing. Putting his foot on the brake he tried again and the engine purred into life, prompting a satisfied smile from him as though he had just invented something new. Slowly he backed the car out of the garage.

Away from the dark hue of the garage, the sunlight of the day made him blink. It was another gorgeous, early autumn day. He pulled the car up next to the Honda and jumped out.

Together they loaded up both cars, splitting the food and general supplies as evenly as possible between the two vehicles,

George taking instruction, but no initiative, while the rest of them, eager to be on their way, worked quickly.

Chloe suggested that she and Lex would take the lead, and she gave Sam a look at the maps she had marked up.

"I'm never going to remember that," he said.

"I know. If we happen to lose each other, just follow the A34. It'll be signposted."

"Okay," he agreed.

Chloe gave him two of the shotguns and five boxes of shells. "Don't give one to George," she warned with a whisper. Instinctively they both turned towards him. He was standing and staring at a point in the distance, his face blank, devoid of expression.

"I won't," Sam promised.

He climbed into the Range Rover, passing the two shotguns over to Sally. He put four of the boxes of shells in the pocket of the driver's door. The other he opened and divided between himself and Sally.

"Put these in your pocket," he advised. She followed his instruction and split the shells between her left and right pockets. Then she settled back in the seat and put on her seatbelt. George got into the rear of the car. If he was annoyed that a stranger was driving his car, or that he was seated in the back, he did not comment.

"Ready?" Sam asked.

Sally glanced back at her father; he was wearing a seatbelt, his eyes glazed as he stared straight ahead. "Yes," she confirmed. She reached over to Sam's leg and gave it a squeeze. "Let's go."

~

It was dusk when they arrived on Friday night. Now it was daylight and the long driveway glimmered in the sun. It looked calm and serene, a normal day. But he was driving a car owned by the man sitting silently in the back. The girl he had shared a tender moment with just shortly before, had her hand on his knee. The day was anything but normal.

Sally's touch felt warm and comforting, yet the trepidation of what they would face on the journey ahead of them built as they got closer to the open gates. "Erm … we probably should have shut those gates," he said.

"God, yes," she replied, the shock at their stupidity evident in her voice, "We need to start thinking more about these things."

"Er yeah," Sam agreed, "Look," He pointed at the solitary figure that was walking slowly towards the cars. The fact it was a zombie was without question.

The clothes were dirty with a combination of mud and blood. The jeans were torn away at the ankle, exposing a large open wound.

An idea occurred to Sam, and he flashed the car lights at the Honda, and pulled to a stop. The car in front stopped a few feet ahead. Sam took one of the shotguns from Sally and jumped out of the car. He jogged quickly over to Chloe.

"Practice," he said with a grin, holding the shotgun up.

Chloe made as though to protest, and then nodded and stepped out of the car. "This is either a great idea or a terrible one, Sam," she said, but he noted the eagerness on her face.

"Don't worry. I'll cover you."

Lex passed the shotgun that she had resting between her legs, to Chloe, who took it and adopted the stance that he had shown her earlier. She assumed a steady aim at the approaching zombie.

"Um, you might want to put a shell in," he prompted, straight faced.

"What? Oh yeah," she replied, taking the shell from him and quickly inserting it into the chamber. She resumed the stance, took a deep breath, and then pulled the trigger. The force of the blast blew the zombie of its feet and a hole in its chest. Chloe turned back to Sam with a grin.

"I hit it," she stated.

"You did, well done… just next time aim a little higher."

"What? Why?" she turned back to face the zombie that was struggling to get to its feet. "Oh. Yeah. Headshots. Give me another shell, and I'll finish it off."

Before Sam could get another shell out of his pocket, Lex jumped out of the car with the axe that Sam had taken from the shed earlier. She ran over to the thing struggling on the ground, and smashed its head with the blunt side of the weapon.

Sam and Chloe watched, dumbfounded as the young girl repeatedly battered the head of the zombie into a bloodied mess. A scream of rage accompanied the relentless pounding.

"Die, you fucker, die!"

"I think it's dead," Sam whispered to Chloe.

"No shit," she whispered back, as they stared at the oozing mess of brains, blood and bone that now took the place of a head.

"Should we do something?"

Before Chloe could reply, and just as quickly as the violent onslaught had started, Lex stopped, wiped the axe on the grass, and calmly got back into the car.

"Right then. Good practice," Sam said and got back into the car too, leaving Chloe staring open mouthed at the mess on the floor.

Strapped back into the driver's seat of the Range Rover, Sam watched as Chloe got back into her car.

"What was that?" Sally asked, a note of concern in her voice.

"Shotgun practice. Chloe demonstrated for us why head shots are important."

Sally snorted a laugh in response, and Sam grinned back at her, "You can put your hand back on my leg if you want," he suggested slyly.

"Okay," she happily agreed.

They saw more zombies on the drive through the village, but Sam decided not to suggest any more practice.

Eventually, they reached the A34. It was a mess. Crashed cars, fallen bodies and blood stains adorned the road. The driving was slow due to the constant need to dodge obstructions. On a clear stretch of the dual carriageway, Sam pulled up alongside Chloe.

"Do you want me to take the lead?" he asked, "This car might be better at clearing some of this crap out of the way."

"Yes okay," Chloe agreed. "I'll indicate when we need to turn off."

"Cool." Sam pulled ahead of the Honda, and they drove on in silence.

"Um, Sam…" Sally started, turning her head from the window to look over at him. "Do you think it's a bit strange that we haven't seen any zombies in ages?"

"I hadn't thought about it, but yeah, I suppose that is weird. I wonder where they've all gone."

"It doesn't matter," a voice piped up from the back, "See them now. See them later. We're all going to die today."

"Dad," Sally exclaims, "that's a horrible thing to say."

"It's true. We will all die. Everything will have been for nothing."

"Stop saying that," Sally turned around to look at her father. He looked back at her with an air of defiance.

"Nothing matters, Sally. Nothing."

"For fuck's sake," Sally screams, startling Sam so much that the car swerves across the road.

"I've been patient with you. We've all be patient. Now you need to snap the fuck out of it and start acting like a man."

George turned away from her and resumed staring out of the window.

"Answer me, goddamnit," Sally shouted, her voice weaker now.

"Sal," Sam said gently, "Leave him be."

"I…" she turned back to face the front again. "Okay."

"It is odd," Sam said breaking the heavy silence, "there are a load of cars and loads of bodies. You would have thought we would have seen some of those things by now."

"Mmm," Sally replied absentmindedly, her anger at her father turning to worry.

"You okay?" Sam whispered.

"Yeah," she nodded, her voice wavering.

They drove on in silence. Sam was actively looking for any signs of life. Nothing.

Lights flashed behind him, and he spotted the flickering light of the left indicator on the Honda. He took the next slip road and joined a single carriageway. The scene was similar to that of the A34. Plenty of debris and destruction. No movement, no zombies.

Sam thought as he drove. He considered stopping the car and saying something to Chloe, but then dismissed the thought immediately. He could imagine her reaction if he expressed concern at not seeing any zombies. Perhaps he should just be glad at their luck. God knew they deserved some.

After twenty or so minutes on the road, the Honda indicated left again, and he pulled off onto a narrow country road. This road was different. There were no cars or bodies, no blood or rubbish. You could be forgiven for thinking this was just a pleasant drive in the country, on an ordinary Sunday in early autumn.

They passed farmhouses and small cottages. No signs of looting. Doors and windows shut. Peaceful. Not even the odd body here or there. There was nothing. Yet Sam felt a growing sense of unease. Other than Lex going crazy with an axe, and George saying all that spooky shit, this journey had been just too easy

Sally's hand was still on Sam's leg, but she stared out of the side window, lost in thought, but not looking unduly worried. Sam kept his thoughts to himself and concentrated on driving.

The Honda indicator flashed again, and this time he took a right turn. After a few miles, Sam slammed on the brakes and came to a sudden stop. Instinctively his hand reached for the hazard lights, but it was too late as the Range Rover was jolted forward from the impact of the Honda hitting it.

Once the initial shock had faded, Chloe checked herself and Lex for injuries then jumped out of the car and stormed over to Sam's window. It took her banging on the window to notice her presence, and when he finally did, he just pointed ahead. Chloe's gaze followed the direction of his finger, and despite the glass separating them, he heard her gasp.

In front of them were hundreds, possibly thousands of bodies. Left. Right. Straight ahead. Bodies. Lots of bodies.

"I told you we were going to die," George stated from the back seat.

Ignoring him, Sam wound down the window, "What the fuck?" he exhaled. Chloe just nodded, unable to find the words to respond. Ahead was a scene of death and destruction. Thousands of people had died here. They might have been zombies when they died, but just a few days ago they had been real people.

"Turn around?" he asked. She didn't respond and instead, ran back to the Honda. She returned quickly with the map. Sam, Lex and Sally all joined her as she unfolded the map on the bonnet of the car.

"We're here," Chloe said, pointing at a spot on the map. "We need to get here," she pointed at another location less than an inch away from where they were.

"We're probably about three miles away. If we can turn around we can go this way." She pointed at a route that had been marked out in red pen. "It would take us about twenty miles out of the way."

"Okay," Sally agreed. "I know it's longer, but we'll never get the cars through that."

"I said if we could turn around," Chloe replied. She pointed back towards the car she had been driving. The front of the car had impacted heavily on the tow bar on the back of the Range Rover.

The front of the car was smashed in. Smoke seeped through the bonnet in a steady stream.

"Is it drivable at all?" Sally asked, knowing the answer, but wanting to be sure.

"I doubt it. I can give it a go," she ran back over to the smoking car, climbed into the seat and started the engine. The car did not respond. Chloe got back out and walked back to the front of Range Rover.

"We can just all squeeze into the Range Rover," Sally suggested, desperation in her voice.

The four of them looked back at the Honda blocking the road. They would need to push it to move it out of the way.

"Did you see any passing spots?" Sam asked Chloe.

"None. So… we'd need to push it at least two miles."

"Shit."

Chloe rubbed at her neck, sore from the impact, "Uphill."

"Shit."

"Yep. Our options are to either push a car for two miles, then drive another twenty miles or walk the three or so miles from here. Across that." Chloe pointed at the sea of bodies.

They stood in silence and weighed up the options. Neither were particularly appealing, yet the lure of being so close to their destination was overwhelming.

"They are dead," Sam stated. 'It can't be that bad. Plus, if it's only three miles, we should be there in about an hour. It will take us longer to push the car back up this road," he paused and stared out again at the scene before him, "I vote that way," he said, with confidence that belied the fear inside.

"Me too," said Sally.

"And me," said Lex.

"George, what do you want to do?" Chloe asked into the back of the car.

"Doesn't matter. We're all going to die," he replied dourly.

Sally glared at her father. "Dad. Shut the fuck up," she said through gritted teeth. "Ignore him. He's been saying that on the way here."

Chloe and Lex stared at father and daughter. Sally just swore at her father, and he did nothing. He didn't bat an eyelid. Didn't flinch.

"It's agreed then," Sam said. "We're going that way."

"Yes," Sally agreed, already moving towards the back of the car to retrieve the supplies. "We won't be able to carry everything. We'll need to be picky about what we bring." She pulled out a bag stuffed with food. "Here, Sam, take this one. Dad, you can take another bag with food. We three will take clothes."

Lex and Chloe hurried to the rear of the Audi. Chloe picked up the bag she had brought from home and Lex chose one that was stuffed full of clothes.

"Do you want the shotgun?" Chloe asked Lex.

"No, thank you. I quite like this axe."

"I noticed," Chloe grinned and winced again at the pain in her neck.

Lex laughed in response. "Yeah, sorry about that. Very stress relieving, though."

"I know. It's awful. It was once a person, but shooting it felt great."

"Yeah, exactly,"

"That looks nasty, are you okay?" Chloe points at a red welt forming across Lex's chest.

"Seatbelt burn," Lex said rubbing it gently. "It's a little sore, but I'll be fine."

They walked back to rejoin the others. Sam and Sally both held a shotgun. George held nothing.

"Erm… I think we have a spare table leg in the Honda, George," Chloe said, adopting a kind tone.

George turned and stared at her, as though she were the crazy one. "You know, for hitting them," the proffered explanation sounded feeble, "a weapon."

"Oh. No. No, thank you," George replied, then muttered something under his breath. Which they all chose to ignore.

"In that case, you can carry another bag," Sally told her father, and threw another bag of food at him.

Rucksacks on. Cars locked. Weapons in hand. Together the five of them stepped into the sea of bodies.

Thirty

I have never seen a sight like this before. I never want to again. It is disgusting. Almost as soon as we started, I regretted our decision. Sure, this is the shortest route, but we hadn't accounted for how slick blood can make the ground. Our feet squelch on the sodden ground. All of us stumble and slip.

I figure that it was the army that caused this mess. Bullet holes riddle the bodies. In many cases, heads have been destroyed, blown apart. Initially, we step carefully, checking for any that might still be alive. Not seeing any, the threat dims, and I stop seeing the bodies as people, just as annoying and totally gross obstacles.

We walk in silence for about half an hour.

The excitement that I might soon see Steve is building inside me and I want us to speed up. He could be so close. We just need to get past these bodies.

"Do you hear that?" Lex asks, breaking the silence. We stop and listen. The sounds of music drifts over the field.

"Music?" Sally asked.

"I think so," Lex says

"Who the fuck plays music in a zombie apocalypse?" Sam huffs, his face already red from the exertion of the walk, made worse by the weight of a bag of tins on his back.

"Someone who likes to get eaten, I guess," I say lightly, and start walking again. It is weird. The only reason I can think that someone would be playing music would be to attract those things. But why? It's hard to get a sense of the direction the sound is coming from, but I'd guess it was coming from the left of the way we are heading. A feeling of deep unease settles in my stomach.

With every step, the music seems to get louder. Then suddenly it is broken by the sound of fireworks. No, not fireworks. Gunshots. Lots of gunshots. Definitely the army. Knowing that safety is so close, I speed up. The others are following behind me, trying to keep up. I can hear them puffing and panting. I do not slow my pace.

Then I hear a sound that makes me stop in my tracks. Groans. Not just one. Lots. I spin around trying to find the source of the noises. It seems to come from everywhere. It permeates the environment, but I cannot see anything. I start walking again, even faster. That uneasy feeling has turned to fear now, because something is wrong; something is very wrong.

I take in the landscape around me, and realise that we have moved off the road and onto a field. The number of bodies scattering the floor makes it hard to tell the difference. My mind solely on Steve, I haven't thought to look.

A sense of panic now accompanies the fear. I've left the map on the bonnet of the car. Stupid. So stupid.

In the distance to the right, I can see a house not too far away. Where there is a house, there must be a road, and I point to the building. "Let's head that way." I can see my fear reflected in their faces. All of them, except for George. He has a resigned, almost knowing look.

As the groans increase, so does our pace. Almost at the house now. I had thought we could follow the road from the house, but now my thoughts turn to hiding. Get to the house. Hide. Wait it out.

We reach the house, and I run up to the front door. It's an old farmhouse, with a solid oak door. Desperation grips me. I bang on the door.

"Help. Please let us in. We just need shelter. Please," but there is no response. Either the occupants aren't home, or they don't want to help us. "Sam, how can we get in?" I turn to him.

"I don't know how to break into houses," he snaps at me indignantly, "Just smash a window."

I search around for a rock or something heavy to throw at the window, but Lex stops me.

"No, don't. It's too late." She points towards hundreds of zombies coming down the road, heading straight for us, "If you break the window they will be able to get in. We need to make a run for it."

"Okay. If your rucksacks are too heavy, throw them away. We are running," I tell the others. I keep my rucksack on my back. No matter what, my last bit of home is coming with me. The others take my lead and stubbornly refused to discard their own. We break into a run. Leaping over bodies, slipping on the blood. We reach a junction, and a quick glance tells me more zombies are coming from that direction too. They are mere metres from us.

"That way," I gasp, my heart thumping, my lungs struggling for air. I hop over a body, but my foot catches on its shirt. I trip and fall. Face down onto the groin of another corpse.

Sam grabs me on his way past and pulls me to my feet.

"Thanks," I pant.

"No problem," he grunts.

The fall has cost me precious seconds, and I can almost feel the zombies from the junction behind me. I risk a glance behind. They are close. Too close. My lungs burn, and I'm not sure if I can run for much longer.

Something grabs at my top, pulling me backwards. I let out a yelp of alarm. Once again, Sam comes to my rescue, smashing the end of the shotgun into its head. The impact doesn't kill it, but it releases its grasp on me, and I manage to get away.

"Thanks again," I say to Sam.

This time he responds with a thin smile and carries on running. The adrenaline from the near miss courses through me and serves to inject extra energy into my legs. I speed up, and the ungainly, meandering gait of the zombies allows me to gain some space between us. Hope floods my senses. We can do this. They are slow. We're fast. We can dodge the bodies. They are stumbling over them.

The problem with hope is that it is fragile. It can be taken away just as quickly as it arrives.

As though in slow motion, I watch as Sally's leg slips from under her. I see her body twist, fall and land with a thud, her ankle bent in an unnatural direction, and her cry of pain pierces my heart. Her pale face shows pain, fear and panic in equal measure.

Hope is now lost.

George casually observes his daughter, making no attempt to help her. He glances at the approaching zombies, then back to Sally on the floor, and he grins, "I told you that we were going to die today."

Thirty-One

George's head snapped back as the fist connected with his cheek.

"Shut the fuck up, old man," Sam screamed, "That is your daughter over there." He rushed over to Sally, and cradled her as she wept from the pain.

George rubbed at his cheek, and stared at the young man holding his daughter. The mist cleared from his mind. The events of the last day were but a blur. All he could see now was that his daughter lay in pain on the blood-sodden ground. He stalked over to her and leaned towards her.

"I'm so sorry," he moaned, and reached out to stroke her hair.

Sam pushed him angrily away, "Fuck off," he spat.

"Guys, we need to move," Lex said, urgency in her tone.

They turned to look at the approaching hoard, "Can you move at all?" Sam asked Sally.

Bravely, she nodded, "If you can help me up, maybe I can walk."

Sam gently put his arms under hers and pulled her to her feet. She tentatively touched the floor with her foot. She screamed with pain and sagged into Sam's arms.

"I can't. I can't do it, Sam. Leave me here. Go."

"No. I can't leave you," Sam sobbed. "Not now," a boom from a shotgun startled them both, and they turned to see Chloe shooting at the encouraging horde.

Lex picked up the shotgun that Sally had dropped, and she took up position next to Chloe. Together they fired into the mob. The repeated blasts stemmed the flow, slowing but not stopping the invasion.

"We can't hold them," Chloe screamed as she picked her next target.

Sam looked at the woman he loved. Then he looked back at George, who paced up and down, staring at his daughter, his eyes clear and focused. Worry emanated from him. Sanity had returned. Sam took one more look at Sally, and made a decision. The tears fell from his eyes and landed on her face. They merged with her own. He kissed her gently on the lips, "I love you, Sally," he whispered.

She offered him a watery smile, "I love you too."

Gently he picked her up and carried her over to George.

"Take her," he ordered. The two men locked eyes. An unspoken message passed between them. Understanding gleaned, and George nodded. Then he took his daughter from Sam. He walked away as fast as he could.

Sam watched them briefly, he saw as Sally's face appeared over her father's shoulder, a look of shocked understanding on her face.

"Nooooo," she howled. His heart broke as he turned away, picking up the shotgun. He joined Chloe and Lex.

"Go," he ordered, "I'll distract them. Just get her away from here."

"Sam, no. You can't hold them," Lex protested.

"Just go," he replied, his lips pursed in concentration. and he took a shot at the encroaching horde.

"Sam … You can't, you'll die," Chloe pleaded, her voice breaking.

"And she'll live. I'm doing this for her. I'm doing this for all of you. Better that one should die and four should live," he turned to Chloe, A look of sheer determination fixed on his face, "the greater good, right?"

Chloe stared at him, then gave an imperceptible nod.

"Go," he ordered again. His tone calm, no trace of fear. Instead, it was the voice of a man, with utter conviction, that the path he had chosen was the right one.

Chloe pecked him on the cheek, "Sam… I… thank you." She choked, then with Lex, she turned to flee.

With the two of them out of immediate danger, Sam grinned manically.

"Come and get me, you fuckers," he shouted. He sprinted up and down the line, dodging away from the arms that grasped at him. The sound of groans increased as the temptation was dangled in front of the crowd of bloodthirsty zombies.

Thirty-Two

Resolve is fixed on Sam's face. How did a jack-the-lad scumbag turn into the brave man standing before me? I know that nothing we say will change his mind. I know that if we delay any longer, we will all die. A glance in George's direction shows me that he isn't making much progress. We need the seconds that Sam's sacrifice will buy us.

I kiss him on the cheek and whisper words of thanks. Words that will never, ever, be enough. I take Lex's hands and pull her with me as I begin to run.

Tears stream down my face as we speed towards George and Sally. I can hear Sally's sobs in front of me; she sounds like an animal in pain. Behind me, I can hear Sam taunting the zombies and the occasional boom of a shotgun. I count the shots. Two spent, four more to go before he will need to reload.

Boom, four left. I risk a glance behind me. Sam is running in a different direction to us.

Boom, three left.

He is trying to lead them away from us.

Boom, one left.

"Fuckers," Sam screams, his voice ringing out, despite the distant cacophony of music and gunshots, and the closer moans of the horde.

Boom. He is out.

I do not turn around. I cannot watch this.

I fix my eyes on George's retreating back. When the attack inevitably comes, Sam screams. A sound that will haunt me until the day I die.

Sally howls as she watches from over George's shoulder. She struggles to free herself from his arms, but George grips her resolutely. He is stronger than she is. She stops fighting him and sags against her father. She watches powerlessly as the man she loves is ripped apart. I'm certain that a part of her dies with him.

But with that death comes life. Sam's sacrifice has bought us the time we need to make ground. Another glance tells me that their progress towards us has ground to a halt. They are falling over each other trying to get to Sam's dying body. Trying to get a taste of fresh meat.

The sight sickens me. Still, I run.

We catch up with George and Sally. Her loud howls turn to silent sobs.

"Let me help you with her," I offer.

The sweat pours from his forehead. His cheeks bright red from the exertion. He shakes his head and holds her tighter. Determined to get his daughter to safety.

I take the knife from my backpack and cut the arms from the one that sits on George's back. He had long since surrendered the bag he held in his hands. The sudden removal of the extra weight allows him to stand a little straighter, to move a little faster.

We jog along together for what seems like hours but is probably far less. I keep a regular check behind me. The zombies are back in pursuit, but they are not gaining on us. Sam's sacrifice has made all the difference.

A new noise interrupts the dull sounds of groans. I realise that I can no longer hear the music. This sound is familiar and offers comfort. It is the sound of engines. I squint into the distance, trucks are moving along a road. Painted in the distinctively dark green colour that is used by the army. I break into a sprint.

The thought of safety pushes me on. I don't notice the tightness in my chest.

I don't feel the ache in my legs. I run. Faster than I have ever run before, and I reach the road.

I am a mess. My hair is wild, my clothes covered in blood and mud. What if they mistake me for a zombie and shoot me? Then I remember the simplest of truths.

Zombies don't talk, "Help," I call out, "Help, please, help," I reach the road. I shout as loudly as I can. I wave my arms frantically. Tears flood down my face. We are so close to safety.

A driver spots me and draws his vehicle to a stop. Through the window, I see him say something into his radio. The whole convoy stops.

Men in uniform get out of the first vehicle. One stays on top with a big machine gun that he points towards the field from where I emerged.

"My friends," I shout, "please help my friends," more soldiers drop from the truck and run past me.

I turn and watch as they drop to a knee and aim their guns at the field. Four of them stay standing, and break off into a sprint towards Sally, George and Lex.

I am pulled roughly into the van. "Have you been bitten or scratched?" a man asks me.

"No," I sob, "I fell. It's not my blood."

"Okay," he points me towards a seat. Gratefully I sit, my breath is gradually coming back. From my position, I watch as the four men reach the others. Two of them take Sally from George and point towards the vehicles. The other two walk slowly backwards, their guns aimed at the horde.

Sally is taken to a separate vehicle. George and Lex join me. They get asked the same questions that I did, and gave the same answers.

"Sally?" I ask when they are finished.

"They've taken her to the medics," Lex replies, tears creating clean streaks down her face as they wash away the dirt.

The soldiers climb back in with us. No one says a word. The vehicles come to life; the sound is deafening as grenades are launched, cracks sound from rifle shots and the machine guns mounted on top of the vehicles kick into life. I close my eyes and bury my head in my hands. I cannot watch. I cannot bear the thought of seeing Sam in that crowd.

The horde is decimated in minutes.

The engines of the vehicles roar back into life. My entire body sags. We are safe. The relief overwhelms me, and the tears begin to fall again.

When we get to the camp, Lex, George and I are checked over, then sent straight to the hospital, where we shower, and get given cleans clothes. I ask a nurse about Steve. He hasn't heard of him, but gives me directions to the admin block, where he says I'll be able to find out.

Before I leave the hospital, I stop in to see Sally. She is awake, and her broken ankle is in a cast.

The painkillers they have given her do little to take away the true source of her pain. Her loss is written all over her face, and my heart breaks for her.

I take her hand in mine, "I'm so sorry Sal."

She looks at me. Her eyes are red from crying. She says nothing in response.

"Sam sacrificed himself for us. He was so brave. The bravest man I've ever met."

"I know," she nods. "I'm lucky to have known him." The tears fall again, "It just hurts so much."

I hold her as she cries into my arms. I can't leave her. I've waited this long to see Steve. I can wait a little longer. I hold her until the sobs turn to silent tears, then finally into silence. The painkillers do their job, and she falls asleep in my arms. I gently release her and tuck her in. I kiss her on the forehead and back out of the room.

George is waiting outside. "She's sleeping. You should go to her. Be there when she wakes up." He nods and moves towards the door. "George," I call out. He turns to me. "You did well today." He smiles sadly and nods again. Without a word, he turns back towards the door and steps inside.

"Chloe?" a familiar voice calls from behind me. My hearts skips a beat, and I spin around.

"Steve," I cry out and fly into his arms, "What … How did you know I was here?"

"I was in the convoy that stopped to pick you up. I saw Sally get taken to the medics. I knew you had to be with her. I would have been here earlier, but we had to go to a debrief."

"It doesn't matter. You're here now," I smile up at him.

"I'm so sorry for leaving you."

"I'm sorry I was angry when you left. I know you did the right thing by coming here."

We speak at the same time. Neither of us replies to the other. The time for words has passed.

I lean in to receive his kiss. When his lips touch mine, the horrors of this new world fall away.

I am safe.

I am home.

One Year Later

I stand and stretch, my lower back aches from being on my knees for the last few hours. Steve will be back soon. He'll tell me off when he knows I've been in the allotments again. He'll remind me that it's not good for the baby, and I'll remind him that the food I am growing will help feed him or her.

Our lives today are unrecognisable from what they once were, yet somehow, I'm happier. Life is simpler, and with little technology to distract us, we spend more time talking, creating friendships. Food and clothing are allocated fairly. Punishment for crimes is swift and harsh. We are all equal.

Of course, I'm nervous when Steve goes out on patrol, zebs massively outnumber survivors, but military casualties are minimal.

Civilians aren't allowed off campus. I do hear rumours of gangs, preying on survivors that haven't found us yet. When our troops encounter them, they are dealt with accordingly. They don't seem to offer any threat to our way of life.

When we got here, it took us all time to adjust. It took a long time to feel truly safe, and the nightmares are yet to stop. Steve's letters give me great comfort in the early hours, when I wake sweating and screaming. Knowing that he was thinking about me in the brief time we were apart is reassuring. I have never told Lex or Sally about those letters. They are mine, private and sacred.

"I thought you weren't supposed to be out here," Sally's merry voice breaks me from my reverie. The girls meet me after work every day, and we walk back home together. We live in the same block, we each have our own rooms but share a communal living area and kitchen.

"Ssshhh, don't tell Steve," I laugh in response.

"Any signs of labour yet?" Lex asks. She leans forward to pat my swollen belly.

"Nope, but I'm sure it's going to be any day now," I say.

Lex is training to be a doctor, which in this new life, means learning quickly and being expected to perform basic medical procedures alone. She works with her new girlfriend and together they are going to assist in my delivery. It will be her first birth, and she's very excited about it. Some of the other new mothers were reluctant to have someone so young and inexperienced, but I would trust Lex with my life. It will be nice to have a familiar face in the room in case Steve is on patrol.

Apparently, paternity leave doesn't apply in an apocalypse.

"How's your dad?" I ask Sally as we head back to our rooms.

"I had lunch with him today," Sally replies, "He's started work on the perimeter extension. Apparently, he was allowed to use a hammer today." She laughed.

"Well that's progress," I chuckle. It's been a standing joke that George hadn't actually built anything since becoming an apprentice. He's spent the past year fetching and carrying for the people who know what they're doing. Yet, he seems content with his new life. While we're a low-grade zone, which means that we don't house anyone important, like politicians or royalty, there is still the opportunity to be influential here. Instead, George volunteered to join the building team. He told Sally that he wanted to do something that would make a difference. That would mean something in the future.

Ironically, Sally works as the assistant to the civilian leader.

She is in an influential position, she helps make decisions on the running of the zone, and she is on first name terms with all the section heads. It keeps her busy and her mind in the present. Her ankle healed well, but she has never been the same since that day. She can be chatting and laughing happily, and then a cloud passes over her, and she will become quiet and withdrawn.

I spot Steve walking towards us up the road. He's home early today, must have been a very quiet patrol. I wave at him, and he jogs towards us, a frown on his face.

"You've been in the allotments, haven't you?"

"No," I answer quickly.

"Liar," he laughs and points at my muddy knees. "Have you told them yet?"

"Told us what?" Lex asks.

"Nope, not yet," I grin.

"What?" Sally demands.

"We've decided on the name," I say.

"But you don't know if it's a boy or a girl yet," Lex says, confused.

"It doesn't matter."

"What, why?"

"Because we're going to call him or her Sam." I watch Sally carefully for a reaction. We chose the name a few weeks ago, and I've put off telling her. With the baby due imminently, Steve and I decided that we needed to tell her today.

"Sam," she says slowly. Tears prickle her eyes, which contradict the smile that breaks out on her face, "it's perfect."

We fall silent and turn towards the door that leads to our block of rooms. As we enter Sally takes my hand in hers, and ever so quietly whispers, "Thank you."

A note from the author

Firstly, thanks to you dear reader for reading Safe Zone: The Greater Good. I really hope you enjoyed this book as much as I enjoyed writing it. I'd love to hear your thoughts, and I can be contacted at Suzanne.sussex@gmail.com.

If you have the opportunity it would be great if you could leave a review on amazon.

My next book, Safe Zone: The Descent, is in progress and will be out soon. For updates please follow me on Facebook.

The Greater Good has been a labour of love, but it would not have been possible without the support of so many;

Thanks to David at DHP Publishing for all the support and encouragement and for taking a chance on me. Thanks to Susan for the fantastic editing and to Claire at Spurwing Creative for the fantastic cover.

A huge thank you to Leon, Jeff, Simon and Joanne for your comments and advice.
Thanks also to the authors that have given me hints and tips on writing. You know who you are. Your help has always been open and honest and I'm so grateful

To Nicola, the best walking buddy and friend a girl could ask for. Thank you for putting up with me going on for hours about the characters and the plot, but mostly for your enthusiasm and belief.

Lastly, thank you to Adam. Without whom, this book would not have been possible. It was Adam that planted the seed and encouraged me to try writing my own book.

So I did, and here we are.